5/20

STAY
GOLD

GOLD

TOBLY McSMITH

HARPER TEEN

An Imprint of HarperCollinsPublishers

Library of Congress Cataloging-in-Publication Data
Names: McSmith, Tobly, author.
Title: Stay gold / Tobly McSmith.
Description: First edition. | New York, NY : HarperTeen, [2020] | Audience: Ages 14 up. |
    Audience: Grades 10-12. | Summary: Told in two voices, Pony, who is concealing his
    transgender identity at his new Texas high school, and Georgia, a cisgender cheerleader
    counting the days until she graduates, develop a complicated relationship.
Identifiers: LCCN 2019040569 | ISBN 978-0-06-294317-0 (hardcover)
Subjects: CYAC: Transgender people—Fiction. | High schools—Fiction. | Schools—Fiction. |
    Family life—Texas—Fiction. | Texas—Fiction.
Classification: LCC PZ7.1.M4648 St 2020 | DDC [Fic]—dc23
LC record available at https://lccn.loc.gov/2019040569

Typography by David DeWitt
20 21 22 23 24 PC/LSCH 10 9 8 7 6 5 4 3 2 1
❖
First Edition

To Mom—your love of books begat my love of books.

PART ONE

NEW KID AND
THE CHEERLEADER

ONE

Tuesday, August 27, 2019

PONY, 8:34 A.M.

Fade in, exterior parking lot. The imaginary director calls action, and the scene opens on New Kid sitting alone in his car on the first day of school. He checks his hair in the rearview mirror. There's a hesitation in his actions. A nervous fidget. New Kid takes a breath and then gets out of his car.

Did the wardrobe department dress New Kid correctly for the scene? He's wearing an untucked, black button-up short-sleeved shirt. Dark blue jeans. His go-to black Sk8-Hi Vans. He studies his reflection in the window of his car. When nervous, I can use too much hair product—I mean, the hairdresser can. But today, it all works. He puts on his backpack and pauses to take in his new school from across the parking lot. (New Kid needs to show up earlier to get a closer spot tomorrow.)

Hillcrest High is an average Texas school. I have seen enough schools—my dad is in the army; we've moved five times—to know what's average. Standard-issue, double-decker, big-box school with faded red bricks and bright white trim. Manicured bushes and trees line the sidewalk, yellow buses line the curb, and an American flag dances proudly over the two huge red doors. From the outside, there's nothing special about Hillcrest.

New Kid makes his way through the massive parking lot. There's a stiffness to his walk. Sweat covers his forehead from the Texas heat. New Kid goes unnoticed by the students in the parking lot. They are too busy reuniting with friends and showing off their first-day looks. And New Kid isn't the kind of guy who turns heads.

But if they were to look my way, what would I want them to see? Nothing more than an average guy of average height and average build, doing average-guy things, living an average-guy life. That's why Hillcrest High School is perfect for me. We are both striving for the ordinary.

Cue dramatic music. New Kid is frozen in place on the curb. He made it through the parking lot but is now stuck. Imaginary cameras fly in to capture a close-up of his face as he looks at the school lawn before him. There must be several hundred kids talking, hugging, and laughing. Why are the guys wearing fishing gear? New Kid is now filled with doubt and terror. He no longer thinks he can pull this off.

The mission is simple: Walk across the cement pathway that splits the school lawn, up the cement stairs, and through the big red doors into the school. For anyone else, this wouldn't be a big deal. But New Kid has a secret to keep. A secret so big that it makes the regular things, like walking past a mob of students, feel like the hardest things he has ever done.

Dream sequence of New Kid comically retreating. He turns around, walks back to his car, and never returns. No one knows him, so no one will notice. New Kid winds up paddling gondolas on the canals of Venice for cash and pizza. End sequence.

I pull my phone out of my pocket. There's a text from my sister: WHO'S THE MAN? YOU THE MAN.

My sister is right (she is always right). I am the man. I can do this. I close my eyes and take the first step, like I'm diving into a cold pool. Once moving, I open my eyes. Keep my head down, my walk cool, and pretend I don't see anyone. Just another average day for this average guy. I hear talking and yelling on both sides of the lawn, but I keep moving forward.

I take the cement steps leading to the entrance with great care. A slip and fall now, with so many eyes, would end my life here before it begins.

At the top of the steps, New Kid turns around and scans the yard from an elevated position. He feels victorious. There are so many new faces. Possible new friends. Possible new girlfriends. *If no one finds out my secret, the possibilities are endless.*

Before turning back around, New Kid spots a girl in the crowd. The Cheerleader. She's beautiful and bored, holding pom-poms and talking to another cheerleader. For no reason but fate, the

Cheerleader's eyes find his. Light shift. Big music swell. Everyone on the lawn disappears. Extreme close-up on the eyes of New Kid. Extreme close-up on the eyes of the Cheerleader. They float up to the clouds, never once breaking eye contact. The world fades away below, and there's only him and her, 'cause she's the love interest and nothing else matters.

Reality comes crashing back when a kid runs into me from behind, almost pushing me down the stairs. I shake my head in disbelief and walk into the school, wondering what kind of guy I need to be to date her.

GEORGIA, 8:40 A.M.

Whoever that guy was, I think our eyes just made out.

"What the what, Georgia?" Mia asks, entering my personal space. "Did you think I wouldn't notice?"

Mia Davis is the head cheerleader and takes her position very seriously. And right now, she's staring daggers directly into my soul. But what did she notice exactly? Me making crazy eye contact with some guy who isn't on the football team? Maybe. I scan my body for error: white cheerleading outfit with red trim, white socks, white Keds with red laces. Couldn't be my look—I nailed it.

"I have no idea what you're talking about," I say, pushing my hair behind my ear. Oh, crap. I was supposed to wear a high-and-tight ponytail with . . .

Mia finishes my thought: "Red bow! Red bow! RED BOW!"

I can't help but laugh. Mia shakes her head in utter disappointment. "This is not funny, Georgia Lynn."

Damn, middle name shade. This situation is severe. It is time to do what I do best: lie my butt off.

"Mia, that red bow, it was ready to go last night when . . . you'll never believe this—"

"Here we go," Mia interrupts.

"I woke up and saw a ghost. A cheerleading ghost! Who took my bow! I was completely frozen—I couldn't fight back. Trust me, Mia, I would have died for that bow."

She rolls her eyes. "As much as I hate to do this, Georgie, I have to give you a demerit."

Cheerleaders are punished on the demerit system. When we do something wrong—like show up late to practice or forget to wear dumb hair bows—we get a demerit. Rack up enough of them and you get sidelined from games and competitions.

"Fine," I concede, and Mia makes a note on her clipboard. What's one more? I'm on track to break the record. I'm the LeBron James of demerits.

A freshman with a fishing net over his head pushes past me. "Sorry," he says with big eyes, like I could ruin his career at Hillcrest. Cheerleaders are highly regarded around here. So I technically *could* ruin him. But I try to use my powers only for good.

"Don't worry about it," I say with a smile. He looks relieved and gets lost in the crowd. This lawn is pure madness, littered with students.

Hillcrest High is home to hundreds of students and thousands of traditions. This school was built with cheap bricks and meaningless rituals. One of those sacred—and never questioned—traditions is Walk of Shame: Fishman Edition. On the first day of school, the seniors dress in camouflage outfits, holding fishing poles and nets, and catch "fishmen" as they walk into school for the first time.

There must be fifty guys running around giving the school lawn a sporting-department-at-Walmart vibe. They have outdone themselves this year, even dragging a couple paddleboats onto the grass. Seniors don't miss a chance to celebrate their dominance and impending freedom. It's loud, rowdy, and smells like worms and Axe body spray.

Hence the cheerleader presence on the lawn. We line up along the sidewalk and serve as friendly faces to the freshmen walking up to the school. Otherwise, they would probably run back to the bus and never return. We smile, say hi, and shake our pom-poms at the frightened kids. So charitable and giving, right? How Michelle Obama of us.

I feel sweat dripping down my back. I am literally melting. Texas summers are twelve months long and scorching, unbearable, oppressive, icky hot. It must be—and I am not being dramatic—at least three thousand degrees out.

Mia finishes noting my gross misconduct in her demerit diary (that she probably holds when she sleeps) and gives me one last look. "Georgia! Chin up and smile ON!"

"Oh, I thought I told you," I say, "I broke my smile last week. Horrible smile-related accident . . ."

Mia crosses her arms. "How tragic."

"Check it out, this is the best I can do now." I twist up my lips, jut out my jaw, and cross my eyes. "Is this better, fearless leader?" I ask while trying to maintain the look.

"You're more beautiful than ever, actually," Mia says, then flashes the smile that won her Little Miss Dallas 2012. Like always, she gives up on me and moves on down the line of cheerleaders. I'm not offended. She's one of my BFFs but can be intense AF. She is actually down-to-earth when not in cheerleader-domination mode.

Mia arrives at a cowering junior and scans her body.

"Emily, how hard is it to match your socks? I'm being super serious because I want to help you. Help me help you on this sock thing, Emily."

I'll admit it, Mia's control issues have control issues. But her heart is in the right place . . . most of time. She's perfected the head-cheerleader look: long blond hair, not a zit in sight ever, dating the all-state linebacker, drives a Mustang convertible, and her socks *always* match.

I watch the freshmen hurry up the walkway and try to imagine what I looked like three years ago. I remember it being terrifying, humiliating, and I basically wanted to die the whole time. My game plan was to keep my head down, walk fast, and then go cry in the bathroom.

Shocking news—I was not cool in middle school. I had braces, loved horses, and started my period at the seventh-grade semiformal. The theme was "Under the Sea," but my theme was "Under the Red Sea."

High school would be a fresh start. I was determined to change my narrative at Hillcrest. On my hurried freshman walk of shame, I was almost to the steps leading to the big red doors unnoticed when a cheerleader caught my eye. She was easily the coolest girl I had ever seen. I stopped cold. I noticed two things: her flawless skin and her pixie haircut.

She not only looked at me. She smiled at me. Time stopped. Birds sang. I felt special. I felt chosen. So special that about a week later, I tried to give myself the same pixie haircut. Want to guess how that turned out?

It didn't matter, I had realized my high school destiny: to be a popular cheerleader.

And here I am, a popular cheerleader. To be honest, I thought it would feel different.

A pom-pom hits my head. I look over and see Lauren in bad shape.

"Georgia, I'm going to toss my cookies," she says with wide eyes while clutching her stomach. *Someone* went out with her boyfriend last night and is hungover today.

I woke up this morning to a flurry of late-night texts from Lauren at some bar, riding—no joke—a mechanical bull. I didn't even know there was a mechanical bull in Addison, but it's

Texas—maybe they're mandatory in every city.

Lauren Vargas is tall and beautiful, with long, wavy black hair. She's a cheerleading wunderkind and insanely smart. We joke that she has the face of a young Salma Hayek and the brains of Jeff Bezos. We have been BFFs since pre-K. Lo knows all my secrets and I know all hers (in case she tells the world any of mine).

She has been with Matt for two years. They are totally in love and totally adorable, and it's totally *disgusting*. Matt is a party animal, which means Lauren parties all the time too. He's captain of the soccer team with the whole David Beckham shaved-head thing.

I snag a selfie with Lauren in the background looking sick as a dog. When I go to post, I count twenty-five new followers. The fishmen are circling.

"Mia!" Lauren yelps. "I need to get out of here."

Mia runs over to investigate. She would go ballistic on anyone else (aka me), but this is Lauren we're talking about—the secret weapon of our team, with the sickest flips and tricks. Mia can't get to the Cheerleading National Championship without her cheer ninja.

Mia feels Lauren's head for a temperature. "Are you going to pass out?"

"Maybe," Lauren mumbles.

Mia puts her hand on her hip. "Didn't you have a date with Matt last night?"

I jump in. "I think her date was with a mechanical bull!"

Lauren shoots me the Look of Death. "That was a secret!"

Shit. I suck at secrets. What can I say? I'm an unreliable cheerleader.

"Ten more minutes," Mia says. "You can do it, girl!"

Once Mia is lost in the crowd, Lauren sits down on the dry brown grass. I throw her pom-pom into her lap. "My bad, the mechanical bull made me say it."

Lauren is nearly perfect but for one small glitch: she won't stand up for herself. Especially to Queen Mia. Lo wouldn't send a meal back at a restaurant if there were a million hairs in it. My girl would eat it with a smile.

A big dancing brown bear emerges from the crowd. That's our mascot, Boomer. The buff bear suit looks like Winnie the Pooh, if he gave up honey and picked up protein powder. He playfully wags his tail in Lauren's face. "Get your butt out of my face, Boomer! Unless you want to take that suit to the cleaners."

"Kelly!" Mia walks over to the bear. "Class starts soon—get out of Boomer. Wow, that suit smells like the boys' locker room. You need to clean it before Friday."

Boomer gives Mia a big bear hug, really bringing her close to the smelly fur. After a couple attempts, Mia pushes the bear away in a playful little scene. Boomer flips Mia off but there's only four fingers on the fur glove, so it looks ridiculous. We all bust out laughing, and Mia feigns offense.

Kelly is hands down the best mascot ever. She has forever been the class clown. Just try to keep a straight face when she's doing her weird dances or spot-on impressions of teachers. It's impossible. I have no doubt that Kelly will be on *Saturday Night Live* someday.

Mia, Lauren, and Kelly are my main mains. We have been through a crap-ton together. The four of us have been almost completely inseparable since sixth grade—no one speaks of the three months during middle school after Mia kissed Lauren's boyfriend. Major drams.

I wave my pom-pom at all my peeps as they head into school. I'm friends with nearly everyone at this school: the theater kids, athletes, activists, gamers, skateboarders, even those girls who throw flags in the air when the band plays. Thanks to my middle school days, I know all too well how it feels to be an outsider. So, I friend everyone. I'm a cheerleader of the people.

The crowd on the lawn thins out, everyone heading inside to make it to class on time. Kelly comes jogging back over—fresh out of the Boomer mascot suit—in a cheerleader outfit. For some idiotic reason, the mascot must wear the cheerleading outfits to school when we do.

She tugs at the skirt uncomfortably. "Why must I wear this polyester prison?"

I laugh.

"It's tradition," Mia says with overwhelming authority. "You know that, Kelly—you've read the Hillcrest Cheerleading Handbook and Bylaws."

"Every night before bed!" Kelly says, saluting our captain.

Here's my least favorite tradition: wearing our cheerleading outfits on the first day of school. And game day. And Flag Day and Arbor Day and . . . you get the picture.

It's the standard-issue cheerleading outfit, complete with an aggressively pleated skirt (short but long enough not to scandalize) and a sleeveless top with *HILLCREST* stitched across the chest. We have five different cheer outfits, all with varying patterns in our school colors: black, silver, and the brightest red that the eye can register. These getups are crazy stiff and starchy. No kidding, the instructions on the care tag reads: *Machine wash cold. Dry by pounding against a rock until the rock breaks.*

"Girls!" Mia yells into a megaphone. "Get your ass to class!"

Finally, into the air-conditioning.

PONY, 8:51 A.M.

After ten minutes of confused wandering, I find my locker. This school is supersize. Four separate corridors—that look exactly the same—and some twisty hallways that lead you nowhere. My last school, about a hundred miles away, was probably half this size.

I enter the combination, the locker opens, and—for the first time this morning—I take a deep breath. I unload the binders out of my backpack, then pull up my schedule on my phone.

I'm zooming in on the school map when a kid knocks into me with brute force—he must have been running. His body hits me like a brick wall, but I manage to stay on my feet. My phone goes sliding across the floor, stopping against the trash can.

Instead of bolting, the kid runs over and fetches my phone, wiping it on his jeans as he returns. Before heading off, he hands me the phone back and says, "Sorry, man."

Man.

Growing up, I wanted to play outside in rock piles with the boys, get dirty, and collect baseball cards. I hated dresses and refused to wear them. Girls made me nervous. I was called a tomboy, which I secretly liked. I pretended that my name was Tom Boy.

Adults mistook me for a boy often. I liked it, but my mom did not. It would embarrass the hell out of her. "She's a girl," my mom would say, and they would apologize, and I would want to disappear. When she wasn't around, I didn't correct anyone. I went along with it.

Then I hit puberty, and my world crumbled. I knew I was a boy, but I kept turning more into a girl. My chest, my face, my voice. My body was revolting against me and developing without my consent. I didn't understand my feelings and had no words to describe them. I couldn't muster the courage to talk to anyone. Not even my sister.

Fast-forward to 2015, the summer before I started eighth grade. I was growing more depressed and uncomfortable by the day. I'd tried to be a girl and do girl things, but it never felt right. It felt like pretending. Or acting.

That all changed the day the *Vanity Fair* issue introducing

Caitlyn Jenner to the world dropped. Jenner—gold-medal-winning reality-TV star, married to Kris Kardashian—came out as transgender. Her very public transition from male to female changed my life. I had heard about transgender people (kind of—Texas is behind), but I didn't fully understand what it meant to be transgender.

My parents wouldn't stop talking about Caitlyn at dinner that night. They were leveled. To them, it was inconceivable that a famous Great Olympian, the very definition of a Man, would "turn" into a woman. "He was on the damn Wheaties box!" Dad said.

My sister, only two years older than me but already an old soul, got pissed and tried to educate them about pronouns—they kept using *him* and *his* for Caitlyn—but it didn't work. She eventually got frustrated at my parents' stubbornness and stomped off to her room. The idea of transitioning gender didn't compute in my parents' old-fashioned brains. To them, it made no sense.

But to me, it made perfect sense. I ran up to my room after dinner and googled articles and blogs about transgender topics until I got to the end of the internet. Everything clicked into place. After so many confusing years, I finally knew the reason for my discomfort. I was transgender. I could change, and I was no longer alone. It was unbelievably exciting and absolutely terrifying.

Maybe I'd always known deep down, I just hadn't been ready to seriously think about transitioning until Caitlyn Jenner. She's not the perfect trans icon—I can't unsee her in that red *Make America Great Again* ball cap—but her level of fame and bravery for coming out under intense scrutiny raised awareness for trans people and cleared the way for more visibility.

When it comes to my feelings, I'm a slow-moving ship. I carried my secret for almost two years before gathering the courage to come out to my friends and family. Two weeks into my sophomore year, I announced my transition in a short email that I wrote and rewrote for a month. Not exactly a *Vanity Fair*–worthy reveal, but big news for me.

When I finally hit Send on the email revealing my truth, I had a full-blown panic attack. I felt vulnerable, exposed, with no control over what people would think of me. I cocooned myself into my bedspread and tried to clear my head.

My sister was the first to respond, in a very sweet text: OMG! YOU ARE MY HERO. I love u, Brother.

Brother.

My parents didn't greet me as warmly when they came into my room later that night. My mom sat on the edge of the bed, her back stiff. "How long have you felt this way?" she asked.

"All my life," I answered. I kept my head down, trying to avoid eye contact with Dad as he paced the room.

"Did something happen to you when you were little?" he asked, trying to find blame.

"No," I said.

"What if you change your mind, dear?" Mom asked.

"I won't."

Then my dad laughed, this horrible venomous laugh that still makes me sick when I think of it. I wanted to say more—I always do. When it comes to trying to explain myself, it's a tangled mess.

My gut had been right: it'd been better to send an email and let my parents have a little time to process my transition—new name, pronouns, and bathroom—without me there. If I had sat them down, I'm not sure I could have handled their first reaction. And we hugged when they left my room.

I don't remember sleeping that night. I was too busy tossing and turning, regretting, and imagining all my friends reading the email and laughing at me. Calling each other and laughing together. Forwarding the email to the entire school, and everyone laughing at once. It was awful.

I finally drifted off around five a.m. and woke up to ten emails with lots of heart emojis. Friends and family started calling, and even a few cards arrived in my mailbox (old-school). I was shocked by the response; I didn't think there would be so much support and love. It made everything easier. I felt loved by the people around me, no matter what.

Cue the movie-makeover montage: Throwing out girl clothes, buying boy clothes. New socks, new underwear. Tons of push-ups. Visiting a doctor. Meeting friends at the LGBTQIA Center. More push-ups. Starting puberty blocking medication until I'm old enough to take testosterone. Even more push-ups.

And the favorite part of the makeover: a trip to an old-fashioned barber to get my first manly haircut.

My whole life before that day, my hair was shoulder-length and never out of a ponytail. Boys would tease me by stealing my hair tie. I would chase them around, holding my hair back with my hand. I couldn't stand my hair down, not even for a minute. It was too girly.

My sister drove me and quickly befriended the barber, Mikhail, who spoke almost exclusively Russian. I didn't know what to ask for, so she instructed Mikhail on my cut—low skin fade with side part. He got out the electric razor and went to work.

During my cut, my sister typed sentences into Google Translate and played the Russian translations for Mikhail. He would listen and laugh wildly. I still have no idea what she was telling him.

Twenty minutes later, Mikhail spun the barber chair around to show me the finished product. I couldn't believe what I saw. I gasped.

For the first time, the person in the mirror was a guy.

I was about to jump out of the chair—ready to show the world the new me—when my sister put her hand on my shoulder, keeping me in the seat.

"Can you give him a hot shave?" she asked Mikhail.

"Not necessary," I said. There was no hair on my face to shave.

"No hair, no need, no hair, no need," he said.

But she stood her ground and typed something into her phone, then played the Russian translation. He laughed and started prepping the shaving cream.

Mikhail leaned the chair back until I was completely horizontal and spread hot foam on my face. He sharpened his blade and rested a perfectly folded white towel on my shoulder. I gripped the chair, nervous, but his hand was steady and precise. In one movement, the razor would drag across my face, collecting the foam and whisking to the towel with a practiced flip of the wrist. It was all so methodical. Mikhail had mastered every movement. He shaved guys all the time, and now he was shaving my (nonexistent) beard. In a way, it was a rite of passage.

After Mikhail finished my shave, he rubbed some cooling oil around my jaw and face. The mint burned my nostrils but felt refreshing, like I had jumped into an ice bath. He popped the chair up, took off the drape, and said, "Ta-da! Brand-new man! No. Brand-new boy!"

I think of Mikhail now, as I put my phone in my pocket and set off to find my first class. Brand-New Boy, indeed.

GEORGIA, 8:58 A.M.

I'm headed to first period—miraculously early—when muscly arms wrap around my waist from behind, stopping me just inches from the door. I look down at the attacker's wrist and spot a Rolex.

Jake Carter.

He's lucky—I was about to throw an elbow. I still might.

"Hey there, Georgie," he says, letting me go. I turn around to a big dopey smile. I wish I could be mad, but he's simply too good-looking. I blame his chiseled face. And curly eyelashes. And broad shoulders. I could go on. Jake is like the sun: you shouldn't stare directly at him for too long.

When it comes to the clichés of Texas high school quarterbacks, Jake Carter checks every box. Popular. King of the keg party. Smart. Perfect hair and teeth. His family is stupid rich. He looks like a young Chadwick Boseman. And his face is nearly symmetrical, which is way more important than you'd think.

Jake and I should be a sure thing, but it's complicated. I promised myself that I wouldn't date my senior year after what went down this summer. And my ex-boyfriend, Anthony, was captain of the football team last year. (I'll admit it: I have a type.) Isn't there some football bro code Jake is violating?

"What happened to you last night?" he asks, upset. "You didn't text me back."

"Oh, right . . . I am so sorry, but my dog . . . gave birth . . . to kittens last night! We didn't even know the pooch was pregnant, and then out popped, like, thirty kittens. Medical miracle. It's going to be in the paper tomorrow!"

"You have a dog?"

"I do now," I say. "And baby kittens. I'm going to be really busy with them all year, actually."

He raises one eyebrow, clearly not enjoying my ruse. "Georgia, you and me? We are it. Just give me a chance."

I should say no and end this. That's what a decent person would do.

Instead I say, "It's you and *I*, Jake, not you and *me*," and walk into class.

Clearly, I'm not a decent person.

Jake yells behind me, "That's a very mixed message, Georgia!"

I walk into class a minute late—damn you, Jake Carter—and find a desk in the back. Mrs. Lunsford is calling attendance: Jenny Fitzgerald, Soo Park, Orion Thompson. I know all these names. I look around at all the familiar faces. We have grown up together, and I will miss them after we graduate. This morning was too chaotic, but it finally sinks in while I'm sitting here—this is the ending of a huge chapter of my life.

I spent most of the summer dreading this day. After what happened with Anthony, I haven't felt like myself. But it's my last year of high school, and I am going to make the best of it. If I can stay away from dating, this could be a fun year.

The classroom door swings open, and in walks an unfamiliar face. He hands Mrs. Lunsford a slip of paper. Wait, that's him. The guy from earlier. Our eyes have been to first base.

Mrs. Lunsford looks up from the paper. "This is your real name, son?"

"Yes," he says, ignoring a few laughs.

"Class, say hello to our new student, Pony!"

Pony?

We welcome the new guy with a few claps and neighing sounds. He's surprisingly chill for walking into a new classroom for the first time. I'd be a bumbling mess.

"Pony," the teacher says, "tell the class about yourself."

And nothing. He just stands there, frozen. "Son?" Mrs. Lunsford asks softly.

"Sorry," he finally says, and the class nervously laughs. "Not much to tell, really."

"No?" Mrs. Lunsford asks.

"I'm from Midland High School. We moved to Addison this summer."

I'm happy to get a closer look at this dude. He's slim, medium height, in a black short-sleeved shirt buttoned all the way up and a pair of bright blue Vans. Freshly cut and styled black hair. He's cute in a soft way, like a young Leo DiCaprio. I'm talking babyface Leo before the *Titanic* went down.

Mrs. Lunsford claps her hands. "Welcome to Hillcrest, Pony. Take the desk in the back beside the cheerleader. Don't worry, she doesn't bite."

"I can't make that promise," I say, and the class laughs.

PONY, 9:07 A.M.

I walk back to my desk and feel every eye on me. Sizing me up. I try to remind myself that it's my first day: they're looking because I'm new, not because I'm transgender. They don't know I'm transgender.

I sit down and think of what I said in front of the class. What a mess. The teacher starts into the lesson, and I slowly feel the attention shifting away from me. I relax my shoulders and secretly text my sister: Smooth sailing so far.

I hit Send and almost instantly get a reply: DON'T FUCK IT UP, BRO!

My sister has a way with words. She doesn't agree with what I'm doing, but she knows it's what I want.

I turn my head and catch a cheerleader looking at me. Not just a cheerleader, *the* cheerleader. I perk up, remembering to square my shoulders and push my chest out. I probably over puff. She's too pretty to be looking at me. *Or maybe she can tell I'm trans?* I play it cool by immediately turning away.

At the end of class, the cheerleader raises her hand. I sneak a look at her while she waits to be called on. She's got shoulder-length brown hair, perfectly straight. Her face is perfect. Her smile, also perfect. Her eyes, freckles, ears, all perfect.

"Mrs. Lunsford," she says without being called on, "just wanted you to know that I volunteer at the homeless shelter at night, so I can't do homework."

The class laughs, and before Mrs. Lunsford can respond, the bell rings.

Everyone files out of the classroom without giving me a second thought—the novelty of the new kid has already worn off. I hit the packed hallway and get lost in the crowd. I'm invisible, like a ghost haunting the school. I have no past here, only future. This is what I have dreamed about for so long. My brand-new life starts today.

I find the boys' bathroom, take a deep breath, and push the door open.

When you're transgender, bathrooms can be uncomfortable.

Keeping my eyes low, I walk past the urinals and feel instant relief when the only stall is empty. Urinals aren't exactly my thing. Matter of fact, they are impossible for me to use. When the toilets are all occupied, I wait awkwardly and hope no one notices me.

But no waiting today. Today feels lucky.

After, I'm washing my hands (something not all guys do) when I hear a deep voice behind me. "What are you doing in here?"

I look in the mirror and see a large guy wearing a football jersey. Our eyes lock in the reflection in the mirror. Panic washes over me, but I stay outwardly calm. I shut the water off and turn around, squaring my shoulders.

"The same thing you're doing in here," I say.

He takes a step closer. "This isn't your bathroom."

And sometimes when you're transgender, bathrooms can be dangerous.

At my old school, I would cross the highway to use the bathroom at McDonald's. In Texas, it's not illegal for transgender people to use the restrooms of their gender—it just made things easier for everyone at Midland High if I never showed up in one. I was the first and only trans student at my old school. It's a lot of pressure to be that special.

After I sent my coming-out email, word about my transition spread quickly around school. Almost everyone was positive and excited for me. People asked questions that felt too personal and kept getting my name and pronouns wrong (saying *she* instead of *he*). I was frustrated and hurt but tried to be patient. It was a big adjustment, and those take time.

There was some bullying. Not surprising—this is Texas. People said mean things and I lost a few friends, but I tried not to pay them much mind.

For the most part, my friends were supportive, but maybe too supportive. I became the token trans person. It was how they introduced me: "This is Pony. He's trans!" Then how they described me: "that trans kid" or "Oh, the trans one?" Being trans became my defining feature. I just wanted to fade into the background.

I read an article last year about transgender people going stealth at work to avoid discrimination. *Stealth*, as I understand it, means passing as your gender and concealing your transition. After a year of too much attention, I just wanted to drop off the radar and be a typical, average—maybe even a little boring—boy.

Going stealth sounded like the perfect solution, and it didn't take long to get my wish. On the last day of junior year, Dad dropped his relocation papers on the table at dinner. *Dad ex machina!*

He's been in the army all my life, so I'm no stranger to moving. I'm usually not happy about starting over, but this time I was boxing up the house a month early. I was ready. This was my chance to go stealth at a new school and live my dream life. A brand-new boy.

But that's over. First day of school and first bathroom visit, and I'm already busted for being trans by this football jock. That was quick. I turn around and face him, channeling Robert De Niro. (Not *Meet the Fockers* De Niro; I'm talking *Taxi Driver* De Niro.) I look him dead in the eye and make sure to use my deep voice. "You going to make me leave this bathroom?"

"Dude. Chill. Freshmen use the bathroom in C wing, by the gym. Hillcrest tradition."

Oh, thank god. He thinks I'm a freshman. I loosen up and take a step back.

"I'm a senior. I'm new here," I say, then lean back on the sink to show this guy just how cool I am.

"Oh shit, my bad. You look young," he says.

"Yeah, I'm still waiting to hit puberty."

He laughs, thinking I made a joke, but I didn't. I need to be eighteen before I can start injecting testosterone to trigger puberty.

"Pony," I say.

"Cool name. Welcome to Hillcrest. I'm Jake."

We head out of the bathroom together, and he points me to my next class. We don't shake hands, but that's fine with me. He didn't wash them after taking a leak.

Did I just make my first friend here?

GEORGIA, 10:59 A.M.

I'm so hungry, I might die. I shouldn't have skipped breakfast this morning. There's a zero percent chance for an on-time arrival to third period. I'm hustling, but I'm also in a weakened state. I would eat a cupcake off the floor right now.

I'm navigating through hordes of kids in the D corridor when I round the final corner and run right into Ms. Randolph.

"Georgia! You startled me!"

I give her a big hug. Ms. R is probably my favorite teacher. As usual, she's wearing a pencil skirt with a white blouse. Her glasses creeping to the tip of her nose. Hair in a tight bun. It works—she is straight-up teacher chic.

"How was your summer?" she asks.

"Fine," I lie.

"Oh, the perils of high school love. It will never be so urgent, it will never be—"

"Did you read the article about Syria in the *New Yorker* last month?" I ask, both testing her and changing the subject.

"I did indeed. It made a few good points. Did you read the piece in the *Atlantic*?"

"No," I admit. She's always going to win this game. When will I learn?

"It's your last year here, Georgia, and the *Hillcrest Reporter* has become more important than ever—"

Ms. Randolph is advisor for the *Hillcrest Reporter*, a weekly newspaper published by the journalism club. She's been trying to recruit me to write for years. First off, the paper needs a new name. The *Hillcrest Reporter*? And, last time I checked, only thirty people follow them online. That's not a paper; it's a sad blog.

And most importantly, I'm not going to abandon an image

that took three years to build. I'm the cheerleader with the funny stories, the cheerleader who dates football guys, the cheerleader who has a pretty good shot at homecoming queen. What would people think of me if I started writing exposés about the cafeteria food?

I cut her pitch off. "Sorry, Ms. Randolph. I am so busy with football season . . ."

"We don't publish articles about the cafeteria food, Georgia."

How does she know my thoughts?

"You can write about anything you want."

Oh boy, she's not going to make this easy. "I'm a reader, not a writer. I'm a cheerleader of words!" I do a couple small *rah-rah-rah* motions to really drive my point home.

"Georgia, the great storyteller, the spinner of tall tales. It's a shame that you're going to sit on the sidelines of life. And why? Because you're afraid to write a story that's true?"

"The truth is boring," I say, rolling my eyes. "Especially if it involves Hillcrest High."

I wave and take off down the hall. Ms. Randolph yells out one last attempt. "Just come to the meeting after school today, Georgia!"

I turn around and say, "Nice running into you! Let's do lunch!"

Ms. R has clocked me correctly—I do want to write. After I finish reading an amazing article, I like to imagine what it would be like to research a story, interview people, and then type furiously on my computer all night—as my editor paces behind me—until, against all odds, I make the deadline. Then I win the Pulitzer, the Nobel Peace Prize, and all the other prizes, no big deal.

This obsession with journalism is my dad's fault. My earliest memories are of him napping on the couch surrounded by newspapers. Even now, there are always rapidly growing stacks of magazines and newspapers around the house. It gives the place a real hoarder feel.

Dad didn't push reading on me, I just picked up a newspaper one day and haven't put them down since. There's nothing like reading an article that broadens my horizons or whatever. So yeah, it would be cool to write something like that. Just not now.

None of my friends know about my secret dream—it's way too nerdy.

I push open the door to Advanced Calculus and immediately spot Pony in the front row. This is our fourth class together. How is that possible? In a school this big, that kind of schedule alignment is nearly impossible. Fate much? I walk past and act like I don't even see him.

PONY, 12:07 P.M.

Here I am, living my dream life, eating lunch in my car. I'll make friends eventually, but I'm dining solo today. I'm fine with it. I'm listening to my favorite movie podcast. It's the one that tells the behind-the-scenes stories of iconic movies. This episode is about one of the funniest movies ever, *The Princess Bride*.

I packed a sandwich stuffed with last night's brisket covered in BBQ sauce. I'm taking my first huge bite when my phone stops the podcast and starts ringing. It's my sister. She made me promise we would FaceTime at lunch.

Two years ago, my sister walked across the stage to collect her high school diploma and kept on walking to the parking lot, drove to the airport, and flew to New York City. My parents lost their minds, but they let her stay. I guess she was over eighteen, and they didn't have a choice in the matter. My sister is a free spirit who reports to nobody.

"Hiiiiyeeeeeee," she says, while moving the phone slowly toward her face, until all I can see is half an eye and a freckle.

"Hi," I say while propping the phone on the steering wheel so I can keep devouring my sandwich. She pulls the phone away from her face, revealing her bedroom—which is also her living room and kitchen. From what she tells me, rent is impossibly expensive in New York City. My sister has a teeny-tiny loft on the Lower East Side. It's so small, she doesn't live in an apartment; she lives in a diorama of an apartment.

"Excuse me, is that a five o'clock shadow?"

"No," I say, a little too defensively.

"Put the phone closer to your face and let me have a look," she demands.

I can feel my face redden. "There's nothing to see."

My sister knows exactly how to embarrass me—always has and always will. I run my hand along my jawline. It's going to be years before I have any facial hair. If I had it my way, I would have the most manly of man-beards. It would be nothing but beard as far as the eye could see. A beard that food gets caught in—not just crumbs, but full pieces of fruit and bread. The kind of beard that would leave no question in anyone's mind that I'm a man. At this point, I'd settle for a soul patch. But it's not up to me.

"Hey," I say, "I was reminiscing about my first haircut. How did you talk that barber into giving me a face shave?"

She acts taken aback that I would even ask. "Pony, that's a secret between me and Mikhail."

"Tell me," I demand, then take a bite of my sandwich.

"Ewwww, don't eat that in front of me. You are aware of my stance against eating meat. Poor cow."

A moment passes. It's clear that she's not going to reveal her secret. I change the subject. "So, sis, what's new with you?"

I ask my sister the same question every time we talk because she's always up to something interesting and weird.

"Well, Ponyboy, I'm glad you asked. There's something I need to tell you . . . I'm a unicorn now!"

I rest my case.

"Congrats!" I say. "When will the horn grow in?"

"Ugh, come on, Pony. The amount you know about this world could fit in a Diva Cup."

Gross.

Her voice takes an educational tone. "Unicorns are the third person in a couple's open relationship. I'm *his* girlfriend . . . and

I'm *her* girlfriend . . . I'm *their* girlfriend!"

"Please bring *them* home for Christmas," I demand, then take the last bite of my sandwich, mostly bread crust and BBQ sauce.

"No way, Pony. The wardens would lock me in the basement and never let me out."

She's correct: my parents are very strict.

"Come on," I beg. "I need the entertainment. It's so boring without you here, Rocky."

It took a month in New York before my sister changed her name to Rocky. To my parents' dismay, her new name was not up for debate. I do feel bad for them sometimes—they raised daughters and now they have a transgender son named Pony and a unicorn named Rocky. They must wonder where it all went wrong.

"And, how did you meet . . . what's their names?" I ask.

"Raul and Amethyst."

"Of course."

"Well, I was at the vegan café in my yoga center after an intense acro session. I was eating a quinoa and tempeh bowl—"

I interrupt. "I understood about three of the words you just said."

"Pony, focus!" She snaps her fingers at me. "I'm sitting there when this attractive couple with the most amazing energy sits down at my table and asks if I want to join them. I thought they meant for lunch, but that's not what they meant . . ."

"OK, no more information is needed, thank you," I say.

"Breakfast time!" Rocky sings as she rolls out of bed. She works until late as a server at a trendy West Village restaurant, so her day starts around noon. I watch her walk the ten steps to the kitchen and pour a bowl of organic health cereal.

"How do you eat that crap?" I ask. "It should be called Twigs and Leaves."

"You'll understand when you're older, Ponyboy. So, how's your first day?"

"Well, I'm eating lunch in my car alone, so that should be a good indicator," I say, turning up the AC—it's extra hot out today.

"It was always like that for me at first," Rocky admits. "Even I had a few car lunches whenever we moved."

I consider revealing the close call in the bathroom, but I don't want to freak her out. I start to tell her about the cheerleader but stop myself. Rocky rebelled against high school clichés, so that would freak her out more.

"You're holding back on me, Pony," she says, waving her spoon at me.

"I think my calculus class is going to suck?"

I'm a chickenshit.

"OK. Whatever." She knows I'm leaving something out. "And what's going on with project stealth?"

"Stealth mode is fully engaged. I'm flying undetected. No one knows I'm trans. No one knows I'm alive, really. I couldn't be happier," I say.

"Well then, I'm happy for you," she admits reluctantly. "Live the life you want to live." She shoves a spoonful of branches into her mouth. *Crunch, crunch, crunch.*

"I have a job interview after school," I say.

"Stop!" She almost chokes on some dry twigs.

"Yeah, I had some time to kill at the Angelika before the movie started yesterday, so I checked out the community board. There was a job listing. Seemed interesting."

"And what was so interesting about it?"

"It said, 'Do you want to work in the movie business?' No name, nothing. Only a phone number. So, I called."

"Yeah, no shit you called, Pony. That's so boneheaded. Do you know what this is?"

"An employment opportunity?" I ask.

"A scam at best. At worst, an elaborate plan to kidnap you."

"I'll be careful."

"You better be careful—" Rocky's buzzer interrupts the I-live-in-New-York-and-know-everything lecture. "Got to go, Pony."

"Who's coming over?"

"Like I'm telling you," she says. "Pony, keep your head up, OK?"

"OK," I say.

"Love you, Bro."

Bro.

It's the little things, like my sister calling me *Bro*. The guy who almost knocked me down saying "Sorry, *man.*" Sure, he almost ended me, but all I'm thinking about is how he said *man.*

Another favorite: "Right this way, *sir*."

Forget whiskers on kittens; correct pronouns are a few of my favorite things. It's like hearing your name pronounced wrong all your life and then all of a sudden, people say it correctly. It's shocking and exhilarating. It's one small victory stacked on another.

The next two classes fly by, and after getting embarrassingly lost, I find my last class of the day a few seconds before the bell rings. I head to an empty table in the back.

Here's an update on the cute cheerleader: she has been in every single one of my classes, but I don't see her here. I'm a little bummed. Using my top-notch detective skills—of listening to attendance getting called in every class—I have discovered that her name is Georgia.

She's cute, but I don't know. A cheerleader? That's not my type at all. I like girls who paint, girls who take photos—photos with real cameras. Girls who want to make the world better. That's my type. I didn't say they were into me, but that's another story.

It's clear that Georgia the cute cheerleader has an easy life. Has she had to deal with a big life problem? Also, I overheard her telling a story about saving a hundred babies from a fire this summer. What was that about?

I'm so wrapped up in my thoughts that I don't notice she's walked into class until she sits down beside me at the lab table. It's a two-person lab table. Just me and her.

"Hi," I say.

"Hi," she says.

How do we have every single class together? This school has hundreds of students—the probability of this schedule coincidence seems so impossible. Yet here we are.

She turns to me. "So, *Pony*, I think you might be following me."

"Funny, I had the same feeling about you," I say. "I cut out at lunch and filed a restraining order against you, *Georgia*."

She shoots me a look. Maybe she isn't used to someone keeping up with her? Not that I've been watching or anything. And she has striking light brown eyes. Not that I care or anything.

The teacher interrupts. "Students, welcome to Chem Lab. My name is Mr. Glover, and we're going to have a proTON of fun!" The class collectively groans. "The person at your table is your new lab partner. Take a moment and introduce yourself!"

I turn to her. "I think Mr. Glover wants us to be friends."

"Should we be friends?" she asks.

"No way," I say. *We should be more.*

"Well, regardless, I guess you're stuck with me, Pony."

She says my name in a way no one has ever said my name before.

"Or until the judge can keep you away," I say.

She laughs. It's a great laugh.

"Georgia, I think you might be trouble."

She smiles. It's a great smile. "You, sir, have no idea."

Sir.

There's only one place to see and be seen in Addison, and that's the Sonic drive-in on Midway Road. Sonic is the best fast-food chain, serving up burgers, fries, and tater tots covered in melted cheese. Also, crazy-good milkshakes and slushies.

At any hour, Sonic is swarming with Hillcresters. This is the spot to meet friends, to show off your date, to experience a life-changing cherry slushy with whipped cream.

It's prime time at Sonic, so the place is extra packed. A post-practice Sonic run is pretty much mandatory. Football, dance, and cheer practices let out at the same time, and then it's a race over here to secure a parking spot. Lucky for us, Mia snags the last one. Once this place is full, cars are banished to park across the street at the Piggly Wiggly grocery store.

Mia rolls down the window of her silver Mustang and yells our order into the crackling intercom box. "Four Diet Cherry Limeades, please."

Lauren taps on Mia's shoulder, all scared. "I want a chocolate shake."

Mia scoffs. "You do not need all that dairy," she says, then returns her attention to the intercom. Kelly, in the back seat with me, starts making fart noises, and we all laugh.

"Lauren, I'm sorry for the near collision at practice," I say with my tail between my legs. I accidently stepped directly in the path of one of her high-speed tumbling passes. Just in time, I leaned back with my arms flailing wildly, like those floppy balloon tube men at car dealerships.

Lauren pats my leg from the passenger seat (she yelled "Shotgun!" first on the way from the locker room). "No problem, girl. You must have been thinking about someone special . . ."

"She was def thinking about Jake!" Mia says, turning down the music.

I *was* distracted, not by Jake but by the thought of missing that journalism meeting happening during practice. I wanted to be there. Maybe I subconsciously threw myself into Lauren's path in hopes of a career-ending injury. I'm having trouble caring about cheerleading.

When I signed up to try out for the cheer team at the end of my sophomore year, I was kind of a nobody. But then I totally killed the tryout, made the team, and overnight, I was kind of a somebody. The invites to cool parties came in, and cuter guys started talking to me. A couple senior cheerleaders took me under their wing and picked me up on the way to school and parties. I'd show up with them, and then, I was someone.

I had leveled up, and it was exciting—so freaking exciting—but part of the deal was playing it cool.

What if I quit cheerleading and wrote for the *Reporter*? People would think I'd lost my marbles. There would be no coming back from that. So I'm kind of stuck here.

"Yes, Georgia," Lauren says, hopping up and down in her seat. "Marry Jake and be set for life!"

Dating in high school can be so predictable, so boring. Mia

is exclusive with the star linebacker, and Lauren is practically engaged to the captain of the soccer team. It's all so *obvious*.

Kelly hasn't dated much. She claims that being mascot takes up too much of her time, but I call bullshit. I have vague memories of a boyfriend in middle school for a month, but she's not interested in all that. She's smart.

"Nothing is happening with me and Jake," I answer. "Remember? I'm not dating this year?"

Lauren waves me off. "Come on, Georgie! Me, you, and Mia could triple-date!" Her eyes get big, realizing that Kelly wasn't in the triple-date equation. She tries to correct herself, "Kelly, you can come too! You can date one of Matt's friends!"

Kelly doesn't even look up from her phone. "Thanks, Lauren, very sweet of you, but I'm going to pass on that tempting offer of eternal love."

I jump in to help. "Don't worry, Kelly. There will be no triple date. You're off the hook."

"Phew," she says.

Mia and Lauren both turn around, focused on me.

"Georgia, Jake is a nice guy," Mia says.

"*Such* a nice guy," Lauren echoes.

"And he likes you!"

"He *really* likes you!"

"Just give him a shot," Mia pleads.

"Fine," I say, just to quiet them down.

Lauren and Mia start squealing and high-fiving. I can't fault my girls—they're just trying to help. I was devastated after the night of Tiffany's party, the ground zero of my breakup with Anthony. I took to my bed for seven days like a character in a Jane Austen novel. It freaked out my dad. I didn't care. I needed to lie flat, feel safe, and sleep until I was human again. On the eighth day, I got out of bed and on with my life, but I'm still working through it all.

The important thing is, who was there for me *every* night with ice cream? Lying in bed with me while I cried all the tears out of my body? My girls. They aren't perfect, but who is? Those girls have my back always. And they enacted revenge on Anthony by keying his truck. Don't cross us, I swear.

The carhop skates up to the window, balancing four jumbo drinks on a tray. Now that's true skill. After Mia pays, we pass around her flask and splash some vodka in our slushes.

Mia raises her Styrofoam cup. "A toast is in order!" We all begrudgingly raise our cups. "Girls, we are seniors! This is our year. Let's do things that scare us! Let's do things that we will regret! Let's do things that will put us in the Hillcrest history books!"

"Like get good grades and go to college?" Kelly sarcastically asks.

"What? Ew. Boring. I have something else in mind," Mia says, pulling a duffel bag from the back seat. "How about we start this year off right?"

She unzips the bag, revealing tubes of plastic wrap, eggs,

and shoe polish. Kelly drops her phone, finally paying attention. "Prank on the first day? Bold move."

Mia nods in the direction of the Piggly Wiggly, where the football guys' trucks are parked, unguarded. "Yes, girl," she confirms.

Another tradition: cheerleaders and football players pulling pranks on each other. Constantly. Last year, the football team stuck thousands of plastic forks and knives into the lawn of the head cheerleader. And I do mean thousands. It took the squad three hours to defork that yard.

We cover all the pranking hits: toilet-papering houses, egging cars, fake kidnapping, whipped cream on lockers. The stakes are high. I hate how much fun it is. But this seems like a suicide mission.

"It's broad daylight. Are you being serious right now?" I ask.

"Ugh, Georgia. We need to go hard this year. Remember?" She pauses and looks me right in the eye. "We made this promise after what happened to you this summer. Revenge is ours."

"I don't know . . ."

Mia hands me a roll of plastic wrap. "G, this will be cathartic."

Kelly grabs two tubes of shoe polish. She is the undisputed champ of writing lewd things on car windows. We all look at Lauren. She's hesitating. Matt's truck is in the mix because he hangs out with football guys. To our shock, she shrugs, pops open Mia's glove box, and pulls out the pepper spray. "Let's do this!"

"I love the enthusiasm, Lauren. I really I do," Mia says as she removes the spray from Lauren's hand and replaces it with a carton of eggs. "But let's start here."

"Look at them," I say. The guys are on the benches showing off for the freshman girls. "They won't even see it coming."

We make a game plan while taking big sips of our slightly alcoholic drinks. The cheap vodka warms my body and gives me courage. This is not our first public pranking—we know how to keep a low profile. It would be too obvious if we all got out at once. Lauren and Kelly exit first and head toward the Piggly Wiggly.

Mia turns back to me. "You doing OK, babe?"

"Better every day," I say.

"You need to move on. That's why we are all Team Jake."

"I'll think about it," I say.

Mia claps her hands, celebrating like a salesperson who just closed the deal. She opens the car door. "And if you need someone to talk to, I am always here for you. I love you, Georgie."

Before I can say anything, Mia gets out of the car and slings the bag stuffed with backup supplies over her shoulder. I follow her lead, and we keep it casual, walking fast but not suspiciously fast, heading across the street to the Piggly Wiggly. Once out of sight of the Sonic, Mia drops the bag between trucks.

Lauren and Kelly find our hiding spot, and we circle up around the bag of tricks. For no reason at all, we're giggling our heads off.

"OK, deep breath. Shhh. Shhh." Mia is trying to send us into battle, but we can't keep it together. "Be fast and effective, and then scatter when the enemy comes running."

"And if you're caught, take your cyanide pill," Kelly says.

"NOW! GO NOW!" Mia screams, and we start running around like crazy.

"I didn't get the cyanide pill!" Lauren yells.

Mia helps me wrap the cars. And by helps, I mean she holds the end of the roll as I run around and around, until the truck looks like leftovers in the freezer. Every few seconds, an egg cracks against a truck. I smell the shoe polish and hear Kelly laughing at her artistry. After the third wrap job, Mia and I stop and snap a selfie with the trucks in the background. We are doing some serious damage.

"HEY! OUR TRUCKS," some dude screams from the Sonic picnic tables.

And that's our cue. Time to get the hell out. I drop the evidence and take off, headed to the 7-Eleven on the corner. I look back and see that Kelly has shoe-polished cartoon penises all over the windows of the trucks. Classic.

Lauren's boyfriend has already caught her. He's picked her up, spinning her around as she's laughing and pretending to escape. *God, they are the worst.* I spot a guy throwing his Sonic cup on the ground, pissed, sending ice everywhere. Some people take the prank game more seriously than others. The guys huddle up to form a plan, and I pick up my pace.

I hit the gas station parking lot and see a familiar face pumping gas. I head over and lean on his car—all chill like—even though I'm out of breath and there are ten jocks on my tail.

"Of all the 7-Elevens in all of Addison," I say with a smile, "you end up at this one."

Pony takes off his sunglasses. "Isn't this the only 7-Eleven in this town?"

"Shhh," I say.

"It must be fate, then," he says, and smiles.

I nod toward his Volvo station wagon. "Get all the ladies with this ride?" I ask.

"Why do you think I had to move?" he asks.

"Weird question, but want to harbor a fugitive for a few minutes?"

Pony returns the gas nozzle to the pump. "I knew you'd ruin me," he says. "Get in."

I duck around to the passenger side of his obvious parental hand-me-down and hop inside. From this spot, we have a great view of the skyline. He starts up the engine, and some indie rock-country band blares from the speakers. He yells over the music, "Rainbow Kitten Surprise!"

"Cool," I say.

He turns down the volume. "Do I want to know what's going on?"

"Definitely not. Let's keep this on a need-to-know basis."

"Will do," he says, then grabs a package of pretzel M&M's from his shirt pocket.

We sit in silence. The sun is setting, staining the sky an unreal watercolor pink. I look over at him. "Pony, if we're going to be friends, I can't have you talking this much. Seriously, it's on and on with you. Story after story. When will it end?"

He laughs. Oh no. He's really freaking cute when he laughs.

"You got me."

"Do I?"

"You wish," he says.

"You wish," I repeat.

He ignores me. "I can be quiet, especially at first."

"OK, then, talk! Tell me something," I say.

"Well . . ." He thinks for a second. "I was just at my first job interview."

"Fancy businessman," I say. "Did you get the job?"

"I did."

"No shit? Congrats, Pony!"

"Thanks," he says shyly.

I'm about to ask more about this job but get distracted by a couple football guys running into the 7-Eleven. I slump down in my seat. Pony looks at me with raised eyebrows. "Your turn," he says. "Tell me something about you. We could start with why you are on the run . . ."

He wants an explanation. That's fair.

"I know we just met, Pony, but I feel like I can tell you this. I'm a spy from Russia."

"Why do you do that?"

"Do what?" I ask innocently.

"That," he says.

I know what he's talking about. My stories. I've always told them, probably since I could form sentences. The stories became more frequent after my mom moved out. And even more frequent after what happened this summer. I turn to Pony, unsure how to answer.

Sounds crazy, but I want to tell him everything. There's this feeling growing in my stomach, warm and happy. I could blame it on the tablespoon of vodka and prank spree, but I think it might be something else.

"Can I see your phone?" I ask.

"Why would I give my phone to a Russian troll?"

"Troll?" I ask, deeply offended.

"Pretty troll?"

I ignore him being cute and grab his phone from the cup holder.

"Give me your passcode," I demand.

"No way, spy."

I'm not getting in this phone, and time is running out. There are only two things you can do with a locked iPhone: call 911 and get into the camera. Calling emergency services seems dramatic. Instead, I slide the camera open, switch to video, hold up the phone so it's level to my face—at a generous angle—and hit record.

"Hi Pony. It's me, Georgia. Four-six-nine-three-two-seven-six-five-five-zero. That's my number. You didn't ask for it, and

47

you certainly don't deserve it, but now you have it. Byeeeee!"

I end the video and toss the phone into Pony's lap. "Guess the ball is in your court," I say, then get out of his car. Maybe Mia is right: I do need to move on. What would she think about me dating the new guy?

PONY, 6:55 P.M.

My windows are down, the volume is on high, and I'm driving way too fast. (Well, as fast as a station wagon can go without exploding.) A girl gave me her number. Not just a girl, a cute cheerleader. I love my new life, and my new school, and the new Pony. I'm bouncing in my seat like I've eaten a pound of sugar.

I pull up into my usual spot on the street by the mailbox. My dad commandeered the garage for his Man Cave of beer drinking and football watching, so the driveway is reserved for my parents. But it's empty. The windows are dark. No one is home. This does not happen often.

This is standard-issue army housing at its finest. A cookie-cutter two-story house with two trees in the lawn, tucked in between two other cookie-cutter houses. The house is painted bright yellow, like the inside of an egg. Mom has been vocal in her dislike of the yolk house, but she knows it's more of a long-stay motel than a home.

She decorates and arranges each house we live in nearly the same. Same couch, coffee table, dining table, all in the same place from house to house. It's my mom who makes anyplace a home.

I drop my bag at the door, no time to waste, and spread out on the couch . . . with my shoes on. I'm a rebel.

Mom is usually cooking dinner now, but she must be out shopping. Probably at Target—that place is like crack for moms. They wheel the big red carts around looking for their next hit of smartly designed wash towels.

I dig the remote out of the couch cushions and put on Netflix. I've been working my way through the cannon of David Cronenberg. He's made movies for decades, but I'm focused on his campy horror films from the eighties. Movies like *Videodrome* and *Scanners* are equal parts awful and awesome. They leave me completely unsettled.

I'm finishing up one of his biggest hits, *The Fly*, the creepy story of a man changing into a fly. I suppose he's also transitioned, M-T-F (man to fly). The scenes really stick with me. There's no way to look at Jeff Goldblum the same after watching him morph into a big slimy fly.

The movie ends and the credits roll. That's my dream—to work on a movie set and see my name crawl across the screen. What job would I do? Who knows. How do I get there? No idea. But I would do anything. I'd even oversee the trash cans full of fake blood and green slime.

It's fair to say that I'm at the obsession level with movies. It started very young with Disney and Pixar and escalated to Kubrick and Scorsese. Movies have helped me get through some dark times. They are my escape from the real world, even for just ninety minutes.

I grab my phone and watch the video of Georgia reciting her

phone number. It's real. And she's real cute. I was frozen when she was sitting in my car, recording it, but now I feel like I can fly. My head is swimming with possibility.

I watch the video again. And one more time to get the number. Now I can reach out to her whenever. Matter of fact, she *wants* me to reach out. I open a text window and stare at the blank screen.

A real man would wait. I learned that during my self-taught boy boot camp this summer. I had some serious catching up to do, especially in the dating department. I spent late nights at my computer poring over girl advice on Reddit and watching rom-coms. I even read some of those cheesy pickup-artist books. Most of the "advice" in the books was bad and borderline illegal, but I did learn some things. And all my research would advise me to make her wait.

Mom comes through the door, arms full of bags from her Target score.

"A little help here, please," she says.

I jump up, pocket my phone, and grab the bags from her arms. It takes five trips from the car to the kitchen to unload everything; it's like a clown car of Target bags. I drop the last load on the table—a month supply of LaCroix—and wipe the sweat from my forehead. Mom is sitting at the dining table, flipping through the latest *O* magazine. She looks up and smiles.

"Thank you, honey. How was your first day of school?"

I got a girl's number.

"Fine," I say.

A booming voice comes from the front door. "I'm home!"

Dad announces himself when he walks in the door after work. Every night, without fail, he comes into the kitchen, gives Mom a kiss on the cheek, loosens his tie, and grabs a beer. He is all army, all the time. Even home life is a routine. He's tall and strong with a tight crew cut, and he walks with a slight limp.

"What's for dinner?" he asks, just like he always does.

"I picked up some Thai on the way home," Mom says, opening the paper bag and filling the room with the smell of curry and ginger. Dad heads upstairs to get out of his work clothes, and I grab the plates and utensils to set the table. Eating a pound of pretzel M&M's won't stop me from enjoying some pad Thai and green curry. Also, family dinner isn't optional around here. We sit down at the table with no TV or phones and eat like a family from 1953.

He reenters the kitchen in full Dad drag—frayed cargo shorts, an *ARMY* shirt stretched over the hint of a beer belly, and socks pulled up to his calves *with* sandals. He's the very definition of a man's man. It was completely naive of me, but I thought he would be happy that I was transitioning into a boy. He always wanted a son, and then he got one.

Once everyone has filled their plates, we go around the table and talk about our days. Answering this can be like tiptoeing though a minefield of potential explosions from Dad. Most nights, I try to gauge his mood and tailor my answer to that.

Tonight, Mom goes first. She is "feeling the heat" from co-ordinating the yearly fund-raiser for Meals on Wheels. That's my mom for you, always thinking about others and trying to help.

They both look at me. My turn to report on my day. Dad seems distracted tonight but generally happy. I swallow a mouthful of creamy chicken curry and blurt out, "I got a job."

Complete silence. Record-scratch moment. This is new information for my parents.

My mom tilts her head. "What will you be doing, honey?"

"I'm working in the movie business," I answer.

They bust out laughing. I realize we didn't discuss my official job title at the interview. I'm terrible at this.

"Personal assistant," I guess. "I'm helping an old actor get his stuff in order."

"Oh! A famous hoarder?" Mom loves celebrities and gossip.

"No, he's . . . dying."

Another record-scratch moment. I'm going for a high score tonight.

"How sad." Mom covers her mouth. "What's his name?"

"Ted?"

She gasps. "Danson?"

"No," I assure her. "I mean, maybe. I don't actually know his last name yet," I admit.

"Why the need for employment all of a sudden?" Dad asks with an ominous tone.

"I need money," I say.

"For what?"

"You know for what, Dad."

"Don't take that tone with me," he says.

Mom jumps in. "Well, I think it's great." She's always quick to defuse a heated moment between me and my dad.

"What does it pay?" he asks.

"Enough," I say flatly.

He grunts. "Sounds weird to me. Some dying old man all alone in some house, and he wants to pay my daughter—"

Not your daughter.

"—to go clean and do god knows what. Helen, do you think she should do this?"

Not she.

My blood is boiling now. All my little pronoun victories from today gone.

"Dad," I say.

"What?" he asks, faking innocence. His eyes meet mine; he's ready for a fight.

Mom places her hand on his. "I'm fine with it, as long as your grades don't suffer."

And with that, Mom has ended this conversation. Dad goes back to eating.

After finishing dinner and clearing the plates, I head upstairs to my room and kick off my shoes. I find myself in the full-length mirror and watch as I unbutton my shirt, revealing my binder. I wear it under my clothes to smooth out my chest.

I had already developed *boobs* when I started taking hormone blockers. I was a year too late. I hate saying boobs almost as much as I hate having them. No, I hate having them more than just about anything.

Gender-affirming compression binders come in all shapes and sizes—the most popular fit looks like a sports bra—but I prefer the more masculine tank top. It's basically a medical bandage undershirt made of thick polyester that's so tight it restricts breathing and squishes my organs together.

Exactly what you want to wear for twelve hours on a hot summer day.

I have read stories about trans men developing medical issues from wearing cheap binders for too long. Serious stuff like collapsed lungs and broken ribs.

To me, it's worth the risk. No matter how much I complain about these polyester torture traps, I wouldn't leave my house without one on. Binders have become my protective layer, my second skin, my shield that makes me feel safe and more myself. This is the discomfort that I put myself through to feel more comfortable.

The term everyone is using now is *gender dysphoria*. It's a fancy way of describing the distress of being in the wrong body. The level of dysphoria that a transgender person feels varies and often causes depression, anger, insecurity, and sometimes suicide.

I bind my chest to ease my discomfort. Chest binders aren't a solution to my dysphoria, just an incredibly uncomfortable Band-Aid. The solution is top surgery, but I would need to rob a bank to afford it.

Removing the binder from my body is no easy task. (Putting it on is no walk in the park either.) I grab at the bottom like I'm removing any other shirt and take a quick breath to suck in my stomach. The trick is to yank the binder up and over my head in one smooth movement. Most of the time, the polyester clings to my body like it has abandonment issues. And occasionally, just to keep me humble, the binder gets caught around my shoulders, covering my face and trapping my arms over my head. I hop around like a bad magician unable to escape his straitjacket.

I count to three in my head and pull. The binder peels off easy this time. My skin goes cold and prickly, happy to feel air. I throw it across the room and take a deep, unrestricted breath. I've been waiting to inhale.

I spin around a couple times, the colors of the movie posters plastering my walls blurring together. I stop and return to the full-length mirror nailed to my closet door. Nothing more honest than a head-to-toe mirror.

My shoulders aren't wide enough, and my posture is hunched from trying to hide my boobs all those years before binders. I wouldn't say my body has curves, but my hips are round. There's no exercise to unround hips; I checked. No body hair. And—I'm missing one important body part.

I hate that I hate my body, but I hate it.

Like Photoshop, I wish my body came with the Copy/Paste function. I'd paste a male chest over mine. Then I would drop in some abs with just a hint of six-pack, broader shoulders, and that trail of hair that starts at the belly button and goes down.

Most importantly, I would add a dick. Any size, don't care.

After that was done, I would cut that body out and paste it on the beach. Swim trunks and no shirt. Girls spread out on beach towels checking me out. I am comfortable and happy and normal. I open my eyes and frown at the mirror. I am so far away from the body I want. This is my dysphoria.

I throw on a shirt and head over to the crown jewel of my room—an extra-large flat screen. My only present last year for Christmas. Worth it. I dig into Netflix and decide on a comfort movie (*Kill Bill*), saddle up to my desk, and crack open my laptop. First stop—without fail—is Twitter to catch up on anything that happened today, but the only trending topics are some celebrity's spinout at a Shake Shack. I move over to Facebook and scan through the posts in a private group for trans teens from all over the world. There's always good discussion on binding, dating, testosterone, and all sorts of random crap. Even though I joined the group over a year ago, I have yet to write one post or even a comment. I guess I'm stealth online, too.

Just for fun, I type *Georgia Roberts* into the search on Instagram. She's got a couple hundred pictures and nearly a thousand followers. For context, I have sixty-three followers. The most recent post is a TBT picture of her at a football game, in which she's getting hugged by a big fuzzy bear—183 likes. And here's one of her at a concert with friends—122 likes. I'm careful to not accidently like any of the photos. And farther down the feed, a picture of some guy—a handsome guy—with his arm around her and a Christmas tree photobombing in the background—270 likes.

Reality comes crashing down on me. There's no chance for me—a secret trans guy who looks nothing like that guy in the picture—with someone like her. I'm mad at myself for thinking I had a chance. I close out of Insta and take a deep, binderless breath.

It's getting late. I'm fading fast. There's one thing to do before hitting the sack. To be honest, I have put it off all day. I open Gmail and click on the email I have been trying to avoid:

FROM: assistant@dallassurgerypartners.com
TO: PonyJacobs@gmail.com
DATE: August 26 at 3:40 p.m.
SUBJECT: Re: Transgender top surgery

Pony,

Thanks for inquiring about gender-affirming chest surgery.

To answer your question, here's the checklist of what you will need to qualify for the procedure:

- **Mental health professional note documenting gender dysphoria**
- **If under 18, letter of parental consent**
- **Gender markers changed on legal documents**
- **Down payment estimated at $12,500 (half of the procedure cost) with the remaining balance to be paid the day of surgery.**

Let us know when you are ready for a consultation. Dr. King has years of experience in this field, and we are confident you will be happy with the results!

Thanks,
Trisha

They do not make this easy.

The doctor's note and having the F(emale) changed to M(ale) on my birth certificate and social security card will be annoying. Lots of waiting in long lines at government offices. But doable. My parents will never consent to the operation, but that won't matter in eight months when I turn eighteen. It's the money. My new job will help, but it's going to take years to come up with that amount. I have begged my parents for a loan with interest to no avail. I can still hear my dad: "Not one of my dollars will go to this, and that's final."

They think I'm going through a phase, and I'll regret any permanent changes. If they only knew how it felt to live in this body, even for a day, they would be writing checks and driving me to the hospital. I hit Reply.

FROM: PonyJacobs@gmail.com
TO: assistant@dallassurgerypartners.com
DATE: August 27 at 10:01 p.m.
SUBJECT: Re: Transgender top surgery

Hi Trisha, thank you for the information.

I will get back in touch when I am eligible for a consultation.

Have a great day,
Pony

I push around the little plastic dog toy on my desk that poops jellybeans. There's only one way to get this surgery. After I graduate, I'm going to delay college and get a full-time job. Otherwise, I will be in binders for at least four more years, and I can't even wrap my head around that possibility.

I get up from my desk, zombie-walk to bed, and spread out on the cool sheets. I crack open the assigned reading for AP English, *The Catcher in the Rye*, but keep reading the same sentence over and over, thinking about Georgia.

My studying is interrupted by shuffling feet outside my door. "Mom?"

She peeks her head in. "Didn't want to bother . . ."

I set my book down. "You're never a bother, Mom."

She comes in and starts picking up clothes off my floor. "So"—she lowers her voice—"are you going to be all right working with someone who won't be around much longer?"

I have only been though one death—my grandma's. She passed when I was a sophomore, and it was awful. It was so sad that Rocky *almost* cried. A sight I have never seen. She might have been born without tears. But I knew Nana all my life and loved her. I won't know this guy, not really. And I need the money.

"Yeah, I guess," I say. "Ask me again in a month."

"I will, honey." She sits down on my bed. "You know, your father tries. He does. It's harder for him."

"I know, Mom," I say, because I love her.

She runs her hand through my hair, messing it up.

"Thank you, Mom." I don't need to explain why.

"I love you, son."

Son.

Wednesday, August 28

GEORGIA, 7:10 A.M.

My phone alarm wakes me—OMG, it's so loud. I'm pushing around the magazines on my bed in hopes of locating my phone and stopping the madness. I zonked out last night while reading an article in the *New Yorker* about the drama behind the curtain of a Broadway musical.

I find my phone (under my pillow), stop the alarm, and see a text from an unsaved number. It must be Pony. On the record, I don't usually give my number to a guy that quick. Off the record, I blame all the endorphins running through my body from the prank. And how cute he looked.

I open the text: Hope u had a good first day, Georgie.

Why would Pony say that? And why would he call me Georgie? We aren't there yet.

Crap. Crapcrapcrap.

I *do* know this number. It's my ex. There's no name saved because I deleted the contact when we broke up. He must have sensed that I was trying to move on. I feel like a freshman caught in a net. Regret kicks in hard. I should have blocked his number.

I bury my face into the pillow and scream for a minute. I flip back over and stare at the ceiling. I am so over Anthony. The night of the breakup was too devastating. It's best told as a dishy gossip column:

HILLCREST HEARTBREAK
Addison, TX, June 28, 2019

Senior quarterback and junior cheerleader go separate ways after a humiliating and public scene unfolded at Tiffany's end-of-school party on Friday night.

Sources close to cheerleader claim the seemingly perfect couple had decided to split when he left for college in August but wanted to spend the summer together. Looks like the quarterback had a different game plan.

Spotted at Tiffany's party, QB invited newly elected dance-team captain upstairs for private talk. In the bathroom! We all know the most meaningful conversation happens next to a toilet! Minutes later, the cheerleader ran upstairs and kicked the bathroom door open, revealing the quarterback and the starlet in a rather compromising position. And if you think that's bad, you'll never believe what happens after that . . .

I don't like talking about the next part. So let's not.

I look out my window expecting to see the lawn covered in toilet paper or some other retribution for yesterday's epic prank. Looks undisturbed. Revenge surely awaits us, unclear when.

I stand motionless in the shower, letting the hot water hit my back, wondering what Anthony is doing right now. He's a freshman at Texas Tech and pledging a fraternity, so he's probably passed out. Ant couldn't wait for college. It was so annoying to listen to him talk constantly about the dorms, the parties, the independence. There's no doubt he was drunk when he sent that text last night. Does that even count?

I try on a few outfits before settling on my go-to blue dress. I'd be down to wear yoga pants and a sleep shirt to school, but Mia demands that the cheerleaders always look as "flawless and fancy" as possible. We represent the squad (and the school, and America). We must dress accordingly.

While driving to school—blasting my air conditioner and Taylor Swift—I think about *why* Anthony reached out to me. I have only seen him once since the shitshow night at Tiffany's party, and that didn't go well either. I told him to stay far away. I was equal parts mad at him and afraid that I would relapse and get back with him. After what he did, there would be no regaining my reputation—or dignity—if I slipped.

I hate myself for saying this, but Anthony swept me off my feet. I dated a couple guys before him, but my feet were firmly planted, and I was in control. Not with Anthony. We met at a keg party in the woods the summer before junior year. I was hanging out with my senior cheerleading friends, celebrating their recent graduation. I did my best to act like I wasn't devastated about them leaving.

Someone started a game of spin the bottle. We all joined in because why not. I dread when this game gets going at parties, but I didn't want to seem uncool by sitting out. I took big gulps of my beer while secretly praying that spinning bottle never landed on me. Making out with some guy as my friends watch? I can think of better hobbies.

My opinion on the game quickly changed when the new senior captain of the football team—this gorgeous guy with big ears and blue eyes—stepped up to take his turn. I wasn't going to be mad if I had to kiss him. He gave the bottle a strong spin, and I held my breath. The Miller Lite bottle made a couple rotations before he reached down, stopped it, and pointed it directly at me. Every part of my body heated up. He walked over, helped me to my feet, pushed my hair behind my ear, leaned in slowly, and kissed me. I could feel his stubble against my face. I could hear my girls yelling and cheering. I could taste whiskey and tobacco. It was intoxicating.

We stopped after a few seconds and both looked around at everyone watching. Getting super shy, I was starting to sit back down when he grabbed my hand and led me into the woods. I was on top of the world. We hid behind a tree and kissed, our bodies pressing against each other.

After that night, we were together. There was no reason to waste time. It was a perfect match: football guy and cheerleader girl. We hung out with other couples, the guys wandered off to play video games, and the girls talked in circles about our relationships and clothes. I didn't care; I did it for him. He got my total and complete attention. I liked making him happy, but I eventually lost myself.

I find my desk in first period and try to forget Anthony. I'm composing mean and super hurtful texts to him in my mind. He's winning when I think about him this much.

I'm spiraling, but just a little. Like, a cute amount.

I feel my calf vibrate. It's my phone tucked into my bag. I reach down, low-key, so the teacher doesn't catch me. Another unidentified number: Look at you, wearing civilian clothes.

There's Pony. *Finally.* I look over. He smiles at me.

Without any thought, I text back: Enjoying the view?

A few seconds later, I hear something hit the ground and bounce a few times.

Someone yells, "New kid dropped his phone!"

And for the first time today, I smile.

12:17 P.M.

At lunch, Lauren and I walk around the school. When we have a problem to solve, we walk and talk it out. It's boiling hot but nice to get some exercise. I'm drinking a Diet Coke and trying to keep up with Ms. Long Legs over here.

Lauren is going on and on about college. I suppose that's a normal discussion topic for two seniors, but it's not where my head is at. Last year, Mia, Lauren, Kelly, and I swore that we would go to Texas Tech. A decent state school in Lubbock, famous for its parties. We would pledge a sorority and keep living our popular-girl fantasy. I'm not against the idea completely—the tuition is affordable, and Lubbock isn't too far from Addison and my dad. But maybe I want to go to a school known more for its academics than its partying.

"You can do better," I say to Lauren.

"But Matt is going to Tech," she argues.

"Lo, you are so smart. That big, beautiful brain in your head could get into any college."

She stops walking to think about it. "Well, my dad is University of Texas alum. It's expensive, but I'm applying for the Hispanic Scholarship Fund. I could go there, but Mia . . ."

"Mia what?"

"She would be so mad."

Which horoscope sign makes you the smartest and nicest person but unable to stand up for yourself? Whatever it is, that's Lauren. "Mia isn't your mommy," I remind her.

"What about you?" she asks.

That's a loaded question. Anthony is at Texas Tech. It's a big school—over thirty thousand people—but that doesn't mean I would be safe from him. I did some research and found out they don't have a strong journalism program. My dream school is Columbia in New York, but that's so out of reach. "I guess I'll go to Tech and get back with Anthony. That's why he reached out, right?"

"No, Georgia. You are done with him. It's that simple."

"It's not that simple," I say. "One freaking text and I'm drowning."

Lauren starts taking big lunging steps. "OK, then text him back and see what he wants." This girl is flip-flopping like a senator. I'm probably consulting the wrong person on this crisis—Lauren and Matt have been together since sophomore year. She's got no point of reference for this kind of pain.

I grunt and stop walking. "This isn't helping."

Lauren puts her arm around my shoulders. We walk over to the steps leading to the gym, and she sits down beside me. "This happened on *The Bachelor* last season. The exact same thing."

I cut in, "I feel so uncomfortable, I just want to climb out of my skin."

"Oh," Lauren says with a concerned face.

"Lo, everyone at school knows what happened that night. I can see them whispering about it when I walk by. Everyone looks at me different."

"No way. He looked like a huge jackass," she says.

"We had a deal. The summer was ours. Then he cheated on me. With *Taylor*. I hate him for that."

"Taylor isn't the problem. And the cheating wasn't the worst part of that night."

I stand up and brush myself off. "I'm mad at myself for letting it happen."

"You think it's your fault?" Lauren asks, hopping up.

"You wouldn't understand. You and Matt are perfect."

"We aren't—"

Lauren stops speaking, and her face goes white like she's seen a ghost.

From behind me I hear, "Hi, Georgia."

Oh no. I turn around and see *her.*

"Hello, Taylor."

She is twirling a piece of hair around her finger. She always does that. It drives me NUTS.

"It's so hot out, I can't see straight," she says.

"You know, that's the first sign of a stroke," I offer. I'd rather run into traffic than have this conversation. Why is she right here, right now? Maybe we said her name too many times and accidently summoned her. If we don't get out of here ASAP, I might say something that I'll regret, like *Why would you hook up with my boyfriend?* for starters.

Taylor lowers her head and kicks the dirt. "Georgia, I just wanted to see . . . if we can talk?"

"That sounds like so much fun, Taylor, but Lauren got stung by a bee and she's allergic to bees. We need to get to the nurse."

Lauren leans in to my ear and whispers, "I'm not allergic to bees."

"OK," Taylor says, "but maybe we can talk soon?"

Maybe never.

"Sure," I say while leading Lauren away.

I'm still fuming about running into Taylor when I walk into the last class of the day, Chem Lab. Rational Me knows that it's not Taylor's fault. But Irrational Me can't get over it. Taylor was fully aware that Anthony and I were together; therefore, I am never ever forgiving her. Solid logic. Maybe I'll show her by getting back with Anthony.

The class has started, and Mr. Glover is warming up his pun game. "*Bunsen burner?* Get it? Hey, that was a chemistry joke! Why no *reaction?* Guys, I'm in my *element* here."

I have zero percent focus. I lean over to Pony. "He's in the zone. The pun zone."

"I'm worried. I think this is a cry for help," Pony says.

I laugh, maybe a little too loudly. Mr. Glover hears me and takes it as validation that his jokes are landing. They aren't, but it's endearing. I have kept my distance from Pony all day, but it's impossible in Chem Lab—we sit two feet away from each other. I look over at him. He's got piercing green eyes.

"You OK, Georgia?" he asks.

"Yes, of course," I say, a little too defensively. He doesn't know me. Why would he know if something was wrong?

"Cool," he says, then returns his focus back to Mr. Glover.

A few minutes later, I elbow him. "Did you know that dinosaurs actually had human skin?"

"You don't say?"

"I do say. Have you seen any pictures of dinosaurs? Pics or didn't happen, Pony."

"Well, scientists have devoted their lives to this kind of research, but please continue . . ."

"Shhhh," I quiet him. "I've read reports that dinosaurs had feathers. Feathers, Pony! How fancy."

Pony tilts his head. "Didn't the *Guardian* prove that wrong?"

That's the sexiest thing a guy has ever said to me. "I think I saw that," I lie.

"Do you believe in the first moon landing?" Pony asks.

"No," I say, because I don't.

He smirks at me. "I know exactly who you are, Georgia."

"You don't know anything about me," I say, returning his dumb smirk.

Mr. Glover interrupts our tête-à-tête. "I'm sorry, is my class *boron* you two in the back?"

We both look up at the teacher with immediate focus and remain still, like wild animals caught eating garbage.

"Hey, Mr. Glover," Pony says loudly, "what do solids, liquids, and gases have in common?"

Mr. Glover thinks for a moment and then takes the bait. "What?"

"They all *matter*," Pony says, and the class laughs a little, but Mr. Glover cracks up. It might be the funniest thing he has ever heard. I'm stunned. Pony is full of surprises.

Mr. Glover collects himself. "Now students, let's talk mitochondria!"

After it's safe to look away, Pony shifts his attention to writing in his notebook, and I'm left to think about what I don't want to think about. I pull my phone out of my bag and conceal it under my desk. I open Anthony's text and stare at the screen, unsure how to respond.

Pony slides a note over to me with a mischievous smile. A written note—how old-fashioned. I drop my phone in my lap and watch Mr. Glover do the Macarena while singing *"Heeeey, Mitochondria."* I don't think he'll notice.

I unfold the paper, and it's a drawing of a T. rex that looks like Mr. Glover—same mustache and everything—covered in feathers and standing on the moon. I start to laugh but cover my mouth. Pony has this big smile with bright, burning eyes.

I put my hand on his shoulder to push him away, but that's not what I want. There's an electricity between us, like that shock from clothes fresh out of the dryer. I let my hand fall down his arm. We both turn our attention back to the teacher, like we just did something wrong.

A few minutes later, I remember that my phone is in my lap. I grab it and read the text from last night: Hope u had a good first day, Georgie.

You know what? I did have a good first day. We pulled an A+ prank that everyone is talking about, and I met someone new. I can do better than Anthony. I put my phone away and sneak a look at Pony.

I'm going to stay right here for now.

THREE

Friday, August 30

PONY, 6:45 P.M.

As I walk up the steps to the mansion, I look at the neighborhood. The houses tower over the trees with big windows and fancy cars in the driveways. Each mansion looks different, all silently competing for superiority. We're not in Addison anymore, Toto.

I ring the bell and hear the echo bounce around the house. After a couple minutes, the actor's assistant answers the door. He seems confused by my presence, even though he interviewed, hired, and told me to be here.

"Hey, Victor, it's Pony . . . You told me to stop by now?"

"Yes, of course I did. Come in, come in, come in!" Victor moves out of the way, and I walk in. "Mr. Pony, we are so glad you will be working for us! Now, let's go to the study. The big guy is up and around. He'll want to meet you."

Victor doesn't walk; he flutters around like a nervous butterfly. He's a small guy—I'm a little taller than him (doesn't happen often). My heart is beating out of my chest. I am ready to meet the mystery celebrity. We walk down an endless hallway, passing by so many rooms. All the doors shut.

"And this is the study!"

We walk into a dark and dusty room. Victor opens the window shutters, filling the room with light. It's stuffy, and the smell of old smoke burns my nose, but—holy shit—there's an Oscar on the shelf. This place is like a movie museum, floor-to-ceiling books and mementos. This is my heaven.

Victor pats the couch, "Sit! Sit, sit, sit!"

He heads over to the bar cart and readies some glasses. "What would you like?"

My knowledge of alcohol is limited to warm beer from kegs and bottles of vodka stolen from parents' liquor cabinets.

"Margarita," I say with the opposite of confidence.

Victor looks at me. "How old are you?"

"I'll have water," I say.

"Water it is," he says while pouring a drink for himself and humming some upbeat song.

Victor hands me a glass and sits across from me. "So, Pony, you are agreed to the terms of the employment?"

"Yes," I say, then take an awkward sip. "Sorry, what are the terms again?"

"Silly boy. You are here to organize and box up Ted London's possessions. And for that we will pay you two hundred and fifty dollars per room."

Per room? That's an odd setup. "I accept your terms," I say, because I'm unsure what else to say. I'd probably agree to anything right now. I'm more focused on meeting a famous person. Should I care? Should I not care? Will he be offended if I don't care? What if he finds out that I'm transgender? I sit up and straighten my shoulders.

The door swings open, and an old man (maybe around eighty?) with a perfect head of hair (probably fake?) enters the room. Big guy is accurate—he's a mountain of a man. "So, this is Pony, I presume," the actor says, coughing. I can't place him, but he's got a great face—it's easy to see the movie-star features buried underneath years of aging. He hobbles over to me and extends his hand.

I hesitate.

"It's not contagious, kid," he says.

I grab his hand and give him a firm shake. A good handshake was something I studied during boy boot camp.

"Lovely to meet you, son. I'm Ted London."

Ted London? The name doesn't ring a bell. I'm scanning my mental catalog of movies but coming up empty. He waits patiently for me to speak.

"Hi, I'm—"

"Pony. Yes, interesting name you've got there. I'm sure there's a good story behind it."

He's right, but I'll never tell him.

A moment of silence passes between us. I listen to him struggle for a deep breath. I wish I recognized him, but I don't watch really old movies. This would be less awkward if I could compliment him on something, anything.

"Victor, you found us a real talker here," he says playfully.

I look down, embarrassed. I worry about my voice. At my age, a guy should be almost finished with puberty and have a deep voice that occasionally cracks. I have learned how to lower my voice and keep it steady, but it takes concentration. Shorter words are easier to keep low. I clear my throat. "Just at first, sir."

"It's no bother at all. I can talk enough for the both of us." Ted London pats me on the back. "Now, young Pony, how about we have a tour of the place?"

"Yes, please," I say, then follow behind Ted as he limps toward the door.

"Have you seen that *Hoarders* television show?" he asks.

"Yes," I say. "Is the camera crew stuck under some boxes around here?"

He laughs. "Would you look at that? He's got a sense of humor."

Ted London leads me from room to room, working up enough air in his lungs to tell me stories of his grand Hollywood life. He drops name after name, and I pretend to know who he's talking about. Each room is jam-packed with crap. This man has saved everything from his life: scripts, props, magazines with him on the cover, costumes, photos, endless stuff that couldn't possibly have any value today.

"Jackpot!" Ted holds up a napkin. "Lauren Bacall wrote me a love note on our last day of filming . . . oh dear, what were we filming? Victor, what was the movie Lauren—"

"*A Walk in the Park*," Victor shouts from the study.

"Ah, yes, it was the bar scene. A camera lens broke into pieces, and we had to wait for hours. Luckily for us, the bar was stocked. We got quite loaded, actually. It helped film the scene, no acting needed."

He hands the napkin to me. I try to decipher what it says, but the handwriting is drunken scribble scrabble. Yet he saved it for years and years. We move on to the next room, overflowing with boxes.

"Look!" he says, picking up a framed picture. "It's me and Ronald Reagan!"

I stumble over a box to check it out. "You met a president!"

"Oh no, this isn't real. The prop department doctored it up when I played the vice president in *End Days*."

"Great movie," I say.

"You've seen *End Days*?"

"No," I admit.

He laughs and leads me into another room. I'm starting to feel overwhelmed. I throw myself down on a beanbag in the corner of the room. To be clear, if there's a beanbag chair, I'm going to sit in it.

"So, Mr. London, what have you hired me to do?"

Ted laughs at the question. "I don't know! How would I know? Call me Ted."

"OK, Ted," I say. He doesn't know what he hired me to do?

"I'm dying, Pony. I don't want to leave this world thinking all my treasures are going to the dumpster. I need you to get it in order, for whatever is next."

He rummages through a box of film canisters in search of another story to tell me. What is this guy's deal? Why does he live in a quiet, rich, gated neighborhood outside of Dallas? Shouldn't he be in Hollywood?

I hear some boxes fall over, and I jump out of the beanbag— not easy to do—stepping over stacks of paper to get to him. Ted is still standing, holding on to a wobbling bag of golf clubs. He's a little spacey. Victor brushes past me and puts his arm gently around Ted's shoulders. "I think it's time for you to rest."

Victor leads him out of the room, and I'm left wondering what to do next. I can barely organize the apps on my phone. I hit the beanbag again and feel my pocket vibrate. There's a text from Max: Dude. What is going on?

Max is my best friend. We met at the back-to-school mixer at the Dallas LGBTQIA Center last year. I'm still shocked that I went to that dance alone. Sometimes I can surprise myself with my courage. Max and I instantly bonded over playing pool, being too shy to talk to girls, and being transgender. It's been helpful to have a friend who is going through the same things as me. He also introduced me to his queer circle of friends.

I text back: Currently at dying actor's house making a few dollars . . .

MAX: Excuse me, what?

PONY: And I think I have a crush

MAX: On the dying actor?

PONY: Ha. No.

MAX: Drop a pin, man. I am on the way to save you!

It's true. If I needed anything at all, Max would be there to help.

PONY: How's your week going?

MAX: Planning a takeover of the Plano community board Monday night!!! The bullying will be addressed!!! You in?

PONY: I would! But I have to work ...

I don't have to work on Monday night, but I am excited to have a valid excuse to get out of things now.

MAX: You suck. What is this job? What is this crush?

I'm not doing this over text.

PONY: IHOP at 8?

MAX: YASSSS!

And another text with ten pride-flag emojis.

I peel myself out of the beanbag chair and immediately knock over a stack of film canisters.

What did I get myself into here? I weave around boxes and trash bags of clothes, trying to find some order in this chaos. A padded envelope filled with yellowing Polaroid photos catches my eye. I fish my hand in, grab a handful of photos, and start flipping through them. A tanned Ted London at a fancy pool party. A satisfied Ted London leaning on an expensive car. A tuxedoed

Ted London at a formal event. The people who surround him are all beautiful and happy and rich. What a life.

I get to the last photo of the pile and see someone I do recognize. I say out loud to nobody, "Holy shit, John Travolta!"

"No, just me, Victor!"

I turn around and see Victor standing behind me with an iced tea in each hand.

"Thanks," I say, still in shock. I reach for the drink and kick over a bag, photos spilling all over the carpet.

"Mr. London was quite famous in his time, yes he was . . ." Victor crouches down and pushes around the photos while sipping his straw. "He knew everybody. Started getting bigger movie roles. He was on his way."

"Then what happened?" I ask.

Victor stops and stands up, looking me dead in eyes. "Not everyone gets to the top, Pony."

"I think I read that in a fortune cookie," I say.

Victor ignores my joke and picks up a photo from the ground. "He had the most beautiful wife," he says, handing me the Polaroid. It's an elated Ted London kissing a blindingly beautiful woman.

"What happened to them?"

"Divorced."

"Too bad. So my payment is two hundred and fifty dollars per room, right?"

"Correct. With my final inspection. I'll pay you at the end of every other week."

I do some quick math: $25,000 (the cost of the surgery) divided by $250. Shit, that's one hundred rooms. "And how many rooms need to be organized?" I ask.

Victor shrugs. "Ten?"

My heart sinks.

He claps his hands twice and says, "OK, get to work!"

I spend an hour stacking boxes and having a panic attack about how much money I need to have my surgery. I sneak out of Ted's house undetected by Victor, but it doesn't matter; I don't have set hours.

Twenty minutes later, I pull into the IHOP parking lot at eight on the dot. As usual, I'm on time, and Max is late. He goes to a liberal arts high school in Fort Worth, about an hour away from me, so we meet in the middle and try new restaurants in Denton.

Max and I have different approaches to our trans identities. He is very out and very proud, and I like to think that he's proud enough for the both of us. Max is always mentoring youth at the LGBTQIA Center or disrupting public hearings. He has a blue Mohawk, and most of his shirts have funny queer slogans. There are social-justice buttons covering his jackets and activist bumper stickers all over his car. It makes buying gifts for him easy.

Ten minutes later, Max walks in and smiles, his lip piercing gleaming. I jump up, and we hug. He lifts me off my feet and shakes me around like a baby. I'm a tiny guy compared to him. We sit down and laugh at how silly that must have looked. A feeling of relief washes over me—I'm happy to be here with my buddy.

I really needed to talk to someone. If my binder allowed a deep breath, I would take it right now.

Our waitress saunters up to our table and asks what we want to drink. I muster up my most masculine voice and order a Diet Coke. She jots it down and turns to Max. "And for the young lady?"

Shots fired. Max doesn't miss an opportunity to educate someone about pronoun assumption. Or gender constructs. Or the best *Black Mirror* episode. Confrontation is not my thing. I freeze up and cover my face with the menu. If there's one thing that gets Max heated, it's being misgendered.

"I'll have a coffee," he says, then returns to the menu. She writes it down and walks off, smacking her gum.

"Max, you feeling OK? *Young lady?*"

"I know, I know. I kept quiet for you, sweetie, and for the kids," he says, winking.

"Thanks," I say.

"Pony, if you absolutely must know the truth"—he feigns frustration and throws his menu down—"I came to the realization at Applebee's last week, when the waitress set my soup down in front of me—"

"Soup in the summer? You're a monster," I say, pretending to ignore the real issue.

He continues, "I decided that the people who handle my food are always right, until I have my food, and then, and only then, will I have a mature and adult conversation with them about their utter ignorance. But not a word until my soup is out of range of their spit."

"Or worse," I say.

"Or worse," he repeats.

It's smart thinking. When you're seen as different, it's best to go with the flow, pick your battles, and plan the right times to push back. Our waitress returns with our drinks. Once she leaves, I raise my glass in a toast and say (but not too loudly), "Here's to being trans in Texas."

We clink glasses.

"OK, enough foreplay, Pony. Out with it! Don't make me beg."

"I kind of want to see you beg," I say.

"TELL ME ABOUT YOUR NEW GIRLFRIEND!" Max says, loud enough to turn a few heads.

I wave my hands in surrender to shut him up and say, "It's new."

"No shit, Casanova. It's the first week of school."

"I don't know how I feel about it yet. Get this—we have every class together. And . . . she's a cheerleader."

"A cheerleader?" Max throws his head back and lets out a wild laugh.

"She has brown eyes that turn golden when the sun hits them, and—"

"Oh, honeybaby." He stops me.

"What?" I ask.

"You're already on the hook," Max warns.

I sit back and fight my impulse to be defensive. I don't feel on the hook yet, but the whole thing is intriguing. And sure, I have imagined our wedding and life together. But that doesn't mean I am on the hook.

"No way. If anything, she's on the hook," I say like a tough guy.

"How much do you think about her?"

Too much.

"Almost never," I say.

"Lie," he says. "How do you feel when she walks into the room?"

My breath stops.

"Practically nothing," I say.

"And does she know you're trans?"

No fucking way.

"I don't think so . . . ," I say.

"Oh shit, Pony," Max says with concerned eyes. "Dude, you need to tell her."

I look around and quiet my voice. "It's too soon. I'll get there when I get there," I say, then take a drink of my Coke. "I'm having trouble wrapping my head around this thing. She's popular and pretty. Why would she waste any time talking to me?"

"'Cause you're a little stud." Max grabs my hand and looks me in the eye. "You've got to believe that you are good enough, and then you will get what you want."

He brings my hand close to his face—I try to pull away but I'm too late—and plants a wet kiss on my knuckle. That's Max, sage advisor and uncomfortable-affection giver. I yank my hand away and wipe it on my jeans, pretending to hate it.

"What's your fear here, Pony?"

"Another Joni situation," I admit.

"Right," he says, understanding.

I met Joni online last summer. She was the first girl I dated after coming out as trans. She's a Goth-lite girl with long black hair and confidence for days. I didn't see her that often—she didn't go to my school—but we were in constant contact. Getting a text from Joni became addictive. Each time my phone dinged, my heart would race. I was acting like those lab rats trained to touch a button to get food. You start off slow and steady, but eventually all you do is touch that damn button. That was me and Joni.

We had something—it felt very real—and I was finally someone's boyfriend. I was so happy, I walked around five inches off the ground until I started to connect the dots. I hadn't met her friends or family. When we did hang out, she always traveled to me. No social-media mentions with me, not even a snap. And then it hit me: I was her secret boyfriend. That sucked. I finally asked her about it during one of our late-night FaceTime sessions.

I'll never forget what she said: "Pony, *I* might be OK with you being trans, but that doesn't mean everyone will be OK with you being trans."

It was devastating to hear that, and I should have ended it, but I didn't. I did start wondering just how OK she really was with me being trans. We hadn't done much beyond kissing. My gut told me to break up with her, but I stubbornly ignored it. A week after that talk, three months into our relationship, Joni disappeared. I wish I could report that I was completely chill about her ghosting me, but I wasn't. I continued texting and calling. It was a low point for me.

About a month later, Joni finally responded: Dating a guy now. Sorry.

Not *another* guy, *a* guy. That small grammatical error (or choice) broke my heart.

"Earth to Pony," Max says while snapping his fingers. I look up and see our beloved waitress staring darts at me and tapping her pen against the notepad. For the first time, I understand what *stink eye* means.

"Burger and fries, no tomato. Please."

We hand her the menus as she smacks her gum and pretends to care. She taps her pen against Max's coffee cup. "Do you want me to top that off, princess?"

Max and I make immediate eye contact. "No, thanks," Max says with a forced smile that makes me bust out laughing as soon as she walks off.

"How's Wendy?" I ask.

"I think she's going to be my life partner."

Max falls in love within minutes of meeting a person. I have seen this cycle all too often. He burns too hot too fast. They will be picking gender-neutral baby names today, and she'll be gone tomorrow. I give this one two more weeks.

"So, you have sex?" I ask as casually as humanly possible.

Max shrugs. "Yeah, we do."

I have another completely casual question that I have wanted to ask for a long time. Sure, I have done my fair share of online research about trans sex, but it's different to talk to someone face-to-face. Even though I can't make eye contact.

"What's sex to you?" I ask.

"What's sex to me?" Max says in mock horror. "What's sex to anyone?"

"A mutual exchange of bodily fluids?" I offer.

"Yes. Gross, but yes. And—connection. Mentally, spiritually, but mostly physically."

Our conversation is interrupted by the food getting delivered to our table. My burger is more tomatoes than meat. I remove them and take a bite. The burger is salty but decent.

Back to the trans-birds-and-trans-bees talk.

"But we don't have the proper equipment," I say between bites.

Max makes a sour face. "What's proper, Pony? Sex is about two, or more, consenting people making each other feel good. Usually naked." He stops and smiles. "Besides, what the lord forgot, the sex shop provides."

"Do you have one?" I ask.

"No, don't be ridiculous," he says. "I have three."

My face gets as red as those discarded tomatoes. Max continues, "When you're ready, I will be your trusted shepherd to the promised land, my favorite queer-owned sex shop in Dallas."

I feel my phone vibrate in my pocket. And again. And again.

I'm dying to check, hoping it's Georgia. I wait until we are done eating and Max hits the bathroom before checking my phone.

GEORGIA: Pony.

GEORGIA: I need a favor.

GEORGIA: You OWE me.

PONY: Do I?

GEORGIA: Yeah you borrowed my pencil today?

For the record, I have ten pencils in my backpack. I was bored to tears in calculus and wanted to talk to her.

PONY: The world will never forget your selfless act of kindness.

GEORGIA: Aaaaand you never gave it back. Jerk.

PONY: Finders keepers.

GEORGIA: A giraffe escaped from the zoo today and destroyed my car.

PONY: And you want me to find the giraffe?

GEORGIA: I need a ride to school on Monday.

A rush of warmth runs through my body. She could have asked anyone for a ride. Could this be happening? My mind is racing. If this was a rom-com movie, I would be running around and high-fiving everyone at IHOP as balloons and streamers fell from the ceiling. I need to play this right—a cat gets bored if they catch the mouse too quick.

I text back: I'm sure there's a bus that owes you a favor, too.

"Who you texting, lover boy?" Max asks as he slides back into the booth.

I pocket my phone and lie. "Mom."

This is my little wonderful secret for now.

America's favorite waitress comes around and drops the check on the table. Max grabs it before I move an inch. "I got this one, playboy," he says, pulling a gold credit card out of his wallet. His parents are mediumly wealthy. He has endless spending money but not enough to completely ruin him.

"Would you look at that?" the waitress says playfully to me. "You gonna let the lady pay for you?"

"OK. Hi. Susanna, is it?" Max says with a frustrated but even voice.

"Yeah," she confirms, then taps her name tag.

Even though I knew this was coming, I want to melt into a puddle and ooze right out the door. Max begins, "I am transgender. My pronouns are *he*, *him*, and *his*. And here's my tip to you, free of charge—if a customer is dressed, *or presenting*, more male than female, then address them with those pronouns. Or use neutral terms like *buddy* or *pal*."

Poor Susanna. I don't know if Max's impromptu lessons help to change the person or further the trans agenda, but he's passionate. She looks over at me with questioning eyes. She's probably wondering if I am transgender, too. There's a silence among the three of us. I have no idea what's about to happen.

Susanna places her hand on Max's arm and says, "I'm sorry, baby." Max puts his hand over hers. *That is not what I expected.* She looks around to make sure no one is listening and says in a low voice, "My cousin is one of you."

"Nope," Max says coolly. "Do you want to try again?"

Susanna tucks her spiral notebook into her apron and clears

her throat. "My cousin is transgender. And the family won't talk to him anymore. I mean, her."

Max smiles up at Susanna, slides over, and pats the booth, inviting her to sit. She shrugs and plops down beside him. My phone starts vibrating again.

"Max, I'll be outside," I say while scooting out of the booth. "Susanna, it was a real pleasure."

I push the doors open and get hit with sticky heat. The sun has set, but the temperature hasn't cooled. On nights with no wind, like this one, the hot air has nowhere to go, so it just hangs around. I park myself on a bench.

GEORGIA: ☹ ☹ ☹ ☹

GEORGIA: ☹ ☹ ☹ ☹

GEORGIA: ☹ ☹ ☹ ☹

PONY: OK, I'll pick you up. My car = my music.

GEORGIA: Thanks, handsome.

Handsome.

I lift my head up and close my eyes. I imagine what it will be like driving to school with her. She jumps in the car and gives me a hug. I can see this being our thing, me picking her up in the morning. The windows are down, and the wind is blowing her hair around wildly. She smiles at me. I say something funny, obviously, and she laughs and places her hand on mine. We make eye contact. We stop at a red light, and she leans in, and . . .

"Dude, you asleep?" Max heads over to me with a swagger.

I snap out of it. "How did it go?" I ask.

"Changing lives every day, Pony."

"You never cease to amaze me, man. I am proud of you."

Max sits on the bench beside me. "I need to tell you, I don't love your stealth thing."

"I know," I say.

"The trans community is less than one percent of the population, my man. We need more voices, not less."

He makes it sound so easy. Small-town public schools are very different from liberal-arts city schools. "You go to a school where it's weird to be straight and cisgender," I try to explain.

"Yeah, buddy, and your new school is exactly where we need more visibility."

I start to talk again, to defend myself and my choices, but he stops me. "I know I can't change your mind. But I needed to say that I don't love what you are doing. But, I love you. Just be careful."

There are a thousand words gathering in my stomach, but I can't get any out.

Max jumps up from the bench. "It's hot as shit. Let's split."

We walk to our cars and hug. He jumps into his Jeep and hangs his head out the window.

"One more thing, Pony. You do need to tell that cheerleader that you're trans. It's the right thing to do."

"I'll get right on that," I say, then watch him drive off. I get in my car, heavy with the guilt Max just laid on me. He's right. It will be over before it begins, but I'll tell her.

FOUR

Monday, September 2

GEORGIA, 8:10 A.M.

Every night before I go to sleep, I set seven alarms on my phone. I can fall asleep on command. It's getting up that's the problem.

The first alarm is an hour before I need to be out of bed—that's intended to start my waking-up process gradually and trick me into believing that I'm getting bonus sleep time, which has never once worked. I'm just too smart for my own tricks. There are five alarms around my target time, and the seventh and final alarm is always for an hour later. If I am not out of bed by that point, there's probably no reason to leave.

This morning, I'm moving on the second alarm. That's got to be a record. No reason, really . . . just excited to get to school. Nothing weird about that. I crank my music in the bathroom while I shower. This has nothing to do with the fact that Pony will be picking me up soon. Back in my room with one towel around my hair and another around my body, I'm singing along with Beyoncé.

I swing open my closet doors with a dramatic flair, but it's aspirational—my closet is nearly empty. Most of my clothes are scattered around my floor and bed. Pushed into my dresser and desk drawers.

As much as I dread the brightly colored polyester prisons, sometimes wearing the cheerleading uniform is easier than picking out the right outfit. Money isn't tight, but I try to be considerate of Dad. Good thing I'm thrifty. I can pull off Hillcrest fashion on a budget. After digging around in a couple piles of clothing—and finding a half-eaten apple—I locate the dress I had planned to wear tangled up in my bedspread. Totally planned that.

Thirty minutes later, I'm polishing off my strawberry Pop-Tart while scanning the headlines in the *Fort Worth Star-Telegram*. Dad comes into the kitchen putting the finishing touches on his tie. It must be a big day—he's trimmed up his beard and even tucked a pocket square into his blazer.

"Thanks for taking the bus today, Georgie."

His car is in the shop, and there's some company-wide finance blah-blah meeting.

"It's cool. I found a ride," I say as nonchalantly as possible.

"Oh, someone I know?" he asks with a raised eyebrow.

"Dad."

"Can we catch up tonight?"

"Dinner?" I suggest. "It's my turn to cook."

That's a joke—it's always my turn to cook. Dad never learned his way around the kitchen. He tried a couple times but burned food that didn't need to be warmed up. I had a cooking intervention, and we ceremoniously retired his apron.

"Sounds good. Love you, Georgie."

"You too, Dad."

He gives me a kiss on the top of my head and takes off.

The house is eerily quiet. This is when I miss my mom most. She filled the place with her boundless energy and enthusiasm about life. Every day felt exciting and new.

Until she moved out two years ago.

I close the newspaper. If her story was in this paper, this is how it would read:

LOCAL MOM HITS THE JACKPOT
Dallas, TX—October 1, 2017

Dallas native Cindy "Cherry" Roberts turned a girls' night out on the town into an upgrade on her life. Cherry and her gal pals hit downtown Dallas on Friday night to celebrate and cut loose with martinis and dancing. Cherry caught the eye of Wayne Gutter, a wealthy real estate mogul, and sparks flew. After several weeks of sneaking around, Cherry traded in her old life, leaving behind her husband and daughter for a life of leisure.

To give her credit, she did ask me to come live with her and Wayne. Living in a mansion with a pool and staff would be rad, but I would never leave Dad behind like she did. I don't think he could have handled losing both of us at once. He's dealt with the divorce with grace—even claims he's not mad at my mom anymore. Can't say I feel the same.

A car honks three times outside. Pony is here. I grab my book bag and take one final look in the mirror by the front door. Looking good, feeling . . . *nervous*. Hello, new crush nerves, haven't felt you in a minute.

"Nice dress," Pony says as I climb into the passenger seat.

"Thanks. Nice shades."

He's wearing a pair of cool vintage sunglasses and a fitted polo shirt buttoned all the way up. I like a guy who can dress himself.

"Mind if we make a stop on the way?" Pony asks.

"Is this when you take me to the woods and murder me?"

"No, that's later. Just to Starbucks. My brain doesn't function until it's been properly drowned in some iced coffee," he says.

"Same," I say. "We are on the same page."

We cover the polite conversational bases quickly: the weather, the news, the weekend—he saw a movie, I hung with friends. There's a lull in conversation as he turns from my neighborhood onto Addison's main road. Strip mall after strip mall, many of the shops out of business or on the way. We pass by all the fast-food joints: Wendy's, Arby's, McDonald's. Sonic, obvs.

I hate silence between two people. It makes me uncomfortable.

I typically just start blabbering. "OK, new guy, I'm dying to know what you think of Hillcrest."

Not my best starter, but it will work. I watch Pony bite his lower lip as he thinks. "It's cool. My dad, he's in the army, so I'm used to moving around."

"A real-life army brat," I tease.

"Big time brat," he says, smiling at me. "This is our fifth move."

"Wow. I've lived in the same house all my life. Could you imagine?" I ask.

"No way. Sounds kind of boring."

Please.

I suppose we were boring until my mom left. "There's a comfort to living in the same house all your life," I admit. "But that doesn't mean nothing happens."

He pulls into the Starbucks drive-through line. We're about four cars back. Not too bad, considering there's only one Starbucks in town. Some mornings the line is ten cars deep and backing up the traffic on the street. I notice that we're sitting in silence again.

"I would hate having to start over every time. I'm exhausted just thinking about making friends and establishing myself at a new school."

Pony tilts his head. "Establishing yourself?"

"Yeah, making a name for yourself? Building a brand?" I realize how silly it sounds as it leaves my mouth. "Maybe it's not the same at all schools, but at Hillcrest High—who you are matters."

"Does it?" Pony questions.

"Yes, sir."

"To who?"

"Everyone, obviously," I say, but don't completely buy what I'm selling.

Pony starts drumming on the bottom of the steering wheel. "It can be tough to make friends, but I'm good at being alone. Starting a new school is like walking on a movie set that's already been filming a long time—there's no place for you, and everyone's story lines are already fully progressed."

"That's sad. Thanks for ruining my morning," I say, but I'm into his honesty. "Well, I'm your friend now." *And maybe more?*

"No thanks," he jokes, then rolls his window down to yell our coffee orders to the speaker box. I try to imagine what it would look like if we were together. What people would think of me dating the new guy? Plot twist.

Once he's done ordering, I say, "So, let's find you your spot at Hillcrest. What do you do? Do you play sports or anything?"

"No," he says. Too bad. Cheerleaders typically date the guys who play football, basketball, or soccer.

"What about theater?" I ask. But honestly, that wouldn't get him far.

"Nah," he says.

"Debate club?" I'm almost out of options.

"I don't really want to be known for one thing," he says.

"Ouch, says the cheerleader."

He smiles. "That's not what I meant. I don't know, I guess I like movies."

"What kind?" I ask.

"All kinds. Mostly horror movies but also documentaries and indie films. I like movies that make me feel something. Even if it's scared out of my mind."

He's getting excited—it's super cute. I can see myself going to the theater with him. Sitting close and grabbing him at those jumpy moments.

"That's cool. Do you want to be an actor?" I ask.

"Hell no. This is not the face for the big screen, or any screen," he says.

"Come on, Pony, a little plastic surgery and you'll be camera-ready!"

He ignores my brilliant joke. "I'd love to help make movies, I just don't know what I would do. Maybe as a camera operator or—"

"Bathroom cleaner?" I offer.

"That might be more realistic," he says, handing me the iced latte of my dreams. We pull back onto the main road, about a mile from school.

"That's cool," I admit. "I'm into movies, too."

"So, Georgia, what's *your* deal?" Pony asks with his eyes on the road. "What do you want to grow up to be?"

"Who knows, who cares," I say.

"So, not professional cheerleading?" he asks.

"No, could you even imagine?" I shake my head and sneak a look at him, his eyes on the road and hands on ten and two. I say, "I'm a writer."

Out loud.

For the first time.

I stare at his face. I need to gauge the shock. I steel myself, ready for him to laugh at me. Instead, he says, "Cool. Anything I can read?"

My body warms. He didn't laugh. He thinks it's *cool*. He wants to read my nonexistent writing. I never actually write the articles. But maybe I could.

"Yeah, maybe—"

"Shhh," Pony says, cutting me off. He bolts upright. Laser focused on the rearview mirror. I look back and see the familiar flashing red lights. Pony slows the car down and pulls over to the shoulder.

"What the hell?" I say. "You weren't speeding."

"Shhhh," he says again.

He's flipping his shit. Every muscle is tight. He can't stay still. What's the big deal? Getting pulled over is business as usual for me. I'm not a bad driver; I'm just misunderstood. Lucky for me, we do a cheerleading fundraiser for the police department every year. Most of the time, I get off with a warning.

"Hey, it's cool. I know most of the cops in town," I say, putting my hand on his shoulder. But he flinches away. "Pony, is there a dead body in the trunk?"

"No," he says.

"Are you lying about your identity and really a criminal on the run?"

He looks at me so seriously I think he's about to admit to it. "No," he says. His jaw clenches.

"Then why so nervous?" I ask.

"Nothing," he says.

Ugh, now I'm nervous, too. We both watch the cop approach from the driver's-side mirror. He leans down, his face shadowing Pony. He taps the glass. Pony fumbles with the switch like it's his first time using a window.

As soon as the window is cracked, I say, "Hi, Officer Dan!"

Pony looks at me with his mouth open and big eyes. The officer takes his sunglasses off, tucks his ticket pad under his arm, and ducks his head into the car.

"Oh, hi, Georgia. And who is your friend here?"

"He's new to town," I say.

"Welcome to Addison. Can I see your license and registration?"

Pony leans over me to the glove box and grabs the registration, his hand shaking. He pulls out his wallet and fishes out his ID. Officer Dan takes a quick look at the registration but slows down on the license. He keeps looking back and forth from ID to Pony and back again.

"You sure this is you?" he asks.

"It's my hair," Pony says, "and I've lost some weight."

"Hmmm," Officer Dan says, unconvinced.

Not going to lie, I'm *dying* to see that ID. Pony couldn't possibly be his legal name. Whatever his real name is, it's right there on that card, and I must know the truth. Also, different hair and weight?

"Do you know why I pulled you over?" Officer Dan asks Pony.

"My plates?" Pony asks. "I think they're expired."

"Bingo," Officer Dan confirms.

"Ding, ding, ding! Tell the man what he's won!" I say, not helping anything. Under pressure, Pony goes silent, and I get louder than ever. We're obviously made for each other.

"I'd normally give you a ticket for this, but you're new and Georgia's friend, so I'll let you off with a warning."

"Thank you, sir," Pony says.

Officer Dan turns his attention back to me. "Georgia, you think the boys are ready for Friday night?"

During football season, the entire city is overly concerned with the football players' emotional and physical well-being. "Yes, sir. I heard they purchased a magical potion from Amazon that has made them superhuman."

Officer Dan laughs. "I'll take some of that! And you, get those plates updated today. Next time you won't be so lucky."

He shakes his head at Pony's ID before handing it back. "Nice to meet you, Sa—"

"YOU TOO, SIR," Pony almost yells.

A clue! His real name starts with *Sa*.

Sam? Sal? Santa?

I'll get to the bottom of this. I love a good mystery.

Pony takes a deep breath and pulls back onto the road. He turns up the volume as *Perfume Genius* scrolls across the radio console—never heard of them. I take the hint that he wants some quiet time. I need to focus on my iced latte anyway.

By the time we pull into the Hillcrest parking lot, he has calmed down. We pull into a spot in the back. No one has told Pony the hierarchy of the Hillcrest parking lot (tradition number 897). Seniors park in the front. I won't bore him with it now.

He kills the engine and turns toward me.

"Georgia, there's something you should know about me."

And then, silence.

He must be messing with me, but his face is so serious.

"Pony, you can tell me anything," I say.

He clears his throat. "I'm different from the other guys you know."

Didn't see that coming.

"Pony, of course you're different. And I bet you'll never hurt me, too?"

His face is blank, hard to read.

I continue, "Are my legs tired? From running through your mind all night?"

"Georgia, actually, that's not what I meant . . ."

"Pony, lame pickup lines? I think you're better than that."

"What I was trying to say was . . ." He stops himself and smiles. He looks relieved. "OK, deal."

"Good." I say.

6:57 P.M.

I wave from the porch as Mia honks and drives off. I head inside—Dad isn't home yet—while finishing off my Strawberry Limeade from Sonic (no vodka this time).

I catch my reflection in the mirror as I close the door. My cheeks and forehead are bright pink. *Dammit, Mia.* She demanded that practice happen outside today. Prep for the game on Friday, Mia said. We're playing Plano, one of our biggest rivals. Hillcrest is rich. Plano is richer.

After washing the vegetables for dinner, I check my phone. A text from Pony awaits.

PONY: Is your middle name Google?

I play along and type back: NO. WHY?

PONY: Because you're everything I'm searching for . . .

Dumb. I text LOL back. I have received a steady stream of cheesy pickup lines from Pony throughout the day. It's been entertaining. I start chopping red peppers and turn on NPR. Dad will be home soon.

In calculus today, I got super bored and passed Pony a note. It said: *Tell me your REAL name or we are DONE.* The curiosity is killing me. I can't help myself. A few minutes later, a note landed on my desk that said: *PONY is my REAL name.*

Touché. I might have to turn to the internet for the answer.

Right on time for dinner, Dad comes through the front door, whistling. He loosens his tie. "Hello, Georgie. What's on the menu tonight?"

"This evening, the chef has prepared a kitchen-sink salad!"

He sits down at the table. "You made a salad in the sink?"

"Needed a big bowl. It was the sink or the toilet . . ."

"Turns out, I'm still pretty full from lunch," he says, patting his stomach.

"Dad, it's everything BUT the kitchen sink." I place the bowl of beautiful greens and reds and yellows on the table. "I used all the veggies from the fridge and topped it off with some leftover chicken."

"Thank you, my favorite daughter." I'm his only daughter. "So," he says, "who is the new fellow who took you to school today?"

"Daaaaaaad," I say, hoping that answer will suffice.

He throws his hands in the air. "What, Dad can't ask questions? I have a right to know!"

"OK, well, he's president . . . of a notorious bike gang. He picked me up on his Harley-Davidson and does not believe in helmets. Don't ask about his face tattoos."

He plays along with my story. "Sounds like every dad's dream!"

"Ugh, fine. I got a ride with a new kid. He just moved here. His name is Pony."

He chokes on his food. "Oh, yeah? Is his dad's name Horse?"

"Very funny, Dad. His name is Pony, for real. I'm dead serious," I say.

He lifts an eyebrow at me, full of doubt. "What happened to the year of no dating?" He loads up another forkful of kale and red pepper slices. "That plan makes my job easy."

I concentrate on my salad, moving it around with my fork. Honestly, I simply stopped thinking about the no-dating thing, and voilà, it went away!

"I met Pony this week. It's brand-new. I'm just getting to know him."

"Look at you, Georgie, you're adulty so hard."

"It's adult*ing* so hard, Dad." He has a unique talent for ruining anything cool. Besides, two can play at this game. "I think it's brave that I put myself out there after getting hurt. When will you be getting out there, Dad?"

He stops chewing and looks up at me. "Soon."

"It's been almost two years," I say.

"I need more time."

"Mom didn't—"

"Georgia."

I went too far on that one.

He softens up. "I think I loved your mother more than she loved me . . ."

"That's not true," I say in a small voice. I shouldn't have pushed, but I want him to be happy. I'm worried about what he'll do when I graduate. He'll go to work, come home, eat things from cans, and repeat every night of the week. Except poker night, but that's once a month. Do I never move away? Attend Addison Community College? Work at the Sonic? I can't skate . . .

Suddenly, the solution hits me—because I'm a freaking genius—and I get up and grab the iPad from my backpack.

"Check this out, Dad. I read an article about an online dating site for people over forty!"

He pushes the iPad away. "No, thank you, I prefer the old-fashioned way: meeting someone in person and talking."

I take the iPad back and start signing him up. "OK, that's charming and idealistic but so very outdated. OUT-DATED. That should be the name of this site."

"One more joke about my age and you'll be grounded until you're forty."

"That's fair," I say, completing a couple steps on the website. I hand the iPad back to him, feeling accomplished. "I uploaded a photo and gave you a name, see?" I point to the username.

"OutDatedDad, very funny."

"Just write your bio and off you go!"

I grab the dinner plates and take them to the sink. As I load the dishwasher up, I think about telling Pony my secret. *He thinks I'm a writer. With things to read.* I don't know what happened. I lost my mind. He is this new person. He's neutral, like Switzerland or beige. I wanted him to see me as more than a cheerleader. And—I felt safe.

Dad takes off his reading glasses and holds up the tablet. "Got it, Georgie!"

I dry off my hands and read his very best attempt over his shoulder.

HI! MY NAME IS ROBERT. SINGLE DAD WITH JOB AND MUSTACHE. EX-WIFE LEFT ME FOR RICH GUY. LOOKING FOR FRIENDSHIP. WILL PAY.

Wow, it's breathtakingly bad. But I need to be supportive.

"Nice attempt! A few notes. The caps lock is a little aggressive. Mustache isn't a selling point. Let's cut the ex-wife thing. And what does 'will pay' mean in your world?"

"I will pay for dinner and such. Just want them to know that I'm a gentleman," he says earnestly.

"That's awfully chivalrous, but that might read as you are willing to pay for more than dinner . . ." I nudge him with my elbow.

"Oh," he says as his cheeks blush up.

I grab the iPad from him. "Delete, delete, delete. OK, that's better." I sit down at the table. Twenty minutes later—genius takes time—I have crafted the best profile possible:

Hello! I'm starting the next chapter in my life and looking for my new love interest. I'm kind, smart, funny, and trustworthy. I have a job and a daughter; all that's missing is you.

He reads it over and allows me to publish his profile.

"All right, you're officially online. The rest is up to you. Just start swiping here," I say, walking him through the website. I wish him well, head up to my room, throw myself on my bed, and unlock my phone. It's time for me to take a step forward, too.

GEORGIA: Are you going to the football game on Friday?

Maybe that was dumb. He doesn't like sports. My phone dings.

PONY: Why would I go to a football game?

I ready my thumbs to type out some silly story but stop.

GEORGIA: For me.

A minute goes by, and it's dreadful.

PONY: Then, yes.

GEORGIA: See you there, handsome.

FIVE

Friday, September 6

PONY, 7:12 P.M.

I feel like the Little Mermaid. She just wanted to be part of our world. Here I am, wanting to be a part of Georgia's world but feeling like my body is all wrong.

I lean against my car in the parking lot and take in the stadium's bright, blinding lights. This isn't some rinky-dink football field with wooden bleachers. This is like a mini pro stadium. I can hear the band from here, playing some fight song. There must be hundreds of people in the bleachers wearing school colors and yelling. No wonder the football players walk around like the kings of everything.

I usually head into Dallas on Friday nights to hang with my friends from the LGBTQIA Center. We go see outdoor movies, bowl, waste a bunch of money at Dave & Buster's. And when I want to go to a party—which isn't that often—Max always has an option.

I am entirely out of my element here. And alone. I should have invited someone, but my old school is hours away, too far for casual hangouts. And my queer friends from the LGBTQIA Center would blow my cover. Max doesn't leave the house without a pride flag somewhere on him. People would wonder about me. I'm tense and uneasy about this situation, but Georgia wanted me here. So I'm here.

I walk through the chain-link fence and pay two dollars to a guy in a booth while a security guard swipes me a couple times with his metal-detector wand. I head toward the concession stand under the bleachers and watch kids balance foot-long hot dogs and bowls of nachos as they return to their seats. I give in to my hunger and get in line.

I don't mind going places by myself, but I prefer low-pressure environments like movie theaters and Barnes & Noble. Chill things. This is a whole different ballgame. Literally. I am very aware of my aloneness and feel like everyone else is aware of it, too. I look around like I'm trying to find someone. I should have spent more time making friends the first two weeks, but I was busy flirting with a cheerleader. I'll put it on my to-do list for next week.

I carry my nachos up the bleachers. It's packed. The band is at full volume, the stadium lights are cranked, everyone is cheering. A heavily padded guy crashes into another heavily padded guy and they roll around on Astroturf. The referee blasts his whistle, and the crowd goes wild. Everything is loud. Everything is bright. This is sensory overload.

I find a seat at the border of the parents' section, around the middle of the field. Seems safe to hang here and get the lay of the land. I dig up a tortilla chip covered in imitation cheese and devour the whole thing. It's too salty and lukewarm and beyond delicious.

The cheerleaders are on the field facing the crowd, spread out side by side in one long line that goes from goal post to goal post. They are wearing matching outfits and waving to the crowd until the blond one in the middle signals them to start a cheer. There's a massive megaphone in front of each girl with their name painted across it in perfect cheerleader cursive. Farther down the field, in front of the student section, I find Georgia's megaphone. She's impossibly cute. The girl, not the megaphone. I really am punching above my weight here. Or possibly, she's just a shameless flirt. Texans are famous for flirting. But it feels like something more.

A macho dancing bear mascot skips over and hugs her until they fall to the ground. They overdo the dramatics, but it's entertaining. Georgia dances with the bear until it struts off to give hugs to the kids in the bleachers.

The parents seated near me are having a ball. The moms are dressed up, Target chic, and laughing loudly while taking big drinks from thermoses. They're preoccupied with talking and gossiping with each other, taking the occasional break to shout words of encouragement in the direction of the field.

The dads, on the other hand, are dressed like coaches and are laser focused on the game. They jump up and down and yell things at their sons. "Get your head in the game!" There's no way the players can hear it on the field. The moms half-heartedly try to calm them down, mostly because they're embarrassed. The dads are wringing their hands like it's the Super Bowl.

As an outsider to this football thing, it seems very foreign and weird. This is what normal people do on Friday nights in small towns around Texas. I guess we're all looking for a community of people who share our likes or beliefs, and this is the equivalent of an LGBTQIA Center for straight people.

To be honest, I thought being a cheerleader was kind of bullshit. I've changed my mind. They flip and throw each other in the air and drop into splits. At times, they are working harder than the football players. I haven't been able to take my eyes off Georgia. She's in her element. Smiling and playing and hyping the crowd. I have a newfound respect. And a deepening crush.

Update: The announcer has declared this a close game, tied at fourteen near the end of the second whatever. There are two minutes on the clock.

Another Update: I'm starting to regret the nachos.

A mom with wild red hair parks herself next to me. "Honey, the kids sit over there," she says, pointing in the general vicinity of the student section.

"I'm new to Hillcrest," I say, having no reason to lie. "I haven't made friends yet."

"Oh? Well, I have a very nice daughter. Maybe she can be your friend?"

"Is she cute?" I ask.

"See for yourself," she says, then points directly at Georgia.

"Georgia?"

"The one and only." She pats my head and gets up. "OK, baby-girl, I need to go."

Babygirl?

"Toodles," she says, then disappears back into the mom mob.

Holy shit, I just met Georgia's mom.

But she thinks I'm a girl.

No, she thinks I'm a *babygirl*.

I'm destroyed.

It must seem silly to get upset about something so small. When I'm misgendered, it feels like I was trying to pull something off and got caught because I wasn't good enough. I failed at passing as male. My self-esteem takes an immediate nosedive.

After something like that happens, I always feel the need to man up. I crank up my stubbornness and use it—like fuel—to power my move to the student section. No more hiding among the parents. I've got to be brave and confident.

I walk over and take a seat on the bleachers right in front of Georgia, about five rows up. She spots me immediately and waves. I wave back and try to act like I don't care about this moment at all.

A loud whistle blows, signaling the end of the first part. The football guys run off the field and the band rushes on. Oh man, it's only halftime. I'm going to be here for the rest of my life.

The Hillcrest Band stands in formation, completely frozen, at full attention. This is their time to shine. The cheerleaders huddle together by the railing, talking, drinking from water bottles, and checking their phones. I feel my pocket vibrate.

GEORGIA: Come here.

I look up, and she's staring right at me. She wants me to go to the railing and talk to her. I get up but take my time, playing it cool. (Pickup artist advice: make her wait.)

I'm dodging the herd of students getting up to hit the bathroom and concession stand during the break. I approach the railing where she's waiting for me. The band has started their show, and the volume is next-level loud.

We both cover our ears and yell.

"LOOK WHO MADE IT," she screams over the blaring horns.

"YOU WERE WAITING FOR ME?" I ask.

"NO WAY. I don't know if you noticed, but I'm pretty busy down here."

I only hear bits of what she's saying but go with it. "I HAVE BEEN HERE THE WHOLE TIME!"

She comes closer to the railing; the band has dropped out, and it's just the drum line beating at the same speed as my heart. We take our hands off our ears.

"For me?" she asks.

"For you," I confirm.

She fights a smile. "So," she says, "what do you think of all of this?"

I look around at her world. "I think . . . you look cute," I say.

She laughs and shakes her head. "I was thinking the same thing about you."

I peek over her head at the group of cheerleaders with every single eye on us. They immediately look away and pretend to talk.

Georgia puts her hand over mine on the railing. "Don't mind them, Pony."

I want to talk, but all I can think about is her hand on mine. I blurt out, "Hey, I met your mom."

She steps from me, pulling away her hand. I feel my eyes go big. Why did she do that? As if perfectly cued, the marching band joins back in with the drummers. The horns come in, loud and strong.

"WHAT?" Georgia asks.

I repeat it louder. "I MET YOUR MOM."

She looks around, confused, and keeps her distance. "MY MOM?"

"WE HIT IT OFF," I scream. *Babygirl.*

Georgia takes another step away. "I have to go," she mouths, walking back to the group of idle cheerleaders. Her posture is slumped, and she's distracted. Well, I managed to mess that up royally.

As chill as possible, I walk back up the steps of the bleachers and try not to fall. The added embarrassment would be too much for me right now. I find a patch of empty bleachers near the top of the stands—not directly in front of Georgia—and sit down to think about what just happened.

I pull out my phone to text my sister. She's the pro on my girl dilemmas. I don't always listen to her advice, but she's always right. The problem with this plan is that I haven't told her about Georgia yet. I'm not ready for the questions. Rocky is allergic to social constructs like cheerleaders.

And she will want me to tell Georgia that I'm trans. Just like Max.

I put my phone away. I can deal with this on my own. Did Georgia not want me to meet her mom? She seemed happy to hang out with me, her new *babygirl.*

I'm lost in thought when an empty plastic cup hits the back of my head.

I close my eyes to hold in the rage exploding in my body. Ready for a fight, I stand up and turn around. Two guys seated directly behind me are watching me. One of them is Asian and extremely tall. He's seated, but you can still tell he's massive. The shorter kid is white with prominent freckles and shaggy hair poorly contained under a dirty baseball hat.

"WHAT THE FUCK?" I say, feeling relieved to have something to take my frustration out on.

"Hey, chill. Our sincerest apologies," the short one says. "We thought you might be jerking off."

The tall one cracks up. "Dude! This is the new kid! He's in my AP History class. Your name is . . ." He's working hard to remember it. "It's Pecker?"

The short one busts a gut. "Pecker," he says between laughs.

"Pony," I say, as steady as possible, and then stand up to leave.

"Dude, calm yourself," the short one urges. "We're just messing with you. My name is Jerry, and this tall drink of bong water is Kenji." Jerry shakes my hand, and Kenji gives me a fist bump. My entire body loosens up, and I sit back down.

"So, Pony, what do you think of Hillcrest?" Kenji asks.

"It sucks," I say, guessing that's what they want to hear.

"Damn right, it sucks. It sucks my balls." It's clear Jerry is the jokester.

"Jerry, no one wants to suck your balls," Kenji says.

"Your mom does."

"I told you to lay off my mom," Kenji says.

"New kid," Jerry says to me, "how are your balls?"

I didn't see that question coming. I quickly realize my boy boot camp missed an important topic: guy talk. I forgot that dudes would assume that I have balls and ask questions and make comments about my hypothetical balls. It feels like I'm on *Jeopardy!* and the final category is balls. Luckily, fast humor is my survival skill. It won't do me any good on a desert island, but it saves my ass in moments like this. Besides, a joke is easier than lying.

"Your mom is very fond of my balls," I say.

Kenji loses his shit and high-fives me.

Jerry laughs, too. "Not bad, Pecker."

Relief washes over me. I move up to the bleachers beside them, and we sit with a foot of space between us, the equivalent of two guys at the movies keeping an empty seat between them.

The game is a nail-biter, but we're busy shooting the shit and cracking jokes. I'm a guy, hanging with guys, talking about guy stuff.

"OK, Pony," Jerry asks, "which lucky lady at Hillcrest will be taking your virginity?"

"I was hoping it would be you," I say.

"Play your cards right, buddy, and it just might be," Jerry says, punching me in the arm.

"Sorry, Jerry, you're not my type."

Kenji asks, "Then who here is your type, Pecker?"

This is a loaded question. Should I tell them the truth? They might have some helpful insight on Georgia, but I don't really know these guys.

Jerry jumps in. "There's my type right there." He points at the mascot. No shit, he has a crush on the dancing bear. It's too good.

Jerry continues, love struck, "There's a girl underneath that mascot suit, and I will win her heart someday."

"But you'll do her in the bear suit, right?" Kenji asks.

"Whatever she wants, you homo."

I look away and try to forget that I heard Jerry say that word. This is guy talk, and there's nothing I can do to change it. Max would be on his feet yelling if he were here. To Jerry and Kenji,

I'm just another guy, and it's cool to talk like that around me. It's conflicting. When I hung out with dudes at my old school, they still treated me like a girl, and I hated it. Not a problem here—these guys are hitting all the notes.

I point to Georgia as she does a high kick and say, "That's my type right there."

"Georgia?" Jerry asks. "You don't mess around, do you? Right to the top!"

Kenji puts his hand on my shoulder. "No offense, Pony. I know we just met, but I think she's out of your league. Like, way, way, way out."

"And I think she's with Jake," Jerry adds.

Before I can respond, the crowd erupts into madness as the announcer screams, "*TOUCHHHHHDOWN HILLCREST! TOOUCCHHDOWN!*"

She's with Jake?

The band kicks in with the school fight song, and everyone in the bleachers is on their feet cheering madly. The touchdown has pushed Hillcrest into the lead, and the crowd is losing their collective mind.

Who is Jake?

I stand up and watch the players slapping the quarterback's helmet and butt. They're all dancing and running around the field. The quarterback takes off his helmet and heads over to Georgia. She jumps into his arms, and he spins her around. The announcer yells, "*ANOTHER TD FOR QB JAKE CARTER!*" It's the end of every episode of *Friday Night Lights*.

I guess that's Jake.

That was my "first friend" who I met in the bathroom. I hate him now. It's official: coming to this football game was a very bad idea. I wanted to get closer to Georgia, but now it's over. Of course she's dating the star quarterback. There's no possible way I could compete with that guy.

"I think I'm done with this scene. Let's split," Kenji says to Jerry. I keep my eyes on the field. I wouldn't mind getting the hell out of here, but I don't want to be that desperate loser who invites himself. I should probably go home and end this night anyway.

"Hey, Pecker," Jerry says to me, "want to hit up Sonic with us?"

I really hope this nickname doesn't stick. I act as blasé as possible. "Yeah, sounds good. I'm starving."

Jerry jumps up. "Great, man. You're driving!"

Kenji gets on his feet, and I am eye-level with his armpit. He must be at least . . .

"I'm six two, Japanese, and, no, I don't play basketball."

"Well," I say, "I'm five six, Irish I think, and I only play your mom."

Kenji gives me a little push, and we head out. He's a gentle giant.

We pass by the bathrooms before the exit. I need to go, but I don't want them to come in with me. I take my chances. "Hold up, I'll be right back," I say.

Jerry looks up and sees the bathroom sign. "Yeah, I need to hit that, too."

"Might as well join you fellas," Kenji says.

I was really hoping they wouldn't need the bathroom. My mind kicks into high gear, gaming outcomes. What if the stalls are all broken? What if they ask me to join at the urinals? I pray to whatever god will listen that there's an open toilet stall.

The bathroom is completely empty, brightly lit, and smelly. Kenji and Jerry make their way to the urinals, and I split off into an open stall. (Thank You, Bathroom God.)

"Pony, you gonna take a dump, man?" Jerry asks.

I stop before going in. "I had the nachos."

They both laugh.

"You'll be paying for that for days," Kenji says.

I slide the tiny push lock in place, pull my pants down, and hover over the toilet. Men's bathrooms are filthy—I never sit down on the seat. I can hear the guys talking as they piss at the urinal. I wish it was that easy.

Jerry's voice fills the bathroom. "OK, Pony, we'll be outside. Holler if you need help."

They laugh more and leave.

A few minutes later, I exit the bathroom, drying my hands on my jeans and trying to act like nothing happened. I don't want them to suspect that there's anything different about me. These guys are bros—there's no way they would be friends with a trans guy. Hanging with them has made my night bearable. It has made the whole Georgia thing sting a little less.

Now this awkward bathroom situation happened. I don't want

them asking any questions. Or thinking about it. I need to create a diversion. I need to appeal to this fraternity of two bros. I walk up, but they don't notice, both their heads down in their phones.

"Ready to go, homos?" I ask, and a little part of me dies.

"Yeah, homo," Jerry says, trying to punch my crotch, going for my balls. I jump back quick, his hand missing my jeans.

I have officially pledged this bro-ternity.

SIX

Saturday, September 7

GEORGIA, 9:37 A.M.

My head is pounding. This room is too bright. My eyes aren't open yet, but I can just tell. I stayed out too late at the after-game party and will pay for it.

Here's how high school parties go down in Addison: fifty kids standing around a warm keg in the woods. The beer is usually courtesy of someone's older brother, who attends the party in hopes of reliving his glory days. It's super sad. The party is over when the beer runs out or when the cops crash.

I open my eyes—it was inevitable—sit up, grab the glass of water on my nightstand, and down the entire thing.

I find my phone, tangled up in my sheet. Nothing from Pony. I looked for him after the game to apologize. I kind of bugged out on him about Mom.

I pull the covers up past my nose and take a selfie. My hair is a wreck, but I don't care. I write the caption *TGIS (Thank God It's Saturday)* and post it.

Saturday is the laziest day of the week. I have challenged myself to do as little as possible. Dad works on most Saturdays, so the house is all mine. I head downstairs in my sleep shirt and slippers to make a little breakfast. I'm a healthy eater most of the time (unless there's bacon in the vicinity), but on Saturday mornings, I make my guiltiest of pleasures: cinnamon rolls.

Sticky, gooey, delicious, pure-fat cinnamon rolls from those cylinder tubes that pop open when you twist them. The POP is so satisfying, and inside awaits raw cinnamon dough buns and a small plastic pot of frosting. I throw the little hockey-puck biscuits on a nonstick pan and do a cinnamon roll dance. I'm tempted to take a bite of the dough but resist. I do have some self-control.

While the oven is preheating, I look up Pony's Insta. He followed me yesterday before the game, and I followed back. There's nothing from last night. No clue why I expected anything to be up—this guy hasn't posted a picture in a month. There's mostly movie memes and selfies. I scroll down and click his first post, a selfie from one year ago. Only one year? Maybe his parents are crazy strict and wouldn't let him have social media. Still— weird.

MYSTERY BOY CATFISHES HOT GIRL
Addison, TX—Saturday, September 7, 2019

*Georgia Roberts, America's sweetheart, has been hoodwinked by
dangerous loner. A young man going by the name of Pony started
Hillcrest High with the sole intention of luring in a cheerleader. A
guy with no past, a name starting with "Sa," and a taste for human
blood. "I had no clue," Georgia said at her own funeral, "that he
was a vampire."*

The oven alarm buzzes, bringing me back to reality. I have
this process down to a science. Step one, I slide the tray into the
oven—top rack, a little to the left—and set my alarm for fifteen
minutes and forty-two seconds.

Step two, check my phone. I have—no joke—ninety-seven
texts. Mia, Lauren, Kelly, and I have an active text thread going.
It's the reason I go over my data plan every month. We might talk
more over text than IRL.

I scroll through the conversation. Looks like Lauren and her
boyfriend went into Dallas after the party last night. There's
picture after picture of them dancing and making out at some
neon light–drenched country bar. I bet her head hurts worse than
mine today. I scroll down to the last text—from 7:25 a.m.

MIA: GIRLS. What time we hitting up Jake's party?

That's Mia, up with the sun and always planning. Do I want
to hang out with Jake? Not really. Do I want to hang out at Jake's
house? Hell yes. His family owns a chain of furniture stores
throughout Texas. They are beyond rich. When his parents leave
town, Jake Carter throws monster parties.

GEORGIA: 8 PM. Kelly's turn to drive. ily Kelly.

I peek through the little oven window. The rolls are rising and browning up. Everything is going according to plan.

KELLY: DAMMIT. Fine.

MIA: No, Lauren can drive.

LAUREN: Ok

MIA: And use that fake ID to get a little pregame?

LAUREN: Sure girl

I shake my head at my phone. We need to find a spine on eBay for Lauren.

Three minutes later, I remove the tray and plate the rolls. My little buns are golden-brown perfection, filling the kitchen with cinnamon-sugar sweetness. I smear icing on top and watch it melt (my form of meditation). To make everyone jealous, I post a picture of my culinary masterpiece.

I sit down at the table and open the *New York Times*. It's not cheap to get the *Times* delivered in Texas, but Dad says it's worth it. I agree wholeheartedly. The Sunday edition is like catnip for me and him.

I bite into the first roll. It's warm and fluffy and spicy and sweet. After reading a couple articles, I pull out my iPad from my backpack and open it. I haven't been the best email checker this week. There's only one that catches my eye.

FROM: Kerry_Randolph@hillcrest.edu
TO: GeorgiaRobertsTX@gmail.com
DATE: September 3 at 12:35 p.m.
SUBJECT: Hillcrest Reporter

Georgia,

I was sorry to not see you at the meeting last week for the *Hillcrest Reporter*. I assume it conflicted with your cheerleading duties. I have a proposal for you. How about doing some freelance writing for the *Reporter*? No pressure, no meetings. You get experience, and we get your point of view. Both important things.

Let me know what you think,
Ms. Randolph

The skin on my arms prickles up. The email literally gave me goose bumps. Could I do this? Could I be a writer? I need time to think. Maybe I should ask Mia? She would hate the idea and find a bylaw against it in the cheerleader handbook.

I grab my phone to text Pony but stop. I got weird on him last night about my mom and didn't see him after the game. I don't really know where we stand. Instead, I grab the Business section of the *Times*.

An hour later, I waddle up the stairs cradling my stomach (filled with cinnamon-roll baby) and crawl back into bed. I have earned some me time. The start of my senior year has been chaotic and every muscle is sore from cheering at the game. Today is all about recharging my batteries by napping and Netflixing.

Before drifting off into my first nap, I think about Pony. I imagine his arms around me. Kissing him. Straddling him and running my hands through his hair. Biting his earlobe. His hands running down my back. That does the trick. I fall asleep with a dumb smile on my face.

7:45 P.M.

The sun has set, and I'm ready to reenter society. I was in slow-mo mode getting ready for the party. It took me two hours and twenty texts from Mia to convince me to not wear sweatpants. I went with black jean shorts and a white shirt with a line drawing of Ruth Bader Ginsburg. The phone buzzes. My girls are here. I fly downstairs, high-five Dad, and run out to Lauren's car.

Jake's McMansion is straight out of one of those fancy-home magazines. It's pretty much a tasteful Dave & Buster's with a batting cage and tennis court. The lawn has real grass that's green (impossible in the Texas heat unless you're rich) and stone fountains. Kids are running around and acting silly, doing cartwheels. I swear, drinking just reverts us back to a younger age.

Kelly pushes open the front doors, and we behold the wealth. No matter how many times I come here, the size of the place still shocks me. It's extra. The living room comfortably fits half the kids at Hillcrest.

We enter like we own the place. Everyone yells and cheers, still buzzing from last night's win. The mood of this town is directly connected to the outcome of the Friday-night game. And tonight, we party.

Jake runs over to us, always the host. "Ladies, you made it! Hi, Georgia."

He gives me a kiss on the cheek.

"Hi, Jake. You're looking rich tonight," I say, and Mia nudges me with her elbow.

"This could all be yours," he says to me with a wink.

I brush it off. "At the very least, whatever fits in my purse, right?"

Mia weaves her arm into mine. "Jake, we're going to find Georgia a drink . . . or ten."

"Solid idea," Jake says. "I'll come find you in a few."

Hate to admit it, but Jake looks kind of cute tonight in his ratty baseball cap and V-neck white shirt. We hit the kitchen and marvel at the rows of bottles and buckets of beer. All that's missing is the bartender . . .

OMG, there's a freaking cheese tray.

Mia finds Red Bull in the fridge. We mix it with vodka and snack on the cheeses. Kelly fishes a beer out of the ice water bucket and joins a game of dominoes at the dining room table. Mia and Lauren eventually get tired of girl time and scurry off to find their boyfriends. How could they leave me . . . and cheese? Their priorities are out of whack. I wander out of the kitchen with my drink and into the backyard, where I watch a heated game of horseshoes.

I find a lawn chair and get comfortable. I lean my head back, close my eyes, and listen to what's around me. There are crickets in the distance, the clanking of horseshoes hitting the metal post, kids splashing around in the pool, a drunk guy talking loudly about some girl.

A couple years ago, I would spend all day getting ready for a party. Stressing about who would be there and what they would think of me. Agonizing over my clothes and hair. Almost not going because of this or that and then showing up and having the best time. I would make the rounds, drink in hand, talking to everyone. Once I got a little buzzed, I would look around and hope that my whole life would be this fun. My phone would fill up with pictures, and I would sneak into my house way past curfew. I thought it would only get better when I was a senior.

"I made you this," a deep voice says above me. *Maybe it's God?*

I open my eyes. Nope, just Jake. He hands me a drink in a coconut.

"Thanks," I say, taking a sip out of the absurdly swirly straw. It's a piss-poor piña colada but a nice gesture. Jake sits down in the lawn chair next to me and uses his hat as a fan. The air is still and stale. I look him over. It's so effortless for him to be gorgeous.

"I see you, Georgia," he says.

"I surely hope so. Otherwise, I'm a ghost," I say.

He laughs. "It must be tough to come to parties, after what happened."

"Impressive," I say. "You must be a mind reader."

"Do you think every guy will do that to you?"

"No, just Anthony," I say. "And maybe you."

He acts offended. "What? Me? Why would I do that?"

Because you are rich and good looking, and what would stop you?

"Maybe I'm a mind reader, too," I say, putting the coconut drink down forever.

"Georgia. I'm nothing like Ant."

Ant is what the football team calls Anthony. I hate that people still like him. When we broke up, I wanted the entire school to collectively unfriend him. It was devastating when they didn't.

Jake scoots his chair closer to me. "Do you remember the first time we met?"

"I don't even remember what I had for breakfast," I say.

Big lie. A whole damn tube of cinnamon rolls.

"It was freshman year. You had the worst haircut," he says.

"That couldn't have been me," I say.

"Like a bowl?"

"No idea. Wasn't me."

Jake shakes his head. He's not going to let me off that easy.

"We had history together. I had the biggest crush on you." He finds my eyes. "And I still do."

He looks at my lips and leans in to kiss me. I move back in my chair and turn my face away. This doesn't feel right. My heart isn't into it. Other parts of me are but that's not enough.

He smiles and takes a drink of his coconut drink. He seems unfazed by my rejection. "Georgia. I get it. Let's make a deal. Are you listening?"

"To you mansplain? Yes, I'm all ears," I say.

"How about we just have fun tonight? No agenda, no end game."

I look at the stars. I'm tired of thinking about my mom. And about what happened this summer. It's my senior year. I should be having fun.

"Terms accepted," I say.

He looks surprised. "OK, then. First stop, dancing."

Jake helps me up, and we head inside to hit the dance floor. I find my girls, and we wild out. Mia and Lo flip when they see me dancing with Jake. I can't even look at them or I'll crack up. Jake is a decent dancer. He keeps the beat sufficiently, doesn't do anything embarrassing or get too humpy.

The music slows, and Jake moves toward me. We're getting closer. And closer. He pushes my hair behind my ear and leans in. "Having fun?"

"Maybe," I admit.

"I'm a fun guy, Georgia."

"Prove it," I say with a mischievous smile.

"OK," he says, then grabs my hand, leading me off the dance floor.

PONY, 9:17 P.M.

I'm either the bravest guy at Hillcrest or the dumbest.

I stay a couple steps behind Kenji and Jerry as we enter Jake's house. This is enemy territory. It's a freaking mansion, packed with rowdy kids. The place smells like expensive furniture and cheap beer. People are scattered around in small groups, talking and laughing. To the left, there's a room that looks like a club, complete with a DJ.

Kenji heard about the party when we were at Sonic last night and invited me. Parties aren't my thing—I get overwhelmed and bored—but I figured Georgia would be here. And seeing how Jake is now my sworn enemy, I need to know what I'm up against. I look around at the sparkly chandeliers and football field–size television. I'm screwed.

On the bright side, I'm here with my new friends. Guys' night. Last night was awesome—after the game, we pigged out at Sonic and made dirty jokes. We even talked to some girls from Plano, in town for the game. They had no interest in our witty banter, but it didn't matter to me. Getting to hang out with guys and talk to girls—who all see me as a guy—is exactly what I have wanted.

Today was brutal. I spent most of the day separating Ted London's possessions into piles and thinking about Georgia. Repeatedly going over the events of last night: meeting her mom, getting misgendered by said mom, Georgia going cold on me when I mentioned her mom, and Jake. Stellar night.

"Let's find the booze," Jerry says, and we follow him toward the kitchen. He's making snide comments to almost everyone we pass. It's clear that Jerry is the funny guy at school. And Kenji is the tall and handsome guy. All the girls are transfixed on him, but he is shy. Not Jerry. He's making farting noises to a group of girls. He needs some help.

I grab a beer (which tastes like moldy bread but is a manly selection) and start wandering around the house. It's not every day that you get to see how the one percent lives. There's a study full of expensive and untouched books. The dust in the room makes me sneeze. I head into the formal dining room, which contains real art in expensive frames. And tablecloths. I try to imagine what a dinner looks like for this family. Much different from mine, that's for sure.

I want to play a few rounds of *Big Buck Hunter* in the game room, but I'm looking for someone. And then, I turn a corner and see her. Dancing with her eyes closed. Georgia moves with confidence, like she likes her body. She's beautiful. I could stand here all night.

She opens her eyes and locks them with mine. Again. The electricity pours through me like it did the first day. My heart races. *This is why I'm here.* She smiles and waves. I think she signals for me to come over, but Jake moves in and starts dancing with her. I can only see his back and backward baseball cap.

I have spent the past couple days in this dream fantasyland where the popular cheerleader falls for the secretly trans guy. The against-all-odds love story. It's pathetic.

I came here to size up my competition. Well, he's right in front of me. Jake is rich, good-looking, fun, and a real guy. Not a freak like me. I can hear Max's voice in my head, yelling at me for saying that, but it's how I feel.

I quick-walk back to the kitchen, looking for Kenji and Jerry, but they are nowhere to be found. I pull out my phone and text: HELP. I'm at party. Big crush on a girl. But she's dancing with another guy. What would Rocky do?

The typing bubble immediately pops up.

ROCKY: WHAAAAAAA?

ROCKY: Go talk to another girl, duh! YOU GOT THIS.

Good plan. I scan the kitchen—no girls. Wait, there's one. She's in the corner, on her phone with disinterested eyes and wildly curly hair. She absentmindedly twists a curl between her finger and scrolls on her phone with her other hand.

I need to be smooth. And calm. Too bad I am neither. My palms are sweating. I wipe them on my jeans and walk over to the sink. I rearrange a few bottles. Look in a drawer. Open the fridge. Open another beer. Finally, I approach.

"Hi," I say.

The curly-haired girl has freckles. They make her even cuter. "Hi," she says without looking up from her phone. Tough crowd.

"Having fun?" I ask.

"Obviously," she says, head still in her phone.

"I hate parties," I confess, leaning up against the wall. No response. She's got bright red Old Skool Vans. "Cool shoes," I say, and she looks up from her phone. Success!

"Thanks," she says, checking out my Vans.

"Daniel Johnston collab," I brag.

"You got style, freshman," she says.

I laugh. "I'm actually a senior, new to Hillcrest."

"My bad," she says, twirling another lock of hair around her finger. "I wish I could be new somewhere else."

I change it up and lean against the chair. "It's not as easy as I make it look."

She smiles. "I'm done at Hillcrest, New Guy. Everybody here knows me for one thing now. The girl who broke up Hillcrest's perfect couple. It sucks. All of me, reduced to one freaking thing. You wouldn't understand."

"You don't know that," I say.

"OK, try me," she says.

A tight voice comes from behind me. "Pony."

Before I can turn around, the curly haired girl says, "Hi, Georgia."

"Hi, *Taylor*."

"Taylor, is it?" I ask without looking at Georgia yet.

"It is," she confirms.

Georgia taps me on the shoulder. "Pony? Can I have a word with you?"

Once again, my sister's advice worked.

"Taylor, the pleasure was all mine," I say, but she's already back in her phone.

I turn around and spot Georgia storming out of the kitchen. I take off in her path. I'm walking a little taller after having a conversation with Taylor.

Georgia stomps all the way out to the backyard. She turns to me with mad eyes and crossed arms. "Look. Pony. If we are going to do . . . whatever this is . . . you need to promise me one thing."

"What's that?" I ask, concentrating mostly on her "whatever this is" comment.

"Please don't do anything with Taylor. Could you just never talk to her? Or look at her? Or think about her?"

"Sounds like a reasonable request," I say sarcastically.

"Pony, please?"

I shouldn't ask, but I do anyway. "What's the deal with you and Jake?"

She pauses. "I don't know. I didn't know you would be here tonight."

"What does me being here change?" I ask.

"Why *are* you here, Pony?"

I puff up, ready to brag about my new friends. "I came with Jerry and Kenji."

She looks surprised. "Those guys?"

And I immediately deflate. "You don't like them?"

"They're cool, I guess."

Two bubbly girls in matching pink dresses approach Georgia to say hello. While they're chatting, I have time to think. Will Georgia tell me the truth about Jake tonight? Probably not. Are they an exclusive thing? Not likely. Could they be close? They were dancing pretty damn close. I need to act quick—I'm walking into the scene late. What does the leading man in rom-coms do when there's a ticking clock? Something big and bold.

"Georgia, do you want to get out of here?"

The girls stop talking. Georgia looks surprised, nervously pushing her hair behind her ear. "How?" she asks.

"Give me five minutes."

"Sure," she says, then returns to the conversation with girls. It sounds like they're thinking of trying out for cheerleading and basically worship Georgia.

I walk as casually as possible until I'm around the house and out of sight. Then I sprint. I need to secure a getaway car. And quick. I'm kicking myself for not driving tonight. I would have ditched those guys in a heartbeat. Steal a car? Too desperate.

I run up to the garage connected to the house. The side door is open. I'm through the door when I see it. Or rather, *them*. Jake and the girl who Georgia just made me promise to never talk to, look at, or think about. I freeze. They freeze. Nothing is happening— they appear to be just talking. Still, I'm guessing Georgia would not be happy to find out this happened. Did she make Jake promise the same thing as me?

"Hey, new kid!" Jake says, smiling at me.

I loosen up. "That's me. And this isn't the bathroom, is it?"

"I would rather that you didn't piss in here," Jake says.

Taylor looks away from me. She seems upset. If this were a movie, I'd be the bumbling guy who tries to stay cool but acts weird and knocks things over.

"Agreed," I say, then start backing out. "Good day to you both." I reach for the doorknob and knock over a stack of books. Without picking anything up, I turn and walk out.

I shut the door and bend over, hands on my knees, taking a few deep breaths. That was weird. Doesn't matter. I accept the truth: I have no wheels. Game over. I stand up straight and start walking back to Georgia, defeated, when I spot something across the tennis court. A beacon of hope.

GEORGIA, 10:01 P.M.

I check my phone; it's been four minutes. One more and I walk away on principle alone.

I hear my name and turn around. Lauren and Matt are standing behind me.

"What are you doing out here alone?" Lauren asks.

I look up at the sky. "Checking out the stars. Just saw a shooting star crash into a still star. Very messy."

They both look up, and just as they do, a golf cart with red-white-and-blue streamers hanging off the back comes sputtering around the corner and pulls up beside me. I duck under the plastic roof and smile at Pony. "Party in the USA?"

"Georgia, want to run away with me?"

I look back at Lo and Matt. They are staring at me. What are they going to think about me leaving with Pony? Word will get back to Mia within minutes. But golf carts are awesome. And Pony is interesting.

"Long story," I say to Lauren, then hop into the cart. We take off slowly, en route to the woods behind Jake's house. I put my feet up on the dashboard. "So, Thelma, where are we going?"

He frowns at me. "I'm more of a Louise."

Pony is flooring the gas pedal, but we're still moving at the pace of an elderly racewalker. We drive off the property and follow a paved path headed toward the lake. I'm nervous and excited about what's next.

He follows the gravel road into the woods. It's quiet. It's too quiet. This is the perfect setup for an ax-murderer situation. Instead of freaking myself out, I pull up Spotify on my phone and start playing my *Chill Out* playlist. The familiar beats fill the muggy air.

Pony looks at me, concerned. "Is Jake going to have me arrested for taking this golf cart?"

"Nah," I say. "I'll make sure he doesn't press charges."

Pony goes quiet. The wheels of the cart crunch over the fallen leaves as we pull up to the lake. The stars dance in the reflection of the dark blue water. Looks warm. Crickets and other bugs sing in the trees around our golf cart. The moon is half full and bright.

"This is White Rock Lake," I say, acting incredibly knowledgeable.

We come to a stop about a foot from the water and stay in the cart. "Interesting fact about this lake, Pony—there are sharks in there. Lake sharks. Those are the worst kind of shark."

"Georgia, what's the deal with the stories?"

"Stories?" I ask, acting like I'm offended.

"I don't know, the way you avoid any real conversation with your wild tales."

I like that he thinks I'm wild. Everyone typically ignores my adorable evasions of the truth. Except Lauren, who falls for most of them (I love her). But no one confronts me about them. "I don't know. It's easier, I guess. Most of the time, the truth is boring."

"You think you're boring?"

"Sometimes," I admit.

Pony laughs. "Georgia, I can't think of a less boring person."

He better stop being cute or I'm going to kiss him right now.

"Fine. Just for you, and tonight only, you can ask me questions and I'll answer truthfully. But . . ."

"There's always a *but*," Pony says.

I continue, "BUT I get to ask you questions, too. And you better not lie."

I stick my pinkie out to make him swear. He thinks the deal over for a second and wraps his pinkie around mine. Game on.

"And what do you call this game?" he asks.

"Truth or truth," I say.

"Nice." He unhooks his pinkie from mine. "I'm first. What's your favorite movie?"

To seem worldly, I would normally rattle off some art house movie that I have never actually seen, but that's not the game. I shrug and tell the stupid truth.

"Love Actually."

"No, Georgia, no! Please lie to me! Anything but *Love Actually*," he says.

"Come on, it's romantic."

He shakes his head. "Let's just agree to disagree."

"OK, my turn." I'm determined to make him regret *Love Actually* shaming me. "Pony, are you a virgin?"

His cheeks get red, and he looks away. "Yes," he says quietly.

"Now I know you're telling the truth."

"Are you a virgin?" he asks.

"No," I admit. "I've been with one guy."

"Oh," he says.

I can't read what his *oh* means. "My turn! All your social media started about a year ago. What's up with that?"

"Stalk much?" he asks.

"Maybe."

"That was my parents' rule," he admits.

"They sound strict."

"Yeah. Dad can be controlling. Probably from his years in the military. My mom is great, but she can't always stop him."

Can't always stop him? That's ominous. I take my feet off the golf cart dashboard and scoot a little closer to him.

"That must be awful," I say.

He scoots a little closer to me. "I deal. Why were you upset that I met your mom?"

"Pony, oh god, I wasn't upset that you met her. I was surprised that she was at the game." I look down and kick my heels. "My parents divorced. Two years ago. Mom ran off with some rich guy. So I don't talk to her much anymore. And she didn't come to a single game last year."

"That's rough," he says. And scoots closer to me. We're almost touching. This honesty thing is kind of fun. I haven't told many people about that stuff. There's just something about this guy. My turn.

"What's your real name?"

"I told you, it's Pony. Are you and Jake dating?"

"What?" I ask, pretending to be offended.

"I saw you dancing earlier. You look like more than friends."

OK, whatever, he saw that. I scoot away, just a little. "Didn't take you for the jealous kind, Pony."

"I just want to know what's up," he says without looking at me.

"What's up is I was born without a heart." Pony shoots me a look. *Ugh, truth.* "I just went through a crazy breakup. My ex cheated on me at a party this summer and betrayed me in a terrible way. I'm not ready to date. I'm not ready to get lied to again."

He bites his lip. I watch his face soften as he thinks about what I said. He grabs my hand and holds it. "I'm sorry, that's awful. I won't lie to you, Georgia."

I know I said I wasn't dating this year. And I know I shouldn't be dating the new kid with no friends. But something comes over me. I lean in and press my lips against his. He hesitates, then kisses me back, and it's *everything.* His lips are soft. He takes it slow. Doesn't overdo it. My body warms up as my heart does flip-flops against my chest. This is more than a kiss—this is a beginning.

After a few blissful seconds, we stop and separate just a little, our faces still close. I nudge the tip of his nose with the tip of my nose, and we smile. Then we both get shy and look away. That was a little too real.

"Georgia?"

I look at him, ready to do that all over again. "Yes?"

"There's something you should know. I was going to tell you, but . . ."

And nothing. He lost his words again. I bet he's about to lay down another lame pickup line. I beat him to the punch. "Should I feel your shirt, Pony? Is it made of boyfriend material?"

"I'm transgender," he says.

"You're what?"

"Transgender."

Transgender? I'm gobsmacked. My jaw is on the floor. I had no idea. Or I hadn't thought about it. Why would I think about it?

I pull away from him completely. "What does that mean?" I ask, even though I understand perfectly what it means. I need to hear him unpack it for me.

Pony clears his throat. "I was born in a girl body, but I'm not a girl. I've never felt like a girl. I'm a boy. Every part of me is a boy, except my body."

I have no words. And that doesn't happen often. A sudden wave of frustration overtakes me. I hop out of the golf cart, feeling the need to stand. I look around, very aware of my surroundings. Is anyone watching? Does everyone know he's transgender? Lauren and Matt saw me leave the party with a trans person? Mia is going to pissed. Are people hiding in the woods laughing at me?

"Georgia," Pony says, pulling me back to reality.

"Why didn't you tell me before we *kissed*?"

He gets out of the cart and stands directly in front of me. "'Cause . . ." He stalls out, pissing me off more.

"Because why?" I demand. I'm so caught up in my tantrum that I don't notice Pony lean in for another kiss. His lips touch mine and I pull away, lose my balance, and fall backward, right on my butt.

"That's why," he says, lowering his head. "I just wanted you to like me."

"I did like you, Pony."

"Did?" he asks.

"I do. Like you."

But that's probably a lie. Who cares? He lied to me. He's the liar here. I just spilled my guts to this guy, and he's been straight-up lying. I get up on my feet and brush the dirt off my jeans.

"Georgia, I'm sorry I didn't tell you sooner. I should have, and I tried, but I didn't. I don't want this to end. More than anything. I'm just like the other guys, I swear. I'm just missing a part."

This is too much. I need time. "Pony . . ."

"Don't," he says.

"You LIED to me, Pony. This whole time."

"No, I didn't."

"You did," I say.

"I just omitted. Delayed. Postponed."

Ugh, I hate how cute he can be—the way he bites his dumb lip and looks at me with his stupid puppy-dog eyes. He weakens my defenses, and I need to stay strong. I'm standing in the middle of a tornado of feelings and thoughts that I've never had to deal with before this moment. I need to get out of here before I say something dumb.

"Pony, I can't do this right now . . . I just can't . . ."

He opens his mouth to talk but changes his mind, turns around, walks away.

And I don't stop him.

SEVEN

Sunday, September 8

PONY, 12:06 P.M.

Victor swings open the door before I have a chance to knock. "You're late!"

I check my phone. "I'm five minutes late?"

"You're two hours and five minutes late, bad boy."

He's right. This has not been my best morning. I woke up with my heart in a clamp. My legs are sore from the long walk home last night. I'm bouncing between extreme exhaustion and a full-on panic attack. The large iced coffee on the way over here probably isn't helping my anxiety.

"I'm sorry. It won't happen again," I promise.

"I'm sure it will," he says with an attitude. I don't think Victor will ever be on my side. "Anyway, Ted is in good spirits today and would like to get to work. Follow me!"

He practically drags me to a bedroom filled with junk. We find Ted sitting on the floor, leaning against a black leather couch, looking at old photos. He's wearing a red satin robe holding a Bloody Mary topped off with celery and olives.

"There you are, son!" Ted motions for me to come over. He's excited to have company, but I've got a hundred things on my mind, and Ted London isn't one of them.

I take a seat on the couch behind him.

Ted hands me a photo. "Look at this woman. Absolutely stunning."

"Yes," I agree.

"She was one of my best friends, Pony."

I hand the photo back. "Not your girlfriend?"

He laughs loudly. "No, no. Just a friend. I miss her dearly. But I'll be seeing her soon, I suppose."

I nod until I realize he's talking about the afterlife and not next Thanksgiving.

"Are you scared of dying?" I ask, triggering another booming Ted laugh.

"Are you?" he asks back.

"Do you have any regrets?" I blurt out. I'm too tired to have a filter today.

"Heavy question from a new friend, but I'll entertain it. The answer is no, I have no regrets. I wouldn't change a thing about my life."

We are sitting in a room full of junk inside an empty house. He wouldn't change one thing? *Not one thing?*

He spreads his arms out like the King of Crap. "And look at what I'm leaving behind. *A legacy!*"

I look around and try to be sincere. "Clearly!"

"Which reminds me, how are you organizing my treasures, Pony?"

"An artist never reveals his process," I say.

Ted pops an olive into his mouth and waits for the real answer. I clear my throat. "Right now, it's divide and conquer. I'm making piles."

"Piles! How charming," Ted says. "Please sir, tell me more about these piles."

"Well," I say, making up the rest as it comes out of my mouth, "there's the movie stuff, photo stuff, clothing stuff, and personal stuff."

He cuts me off. "Personal stuff?"

"Like old bills and press clippings and letters," I say.

"Pony, I trust that you will not read my personal letters."

"Why would I read your letters?" I ask defensively. I am punchy from lack of sleep and rejection.

"Thank you for understanding, my boy," Ted says, while using the couch to pull himself up. I try to help, but he waves me off. "I'm headed to the backyard to get some sun. Come out and take a break with me later?"

"Actually, I am going to—"

"Wonderful. Why don't you bring out one of my treasures, and I'll tell you the story behind it? Show-and-tell, Pony! How much fun will that be?"

"Fun," I confirm. I need to renegotiate my contract to include friendship hours. "And maybe I can have a Bloody Mary?"

Ted London flashes his Hollywood smile at me. "Not a chance, kid."

Victor appears, and they head outside, leaving me alone with all his stuff and all my thoughts. I sit on the cool leather couch and shut my eyes.

Last night was messy. It was too much, too fast. I froze up and became the spinning pinwheel when the computer gets overloaded. Too bad I can't just reboot last night.

I stretch my sore calves. Can't believe I walked away from Georgia. And all the way home. Both dumb decisions. I couldn't bring myself to go back to the party and find Kenji and Jerry. On the bright side, the two-hour walk (through the woods, backyards, and strip malls) gave me plenty of time to mentally beat myself up. I'm lucky that I didn't cross paths with a rabid racoon or armadillo.

There's so much I should have said to Georgia. But as usual, I didn't. Why do I get so tongue-tied? Technically, my tongue isn't the problem. The words get tangled in a ball at the bottom of my stomach. My sister always screams, "USE YOUR WORDS!" but it never helps.

I've been daydreaming that I would tell Georgia I'm trans, and it wouldn't matter to her. She would look at me with the kindest eyes, hug me, and tell me that nothing could stop her from liking me. What an idiot I am.

I know I didn't choose to be transgender, but it doesn't seem fair. Why couldn't I have been born in the right body? This would all be so easy. Last night would have been perfect. But I'm not normal. And I never will be.

On days like today, I wish I could reboot my life.

But maybe if I use my words, she'll come around. I can't give up now. I open my phone and pull up Gmail.

FROM: PonyJacobs@gmail.com
TO: GeorgiaRobertsTX@gmail.com
DATE: September 8 at 12:55 p.m.
SUBJECT: About last night . . .

Georgia,

There's a few things I wanted to say to you last night.

I'm sorry that I didn't tell you earlier that I'm transgender. I tried once, after we got pulled over on the way to school. Doesn't matter now.

I messed up. I like you. I like what's happening between us and I don't want it to be over.

Can we talk about this face-to-face?

You're magic.
Pony

I reread the email, imagining what she will think when she reads it. It's not quite a declaration of love, but I used some of my words. That's progress. I hit Send. Look at me, stepping out of my comfort zone. I'm about to get up from the couch when my phone dings.

FROM: GeorgiaRobertsTX@gmail.com
TO: PonyJacobs@gmail.com
DATE: September 8 at 1:01 p.m.
SUBJECT: Magic, you say?

You think I'm magic, Pony? That's funny cause I'm the one who got TRICKED.

UGH, Pony. I'm mad at you. And confused.

G.

Downside: Anger. Upside: Levity. She's making jokes. This can't possibly be over. Hope expands my heart, pressing against the clamp. Against all online dating tips for bros, I hit Reply immediately.

FROM: PonyJacobs@gmail.com
TO: GeorgiaRobertsTX@gmail.com
DATE: September 8 at 1:04 p.m.
SUBJECT: M-A-G-I-C

Are you a magician? Because when I look at you, everyone else disappears . . .

Can we please talk?

For the record, I'm really bad at magic (I once pulled a hat out of a rabbit), but I have been creating an illusion of a regular guy, and now someone knows my secret. And I have feelings for that somebody.

My phones dings.

FROM: GeorgiaRobertsTX@gmail.com
TO: PonyJacobs@gmail.com
DATE: September 8 at 1:07 p.m.
SUBJECT: You're a dork

I'm not ready.

G.

The clamp on my heart tightens, destroying hope. I'm stuck in purgatory with no clue what she's thinking. I pocket my phone and stand up. I know exactly what I want Ted to tell me about.

I head to the backyard with a paper bag that I'm extra careful not to drop. The patio deck is wrapped around a large pool with cool blue water; there are ceiling fans and matching patio furniture. Ted is reading a book in a wicker chair with an unlit cigar hanging from his mouth. I sit down in a rocking chair beside him, looking out to the water.

"This would be a great place to have a party," I say.

"Pony, if I told you the things that happened at the parties in Hollywood back in the day, I'd have to kill you."

"Try me," I say (it might be worth dying to hear).

Ted laughs, snapping out of memory land and back into reality.

"What did you bring me, Sir Pony?"

I put the paper bag on my lap and pull out his Oscar. Ted wants to talk. I want to hear this story. And—I want to hold a real Oscar. So win, win, win.

"That's my boy," Ted says. "Going for the gold!"

"Story of my life," I joke.

"Well, then. That beautiful piece of metal in your unworthy hands is the Academy Award for Best Supporting Actor, 1956. The movie was *The Gigantic*, a surprisingly smart Western thriller starring James Dean, Elizabeth Taylor, and up-and-comer Ted London. I was twenty-two at the time and unstoppable."

Ted reaches for the trophy and bounces it around in his hands. He continues, "Working on *Gigantic* was truly remarkable, like the stars aligned for the eighteen days of filming. No dramatic actor blowups halting production, no punishing director doing every scene over and over again. It was a good time for all."

I get chills thinking about working on that movie set. "James

Dean died in that tragic car accident after we shot the movie. He never got to see it."

He hands the Oscar back to me. Almost like the weight of it was too heavy for him. "How did you get into the movie business?" I ask, hoping for a clue.

"Well, aren't you a little Barbara Walters?"

"Who?" I ask.

"Dear lord, kids today. OK. How about Anderson Cooper?"

"Reporter. Got it. Not looking for an interview, just curious," I say.

Ted sits up. "My family was working class, so I worked as soon as I could. They didn't have rules about kids working at that time. My first job was an usher at the only movie theater in town. They played black-and-white talkies. Could you even imagine such a world, Pony?"

"Sure," I say.

"Bloody liar! Anyway, that's when I fell in love with films. I moved to LA with one dollar in my pocket when I turned eighteen. Sounds crazy, but I made it work, because that's what working-class people do."

I hold up the Oscar to get his attention. "Was your wife there when you got this?"

"My wife?" Ted looks stunned.

"You were married?"

"Oh, yes, my wife. No, that wasn't until later."

"Cool," I say, wondering what Anderson Cooper would ask next.

"Pony, do you have a girlfriend?"

"It's complicated, Mr. London." It feels weird to call him Ted as I hold his Oscar.

"What love story isn't complicated?" he questions.

"There's a girl. And she's amazing. But she just found out something about me last night, something that I was hiding, and I don't know what she'll do now."

Sure, I have no problem telling this movie star how I feel, but put me in front of Georgia, and I'm Silly Putty.

"Oh, what a movie this will make someday! How will it end, Pony?"

"With me dying alone," I say too quickly to stop myself.

"What a twist!" Ted says, either ignoring the comparison, or not caring.

I correct myself. "We will end up together, obviously."

"Obviously," he repeats in singsong. "Does she know that?"

"No."

Ted takes off his sunglasses and looks me directly in the eye. "Pony. You must tell her how you feel. Perhaps it will help her make a choice?"

"Sounds easy enough, but the words tend to get stuck."

He thinks for a second. "When I have trouble remembering my lines, I simply start speaking, and eventually my brain catches up. Same thing here—just start speaking and let your heart catch up to your mouth."

"That's brilliant," I say.

"Fake it until you make it," Ted says.

"Is that an acting technique?" I ask.

"Alcoholics Anonymous," he says, then takes a drink. Ted puts his sunglasses back on and settles into the chair. That is the conclusion of this Ted talk.

GEORGIA, 5:54 P.M.

I'm tired, cranky, hangry, and ready to go home. Too bad I just got here.

Mia opens her door. "Girl, you're late!"

She hands me a flute of champagne and ushers me into her mini mansion. Mia lives in one of the rich neighborhoods. Her mom is set for life from the divorce of her wealthy lawyer husband (Mia's stepdad), after finding him with another woman.

Most Sunday nights, the mains—Lauren, Kelly, Mia, and I—gather for dinner and debriefing. Nine times out of ten, we meet at Mia's house because her mom looks the other way while we responsibly enjoy a glass of wine or champagne—or two.

Only problem is Mrs. Davis tries too hard to be the cool mom, insisting that we call her Connie and gossip about the guys at school. *Gross.* We have heard too many stories of her wild times as a cheerleader at Hillcrest. Mia and Connie are more BFF than mother-daughter. It's a little odd to me, but they are thick as thieves and happy.

Mia and I enter the dining room, where everyone is waiting. Including Connie.

"Georgia, that top is everything," Connie says. "Where did you get it?"

I look down at my shirt. It's nothing special.

"Target, maybe?"

"Girl!" She snaps twice, shaking all the bracelets on her hand. "I love me some Target fashion!"

Connie is coming in hot tonight. I hug Lauren and Kelly and take a seat at the table.

"Mom," Mia demands, "could you get dinner? I am running on empty."

"Yes, girl," Connie says, then heads into the kitchen. "Y'all are not ready for my chicken and dumplings."

Once it's a Connie-free zone, Mia gets down to business. "Georgia, dish right now. Lo told us that you left *in a golf cart* with that new guy last night," Mia says.

"We have been texting you all day," Lauren adds.

Mia shakes her head. "And Jake has been worried sick!"

I am outnumbered. I look over at Kelly. Maybe she can help. "Kelly?"

She looks at me with teasing eyes. "I, too, am interested in your whereabouts."

There's no way I can tell them what *actually* happened. Could you imagine unleashing that kind of juicy secret on a group of gossipy cheerleaders? The entire school would know that Pony was transgender before I finished my sentence.

I don't want to hurt Pony, but I'm not known for my secret-keeping abilities. I'm literally sweating. I can feel the secret in my throat, begging to be told, like an itch that needs to be scratched. But this isn't gossip, it's a secret. I need to be strong.

"I was abducted by aliens," I say.

"No way," Lauren says. "Wait, were you really?"

"Lo, no, she wasn't," Mia says.

"How was the anal probe?" Kelly asks, and we all laugh. I can't decide when she is funnier, in the mascot costume or out of it.

"Our sweet Georgia was abducted, but not by aliens," Mia says, flipping her hair. "Is this new guy going to be a problem for us?"

"Georgie," Lauren says, "we have decided on Jake for you. But the new guy is cute."

Mia jumps in. "A little weird, though. Always alone."

I perk up, ready for a fight. "He literally just started in a new school. What do you expect?"

Mia takes a sip of champagne. "Georgia, really? That kid is a nobody. He doesn't make sense for you."

"G," Kelly finally jumps in, "I support you dating Pony. Just don't forget a saddle."

"We are not dating," I say, hoping to end this conversation.

"Good," Mia says, like she influenced that decision. Whatever.

The savory smell of creamy chicken goodness fills the room. Connie enters wearing a bright pink apron and matching oven mitts, holding the piping hot casserole dish. I almost faint from excitement. I might have forgotten to eat today. That happens when I'm upset.

"Dinner is served, y'all!" Connie says, and we clap in appreciation.

Mia turns to Lauren. "Lo, fetch the plates and utensils?"

I look at Lauren with big eyes. Now is her chance to stand up to Mia. She can get her own damn plates.

"Sure," Lauren says, then heads off to the kitchen. I slump in my chair in defeat. How do I help her with that?

Connie sets the dish in the middle of the table and fans the steam with her oven mitt. When Lo returns, we take turns ladling dumplings and bits of chicken swimming in cream sauce onto our plates. Connie takes a plate and heads to the living room. "I'll be watching *Real Housewives.* Holler if y'all need me!"

There's silence for several minutes as we devour the dumplings. Just a bunch of "mmmm" and "ahhh" and "ouch" (when Lauren burns her tongue). I start to feel better. They call it comfort food for a reason.

"I heard a rumor," Mia says, ending the silence. "Chuck told Angie that there's a *lesbian* on the cheerleading team." She looks at us, one at a time, with her openmouthed OMG face, expecting a similar reaction. No one returns it.

This is Mia's drama dragon rearing its head. She is the primary power source of Hillcrest's gossip. If some guy has an accidental boner in front of the class, she knows. If someone is hooking up with someone they shouldn't, she knows. If there are whispers in the hallway, you can bet Mia had some part in them.

"Who could it be?" Mia asks.

Lauren jumps in. "I think it's Zoe. She is always lingering in the locker room."

"I don't think it matters," I say. But it does matter to them. Just wait until they find out about Pony.

"We can figure it out. There are only twenty cheerleaders," Lauren offers.

"Keep your eyes out. Stay sharp," Mia urges.

"And then what?" Kelly finally enters the conversation.

Mia tosses her hair. "I don't know, have a talk with her?"

If I was to date Pony, and he was born in a girl body, would that make me a lesbian? I don't understand the sex part of this situation. But I did like kissing him. My mind drifts to that kiss, the moment before everything fell apart.

"Jerry asked me out," Kelly says very fast.

Mia drops her fork. "Jerry Goldberg?"

We exchange glances around the table, deciding how to react. We are happy that Kelly is dating, but Jerry is a total dud. She can do better, although he's funny and she's funny. And who am I to judge? I may or may not be dating a transgender guy.

I finally roll myself out of Mia's house an hour later with a to-go cheesecake slice on a paper plate. Sunday supper was a welcome distraction to my all-day pity party. I have been going back and forth about Pony, but this night helped convince me. I start my car and head home, jamming some sad songs.

I pull into the driveway, somehow beating my dad home, and kill my headlights. I unlock my phone and reopen Ms. Randolph's offer to be freelance writer. I've done some thinking today. I know what I want, and I know what to say.

FROM: GeorgiaRobertsTX@gmail.com
TO: Kerry_Randolph@hillcrest.com
DATE: September 8 at 8:12 p.m.
SUBJECT: Re: Hillcrest Reporter

Ms. Randolph,

Thank you for never giving up on me.

I would like to take you up on your offer to freelance for the *Reporter*. But I checked the cheerleader bylaws, and I can't write for the paper and be a cheerleader. How archaic is that crap? Can I write the columns anonymously?

Yours,
Georgia

I gather my stuff and get out of my car. I am more than ready for a good night's sleep. Our porch is pitch black—the light has been broken for weeks—so I'm really flexing my unlocking-the-door-and-balancing-cheesecake muscles.

From my left, in the dark, I hear, "Hey, you."

I jump and scream. The old jump-and-scream. With bonus points for dropping the cheesecake on the ground. I look over and see a dark figure sitting on the bench.

"Pony?" I say, hoping that it's Pony.

"Yeah, sorry, didn't mean to scare you."

"Maybe less creepy next time," I say, bending down to clean up the fallen cheesecake. He stands up to help me, too. That piece of cheesecake was the brightest part of this dumb day, the only thing right in my life, and now it's facedown on the porch.

I stop cleaning and sit down on the welcome mat, my back against the door. I'm just so fucking frustrated. I don't want to do this now—he's forcing my hand. A couple anger/exhaustion tears run down my face. I'm glad it's dark and Pony can't see. He's preoccupied pushing white mush on a paper plate anyway. I wipe the tears away, unnoticed.

Pony helps me up and hands me the plate. "Thanks," I say. We sit down on the bench. I start to say, "Pony—"

"Georgia, before you say anything, I need to tell you a few things." He's wringing his hands and slumped over. "I'm terrible at this, obviously. But Ted London said to tell you how I feel before it's too late."

"Who is Ted London?" I ask.

"Ted is the actor, the one who's dying?"

"You told him about us?"

"Kind of," he admits.

"Does Ted London know you are transgendered?"

"Not really. And it's transgender, present tense."

I'm annoyed and glad he's is here right now. I have questions bouncing around in my head. If I can't have cheesecake, at least I get some answers.

"Pony? Are you lying to everyone all the time?"

He looks away. "And you aren't? With your stories?"

"This isn't about me," I say.

He lets out a breath. "I started my transition at my old school. Everyone knew. Some people had a problem with it and were vocal at the school board meetings."

"What? That's disgusting," I say.

"Well, it's Texas," he says. "There were some supportive people. But I hated all the attention. I was sick of only being known as transgender. I didn't want to be scared to walk into a bathroom."

He pauses. I push. "Did something happen in the bathroom, Pony?"

"Nothing serious," he says, and then sits back, staring straight ahead. I follow his lead and sit back as well. We both look out at the lawn.

"There was this one kid. Chip," he begins.

"Ugh, *Chips*," I say.

"Yeah. His dad was not OK with me using the boys' bathroom. He was the loudest at the public hearings. And when that didn't work, he sent his son to spread the message. Chip would follow me into the boys' bathroom and start yelling that I was a girl and other things."

"My god, Pony. That's awful," I say, grabbing his hand. "What happened?"

"I stopped using the bathrooms at school," he says, then goes quiet.

I'm sad and mad for Pony. That must have been tough. I squeeze his hand.

He looks back over at me. "I just want to be normal."

"What's normal?" I ask.

"You," he says. "You're normal."

I laugh, loud. "I'm your standard for normal?"

He shrugs. "I want to walk into a room and not have everyone know I'm trans."

"And how's that working out for you?"

"Not bad. No one stares at me. No one whispers behind my back. I made a couple friends. We talk about guy stuff, like balls."

He's all excited. I laugh and give him a push. "TMI, Pony."

"And . . . I met this girl."

"Careful, I hear they are nothing but trouble," I say, letting go of his hand.

"Tell me about it," he says, then finds my hand again.

"No, you tell me about it."

Pony smiles but tries to hide it. "OK. This girl. She's something else. The first time our eyes met, I was on the hook. She's the smartest person in the room but hides it. I don't know why she does that. Her brown eyes make me happy. Her smile makes me happy. I'm just getting to know her, and that makes me happy. I don't even care that she's a cheerleader."

I give him a soft punch on the arm for that one.

Pony continues, "I'm talking about Mia, of course."

I hit him again, harder.

At the worst time, car headlights blind us as my dad turns

into the driveway. I let go of Pony's hand. I guess Pony is about to meet my dad. We watch silently as he gets out of the car and walks up the steps to the porch.

"And why are you so late?" I ask.

"Oh, Georgia," he says, straining his eyes to decipher the shadows in the dark. "And friend?"

"This is Pony," I say.

"Ah, the infamous Pony," he says. I'm counting my lucky stars that no one can see me blush.

Pony stands and shakes my dad's hand. "Nice to meet you, Mr. Roberts."

"And you, Pony. I might have some carrots inside, if you're hungry?"

"Very funny, Dad." I can't with his dad jokes. "Where were you?"

He puffs up, all proud. "I was on a date with the internet."

Pony shoots me a wide-eyed look.

"You mean, you met a woman from the internet?"

"Correct. We met for drinks at the Mucky Duck."

"Romantic. And?" I'm dying to hear the play-by-play, but the timing is not ideal.

"She was lovely. She listened to all my stories. We had so much fun. At one point, the bartender asked if we were on an internet date! Everyone could tell!"

Oh, boy.

"OK, Dad, can we finish this later?" I say, hoping he takes the hint.

"Right-o, I will head in. Five more minutes out here, Georgie? It's getting late."

"You got it, dude," I say.

Pony and I watch him go into the house. Then Pony turns back to me. "Georgia, I like you. And before you knew I was transgender, I think you liked me. I'm the same person. Nothing has changed about me. Let's keep getting to know each other."

He reaches for my hand, but I move it away. I can't do this. All I want to do is tell Pony about my new freelance gig and kiss him again. I'd like to believe that I could date him and not care what people thought of me, but I know me. I would be paranoid that his secret would get out. What people would think of me.

And I'm not a lesbian. Or whatever I would be if I dated a trans guy.

But I can't tell him that. I need another reason why we can't be together. Something that won't hurt him.

"Georgia, I'm sorry that I lied to you."

Bingo.

"Pony. My ex-boyfriend lied to me. Big time. And probably multiple times. My trust in guys? It's ruined."

"Would you have kissed me if you knew I was trans?"

"I don't know," I lie. He lowers his head, looking defeated. "Pony, I did like you. You came out of nowhere, all cute and funny. I was open to the possibility of something." I pause, wondering if I should tell him the next part. "I even started writing."

"Because of me?" he asks, fighting a smile.

"You helped. But you also lied to me. If I can't trust you, I can't be with you. That's my bottom line."

Pony gets upset, shifting in his seat. "And you can trust Jake?"

"He hasn't lied to me like you have."

"Yeah, well, I saw Jake and Taylor talking last night. Alone. There, now you can add Jake to the list of guys you can't trust."

My dad knocks lightly on the window behind us. *Saved by the dad.* I stand up. I need to get out of here. "Pony, I'm sorry, I really am. I'd like to still be . . ."

"Don't say it, Georgia."

I have to say it, because it needs to be said. I also know it will hurt Pony, and he just hurt me. So I say it:

"Friends."

PART TWO

THE FRIEND ZONE

EIGHT

Sunday, September 22

PONY, 6:35 A.M.

"Hey, Fartface."

"Morning, Rocky."

Even though it's way too early, I'm happy to connect with my sister. It's been impossible to talk since she picked up a second job as a performer at some artsy burlesque space. Rocky serves dinner at an Ethiopian restaurant in the West Village and then heads into Brooklyn to dance until the sun comes up. About once a week, I get an early-morning call when she's about to go to bed and I'm about to wake up.

I lie back down and rest the laptop on my stomach. Thanks to the magic of Skype, I'm watching Rocky remove her makeup. To be fair, it's more glitter than makeup. She pulls a tissue out and starts wiping off her bright green eye shadow. "So, bro, how many girlfriends you got?"

"Same as last time you asked—none."

Georgia and I kissed fifteen days ago. Or three hundred and sixty hours. Or one hundred and forty-four showings of *The Shining*. But who's counting? Not me.

"Pony, Pony, Pony," Rocky says. "You need to emotionally detach from Georgia with love."

"I'm over her," I lie. "Georgia who? You keep bringing her up."

My sister knows firsthand how upset I was about Georgia. When I got home that night, I called her, crying like crazy. Sometimes, hope is a curse. The next day, I woke up and deleted Georgia's number and our text thread—after reading it once or seven times—and unfollowed her. I needed to put her behind me. I don't want to be friends with her. Never ever.

"Pony, no offense, but you're seventeen. They will all feel like *the one*."

"Says the nineteen-year-old."

"Whatever. I'm worldly as fuck!" she says, snapping her fingers into the camera.

"What's new in your dating life, sis?"

Rocky recently retired her unicorn status, after the couple she was dating got too "needy" by offering her their spare bedroom and tropical vacations. My sister gets bored easily.

"I have an overwhelming crush on a flame dancer named Eric Divine!"

"Actual fire dancing?" I ask.

"Pony, yes. And don't you dare make fun of him—it's so sexy.

Eric is one of the best in the world. He invited me to Burning Man next year!"

"Burning Man?" I ask.

"It's a nine-day outdoor arts and culture festival in the middle of the desert, with no running water or electricity. Want to come?"

"Hard pass," I say without hesitation. I am not an outdoorsman. I like showers and toilets and sleeping as far off the ground as possible.

Rocky is applying lotion to her face. "Ponyyy," she says. "How's school?"

"Really great. No one stares when I go to the bathroom. People treat me like I'm just another guy. I'm making friends. I'm happy, Rocky."

And I'm not lying to my sister. I am ten times happier at Hillcrest than my past school. I wish I didn't have to spend so much time thinking about keeping my secret a secret. Always on guard, but it's worth it. And Georgia? She was just this bright, burning flame. I wish she weren't in all my classes, but nothing I can do about it.

Rocky combs her hair and yawns. "Pony. Do me a favor?"

"Maybe."

"Talk to someone about how you're feeling. A friend? Don't bottle it all in. That's not good for you. Your chakras are blocked."

"Rocky, you be careful with the flame dancer. Don't get burned!"

"I hate you. And I love you. Bye."

My depression sneaks back in as soon as I shut my computer. I pull the covers over my head and hide from the world. I should get over my crap and be friends with Georgia, but I can't let go of the anger and rejection.

I wake up a couple hours later to my dad pounding on the door: my weekend wake-up call. I have the whole day ahead of me with not one plan. I should go work, but I need a break from the dehoarding of Ted London. I have cleaned five rooms so far. Only ninety-five more before I can afford my surgery. Too bad there's only five left.

I check my phone. One message.

Max: DUDE. EPIC SUNDAY. Working at Ellie's. Come thru. Let's hit up the fundraiser carnival at the Center!

Max works the brunch shift at Ellie's Café, a queer-owned restaurant in downtown Dallas. It makes for great people watching, always packed with colorful and creative types.

I make it from bed to brunch in under an hour. The small café is wedged in between two towering condominiums and painted the colors of the pride flag. The gravel parking lot is littered with garden gnomes placed in sexual positions. As my mom would say, this place has character.

I walk in and get hit with the smell of pancakes and patchouli. The place is tiny, probably seats thirty queers and their allies. I saddle up to the only seat left, a stool connected to the small wooden bar. Max is in top form, cutting through the aisles and making people laugh and smile.

"Well, look who it is," he says, hugging me. "Everyone," he announces to the place, "this is Little Man!"

And the whole place says in unison, "Hey, Little Man!"

Ellie wanted to create a space that felt inclusive, so every customer is appointed a nickname by the server and greeted in unison. I guess I'm Little Man today. This place has heart, that's for sure.

"What will it be?" he asks as he pours me a cup of coffee. My hero.

I have eaten here enough, I don't need a menu. "Steak and eggs, side of bacon."

"Right on," he says. "Gluten-free pancakes and tofu scramble coming up."

Did I mention this was a vegan restaurant? Max struts off to place my order. The place is alive with bubbly energy and chatter. Friends catching up, couples being cute. The mimosas help the spirits. Are they vegan?

I pull out a tattered paperback from my bag and open to the dog-eared page.

Lately, I have two different books going at the same time. When I'm in stealth mode, I read Harry Potter. An online dating thread suggested reading Harry Potter in public because girls will come up and talk to you about the book. Sadly, Harry hasn't worked his magic for me yet.

When I'm in a safe space, like Ellie's, I am reading Michelle Tea, Eileen Myles, Armistead Maupin, or some other queer writer.

I get lost in the book and don't look up until Max drops a plate of beautiful fake pancakes and fluffy fake eggs in front of me. Vegan food always looks better than it tastes. Max comes up behind me and gives my butt a pinch. "You've lost weight," he says. Max knows that I don't eat as much when I'm upset. My anger gets caught in my stomach, leaving no room for food.

Before I can answer, he shouts, "There she is!" and takes off in the direction of the door. A short Asian girl dressed in a Goth Sailor Moon costume has walked in. Max kisses her on the cheek and yells out, "Fam, this is my dream girl!" The remaining patrons yell out, "Hey, Dream Girl," and laugh. Max excitedly ushers her over to the now-empty barstool beside me and runs off to finish refiling the ketchup bottles and change clothes.

"Hey, Wendy," I say as she gives me a big hug.

"You look like crap." She picks up my coffee cup and takes a drink. We have only met twice, but I guess we are on that level of friendship. A couple minutes later, Max returns wearing an ill-fitted suit with his hair greased back. He's dressed like Sailor Moon's love interest. "Tuxedo Max, here to serve!"

Wendy looks at me, disappointed. "No costume, Pony?"

"It's a carnival fundraiser?"

"And?" she asks.

We walk the five blocks to the LGBTQIA Center with Max in the middle, his arms around both of us. I try to explain my reasoning about going stealth at Hillcrest. "Pony goes to one of those small-town schools," Max informs Wendy.

She tugs at my sleeve. "Pony, you should transfer to Booker and be with us."

"That would be fun, but I think I'll stay put."

"How many trans kids are at your new school?" Wendy asks, always an ally.

"None," I say.

"Well, there's one," Max corrects me. "And it would help things if you were visible."

"Maxy," Wendy interrupts. "Not everyone can be out and proud. Sometimes it's dangerous."

"I get that, Wendy-bear," Max says.

"And not everyone has to be out," she adds. "Pony will come out when he's ready, or not, and that's fine, too."

"And I get that." Max is flustered.

I jump in, trying to help. "I want to be known as the sometimes-funny, sometimes-cute new kid."

"Why can't you be the all-the-time cute and funny transgender new kid?"

I shake my head. "The transgender part can overshadow the other parts."

Wendy ruffles his hair. "It's a personal choice, and this is what Pony wants right now. We should support him."

"You're probably right, Wendy-bear," he says.

I smile at Wendy. I'm starting to really like her for Max.

We arrive at the Resource Center and run up the steps. It's a funky-looking building offering medical and dental services, classes, counseling, and social events for the LGBTQIA community. This is where I met Max, actually. The place of our meet-cute.

We skip down the corridor to the youth center and swing open the door, making a grand entrance. It's a huge room with video games, stacks of board games, and a pool table. The place is packed wall-to-wall with queer kids. They host events like dinner parties, game nights, and dances. Today is the annual fundraiser carnival. When we are older, we will be hanging out at queer bars, but for now, this is our playground.

After writing our names and pronouns on name tags and sticking them to our chests, we hit the refreshment stand and try to orient ourselves to the chaos. There's all sorts of stations set up—games, crafts for sale, and face painting. No alcohol here, just teens fueled on sugar and the excitement of being surrounded by their chosen family.

After they procure sodas and Junior Mints, Max and Wendy wander off to get matching temporary tattoos. I walk around looking for my other friends, but I don't see any familiar faces. Finally, I see an old friend. Dylan is nonbinary, tall with short black hair held back by two pink barrettes. I read the pronoun sticker: they/them.

"Hey, Dylan," I say, and we hug.

"Pony, where you been? Haven't seen you around the center."

Guilt sets in immediately. I have been caught up in my stealth life. "Yeah, bud. I started at a new school. It's been keeping me busy."

"Yeah, I heard."

"You heard?" I ask.

Dylan shrugs. "I'm hosting a queer open mic next Wednesday. Can you come by?"

"Maybe, I might be—"

"Busy?"

"No," I try to explain. "I think I'm working."

"Sure, I get it. New life, new friends. No need for us anymore, right?

"Not at all," I say. My guilt has turned into anger. They walk off, revealing another familiar face about ten feet away. This one from Hillcrest. I duck down like a complete lunatic and peek over the table. I watch Kelly thumb through a box of old records. Kelly, the mascot. Kelly, Georgia's friend. Kelly, the girl who Jerry has been dating. What the hell is she doing here? She turns around to talk to a girl, and I duck back down.

I hear a voice above me. "How long are you planning to hide out at my table?"

I look up at the girl sitting at the table that I'm using as a body shield. She's got long black hair and a sexy, witchy look. Not sure if it's a costume.

"Sorry," I say, "just a minute more."

"Whoever you're hiding from, she walked away. You're safe. Would you like me to read your tarot cards?"

"Sure," I say, then slide into the empty chair across from her.

"It'll be five raffle tickets."

"Oh, sorry, I don't have any." I start to stand up.

"No, stay. The first reading is free for cute boys." She winks at me and begins shuffling her cards. "I'm Gretchen."

"Pony," I say.

"Ask the universe a question to set the intention of the cards."

I pretend like I'm narrowing down the options in my head, but there's only one thing I want to know about.

I close my eyes and think: *What will happen with me and Georgia?*

I open my eyes, and Gretchen spreads the cards out in front of me.

"Now, select one card, and I will tell you the answer to your question."

I move my hands across the deck and flip over a card at random. It's got a heart on it with three swords piecing through it. That can't be good.

"Pony. You have selected the three of hearts. The card of betrayal. The card of heartbreak. The love triangle card. Whoever you were thinking about, this will not end well for you."

"Oh," I say, then sit back in the chair. The reality sinks in, sending chills down my back. I say it again for good measure. "Oh."

"I'm sorry to tell you that bad news." She grabs her pen and starts scribbling on the heart card. "Promise to not hold it against me?"

"I hold you personally responsible," I say.

"Pony, these cards are only guidance. Your fate isn't sealed. You decide that."

I get up to leave, and she hands me the heart card.

"Take it as a reminder."

I look down at the card. She has scribbled her phone number on the edge of it.

"And call me when you're ready to move on."

I pocket the card. I turn to walk away but stop. "Gretchen, I'm trans."

"Pony," she says, "that only makes me like you more."

"Cool," I say, then walk out, head down, praying that I won't run into Kelly. It sucks that I'm ditching Max, but I can't get spotted. Even if she is an ally, I can't run the risk of being outed. Before exiting, I turn around and see people having fun. I can't help but feel on the outside of it all.

NINE

Wednesday, September 25

GEORGIA, 6:10 P.M.

Stop eating my tots. Stop eating my tots. STOP EATING MY TOTS.

"You don't mind, do you, sis?" Izzy asks, ten tots too late.

"Have as many as you want, sis," I say through clenched teeth.

"Truth," she says.

Cheerleader tradition #3478: Seniors mentor sophomores, sister style. Izzy is a decent "li'l sis," and I'm a terrible "big sis," but I'm trying to make things right by taking her out after a brutal practice. The cheerleaders have commandeered a picnic table in the middle of Sonic at peak time. The whole team is spread out and having a ball.

I'm dedicating time to Izzy and her future. Mentoring today's youth is a selfless act on my part, but it's cool; I have plenty of time lately. I have been boy-less since Pony rejected my friendship and dropped the bomb about Jake and Taylor. The universe is making sure that I keep my "no dating for a year" promise whether I like it or not.

Football season has kept me busy. And school too, I suppose. But my time and energy have been devoted to my undercover writing for the *Reporter*. Ms. Randolph agreed to let me publish without a name attached. She thought it might create mystery.

As a joke, I turned in five hundred words about the cafeteria food. To my surprise, the searing op-ed of Sloppy Joes Monday— which I wrote like a fancy restaurant review—was published (by "Anonymous") the next week. Seriously, no one reads the school newspaper, but it felt like I was walking on water to read my words out there in the world.

After that, I met with Ms. Randolph, and we came up with some story ideas. She told me that my sloppy joe piece had the highest click-through rate ever. I can only imagine what that means. Ten clicks, maybe? Couldn't be more than eleven. I've had another article published, and I'm working on another one demanding goat yoga during gym class once a week.

Mia yells my name, bringing me back to earth. She's at the other end of the table, waving her hand and holding up her phone. Picture time. I put my arm around Izzy and smile. Mia snaps a couple and gives a thumbs-up. Time to impart some wisdom on a young and still-forming mind. "Izzy, you are a great cheerleader. You have a bright few years ahead of you."

"Truth," she says.

I remember being in Izzy's shoes. Trying to be cool to impress the seniors. Saying whatever I thought would get me there.

"Iz, do you have any hobbies? Things you do outside of cheer-leading?"

"Um. I hang out. Talk to guys. My parents make me spend time with them. Is that what you mean?" she asks, then takes another damn tater tot.

"Kind of," I say, moving my tot tray out of her reach. "I just don't want you to have any regrets about high school."

"Regrets?" she asks with crumpled eyebrows.

"Yeah," I say. "I have a few."

"G, we all heard the story about the party last summer. But whatever. You shouldn't regret that," she says.

Is my li'l sis trying to comfort *me*? Gross. No.

"I'm just saying, don't get consumed with cheerleading. It's not everything."

Izzy looks at me and nods like she's getting it. Then she lets out a loud laugh. She thinks I'm lying. "I'm serious," I say.

"Georgia? Cheerleading is going to pay for my college. My friends are cheerleaders. I am proud that this my life. It's who I am."

"But you might wake up and realize you wasted your time."

"Have you?" she asks.

"No," I lie.

I feel a tap on my shoulder, and Izzy goes quiet. "Georgia?"

I turn around. "Jake?"

We haven't talked in weeks. He looks cute in his white shirt, unbuttoned flannel, and letter jacket. "Hi, Georgia. Can we take a walk?"

"To where? The pawnshop across the street?" I ask loudly. The entire table has halted all activities to stare at Jake. *Real casual, gals.* He smiles uncomfortably and waves at them. Under his breath, he whispers to me, "Please?"

I stand up and act like I don't care. "Izzy, if I'm not back in twenty, then Jake has pawned me off for quick cash."

"Truth," says Izzie.

Kids these days.

I follow Jake to the parking lot, headed toward his truck. Whatever is about to happen, it's not going to work. I can't deal with Mr. Richpants having secret conversations with Taylor. Major red flag. I ghosted Jake hard after his party—so hard and for so long that he eventually gave up. Now that I think about it, I was doing Jake like Pony did me. Anyway, Pony sucks. Why can't we just be friends? Was all he wanted from me sex stuff?

Jake lowers the back door of the truck, revealing two lawn chairs and a bottle of champagne in a bucket.

"Do you always drive around with this spread?"

He jumps up on the truck and extends his hand. "Ten minutes?"

"Ten minutes," I agree, taking his hand.

We sit on the chairs, and Jake pours some champagne into red Solo cups (we can't be too obvious about our underage drinking).

"Georgia. Can we talk about what happened? We were having fun at my party, and then *poof.*"

"Poof," I repeat.

"What did I do to you? It's killing me. I just need to know why," Jake says.

I take a big gulp of the bubbly drink. It tastes expensive. The sun is half gone, setting earlier and earlier in prep for the winter. The sky lights up red and pink and blue; it's one of the few things I will miss about Texas.

"Jake, I'm going to become a nun. I need to cut earthly ties."

"I'll become a priest, then!" he offers.

"I don't think it works that way," I say. "OK, fine. Pony saw you talking to Taylor alone at that party. In the garage? So, for all the obvious reasons, I split."

Jake laughs and then tightens up. "The new kid? He tattled on me?"

OK, that was probably a mistake.

"I wouldn't call it tattling. He just mentioned it. He didn't know about us." Lie, lie, lie.

"Georgia, I promise to god that I will never hook up with Taylor."

"Dude. How could I trust you? What were y'all talking about?"

"Can't you just trust me?" he asks with sad eyes that only make him cuter.

"It's not you, Jake. You can thank Anthony for this."

He puts his head down, like he's trying to think big thoughts. *Good luck, buddy.* There's nothing he can say right now that would make me change my mind.

"Taylor is my half cousin," he mumbles.

"Excuse me, your what?"

"My uncle married Taylor's mom, but he's not her dad. We don't advertise it. It's a family thing."

"Why? That's silly."

"Taylor doesn't want people to know she comes from money. She tries to hide it."

"Oh," I say, trying to process.

Jake stretches his arms above his head. I can behold all his muscles through his tight shirt. "It must look great from the outside, to come from a rich family," he says. "Living in a giant house. Doing whatever I want. This truck."

"I'm struggling to have compassion here," I report from obvious town.

"Having money doesn't mean there aren't problems," he says, refilling his cup. "And people just see me as the rich kid. That's boring. I can't tell if they like me or my money. I don't even care about the money."

"I'll take it off your hands," I offer.

"I didn't choose this life. This is the life I was born into. What would you do?" he asks. My family is not rich but not poor. I haven't been spoiled, but I don't want for anything. Well, more clothes. And a better car. Nicer house? But nothing else. I guess it would be weird to be known for having large amounts of money.

"Yeah, fine. Point taken," I say, then take a deep breath. I'm relieved that he's more real than I thought, and that Taylor is off-limits. Legally. "Look, can you just not be mad at Pony?"

"Depends," he says with a big mischievous smile.

"On what?"

"On you being my date to homecoming."

This guy could date any girl at school. Correction, this guy could date any girl in Texas. But for some reason, he wants to date me. It's flattering. And I need him to leave Pony alone. It's the right thing to do. Me and Jake, we're supposed to be a thing. I should go with it. "Yes," I say.

"Yes?" he asks, surprised.

"I will go with you to homecoming, Jake."

"Great," he says. "Great, great, great."

This is all so sudden. It doesn't make sense. "Homecoming is a month away. Why now? At the Sonic?" I ask.

He sits back in his chair and motions his head in the direction of the picnic table overflowing with cheerleaders.

"'Cause why?" I ask.

Jake shushes me. "Just watch."

I roll my eyes to let my frustration be known and focus on my friends. Out of nowhere, a group of guys wearing black clothing and ski masks emerges from in between cars and descends upon the cheerleaders. Once close enough, the guys start launching water balloons. Cue the high-pitched screams. Spilled drinks. The girls are trying to shield themselves with binders and backpacks. A couple brave ones stand tall and throw food at the guys. Classic water-balloon prank by the football team. Well played.

I turn back with my mouth open in shock. "That's why you wanted to talk now?"

"Yeah," Jake says. "I wanted to protect you." He smiles, revealing his one dimple. He has one damn dimple.

I finish what's in my cup and get up. I'm glad to not be soaked from water balloons right now. "Really smooth, mister," I say, then jump off the truck. "I need to go help my friends. You're sweet, Jake."

From behind I hear, "I'm just getting started!"

TEN

PONY, 12:35 P.M.

"It's puff, puff, pass, Pony!" Jerry says, handing me a poorly rolled joint. "Not pass, pass, pass!"

"I do not succumb to peer pressure," I say, handing the joint to Kenji. I had a couple hits and already feel light-headed. Any more and I'll be too paranoid to go back to school. I don't love getting high, but I guess I do, in fact, succumb to peer pressure.

I ran into Kenji in the parking lot this morning, and he invited me to lunch. He said they were getting baked pizza. I'm interested in pizza, so I agreed. Turns out "baked pizza" is smoking pot (getting baked) in an abandoned lot across from school and eating cheese pizza from Papa John's.

We're sitting on large rocks pushed into a circle with a burnt fire pit in the middle. I snag the pizza box off Kenji's lap and lift the top, revealing the gloriously greasy cheesy perfection. It's still hot. I have never been hungrier in my life.

"How's Emma?" I ask Kenji after polishing off the crispy crust. He's been hanging out with an exchange student from Paris.

"She's cool, man. I have no idea what she's talking about most of the time, but we speak the language of love."

Jerry jumps in. "Slipped her your baguette yet?"

Kenji and I exchange looks and shake our heads. "What's up with your girl, Jerry?" Kenji asks. "You slipped her your pencil yet?"

Jerry drops the roach on the ground and stomps it out with his foot. "We hang out."

"And hook up?" I ask. I don't usually get personal, but I'm curious about their relationship after seeing Kelly at the LGBTQIA Center. Jerry grabs the pizza box from my lap and looks at us, deciding how much he can embellish.

"We made out," he says, then takes a bite of pizza. "Once."

Kenji folds over in laughter. He might fall off his rock.

"Look," Jerry says, "we're taking it slow. I think that's cool. I think she's cool. So I don't care what you fuckers think!"

Kenji regains composure. "Dude, it's chill. You do you."

"'Cause she's definitely not doing you!" I say, and they both laugh. Best feeling.

Kenji kicks my shoe with his size-15 Jordan. "So, playboy, you make any progress on the cheerleader?"

I never told them about The Kiss. I could earn so much respect, but I didn't want to open myself up to their questions. "I'm over her," I say.

"Good, man. You dodged a bullet."

"Why?" I ask, truly stunned that Kenji would say that.

He shrugs. "I don't know. Something about her—she's fake."

"Fake who? Fake how?" I am forgetting to keep it cool.

"Dude, I don't know. She's always telling those stories. Pretending."

Have I been blinded by like? Do I not see what other people see? Am I too high?

"And," Jerry adds, "what went down this summer."

Kenji nods. "Yeah, man."

I'm about to get *the* story. Am I ready for it? There's a possibility what I am about to hear will change the way I think about her. What if she went super nuts? This could help me move on. "What happened that night?"

"He doesn't know the story!" Jerry says, and they punch on each other with excitement to tell me what went down.

"I was there," Kenji begins.

"And I was not invited," Jerry says.

"I was chilling with Amber on the couch and making good progress."

"Dude, you didn't have a chance," Jerry says. "Amber is going to be a famous actress, and you're going to be Kenji."

They start bickering. Sometimes, I swear they act like an old married couple. I am at the edge of my rock, dying to hear the story. It feels wrong. I should hear this from Georgia, not them. But I can't stop myself. I need closure. I have tried everything to move on, but maybe this will do the trick. "Hey!" I say. "Can we focus?"

"Right." Kenji shifts his attention back to me. "OK. The party was winding down. There were probably five of us still there, just chilling. From the couch, I can see Taylor leading Ant upstairs. We all know Ant is with Georgia and shouldn't be going up there with Taylor. But what could I do? Nothing. So, I return to Amber. A few minutes later, Georgia comes storming through the living room and up the stairs. The whole room goes quiet. We all need popcorn, you know? We are there for the show."

Kenji stands up, all excited, getting ready to act out what comes next. "We hear knocking, and then pounding, and then kicking. And then nothing. And then yelling, screaming, a slap. Something breaks, like glass. Georgia comes flying down the stairs, and she's crying and yelling."

"Damn," I say. "Was she OK?"

"Definitely not, bro," Jerry answers.

"Shut up. You weren't there," Kenji says.

"And?" I ask.

"And she stops and looks at us with big, wide eyes. And we're looking back, staying still, like she's a wild animal that might attack."

"Rabid raccoon on the loose," Jerry adds.

"She wipes her eyes with her hands and yells, loud enough so they can hear upstairs, 'ANTHONY HAS A TINY, CROOKED DICK,' and then runs off. We all lost our shit."

"I've seen it in the locker room. I can confirm that report," Jerry adds.

Kenji continues, "Ant comes stomping downstairs, clearly pissed. He gets in front of the room and mirrors his phone on the TV, so we can see his screen, pulls up a video, and hits Play. And dude, it was Georgia and him kissing and messing around, with full shots of her—"

"BOOBS!" Jerry says.

"Ant keeps saying, 'Look at those small tits' and 'Good riddance' and then walks out. By the next morning, everyone knew what had happened."

That's terrible. I feel sick, the pizza grease revolting in my stomach.

"I would pay to own that video for private viewing!" Jerry says.

I hope I never meet Anthony. I feel an anger growing inside me. That didn't help at all. Now I feel bad for her. "Let's get out of here," I say, standing up. "I need to take a piss."

"Dude, go over there," Kenji says, motioning to the bushes about ten feet away. That would be a fine solution if I could pee standing up.

"Can we just get back?" I ask.

Jerry gets up and takes a step toward me. "Pony needs to rub one out after hearing that story," he says, grabbing at my non-existent balls. I jump back quick enough to avoid his reach, then lunge forward, pushing him. He stumbles backward but regains his balance.

He comes back at me and squares off. We are almost nose-to-nose. "What you going to do about it, Pecker?"

I have never punched anyone before, but this might be the moment.

"Easy, cowboy," Kenji says, putting his hand on Jerry's shoulder, pulling us apart. "Let's get out of here. Lunch hour is almost up."

I pick up the pizza box and walk right past the car. I need space to clear my head. I cross the street as Kenji's car pulls out of the lot. Jerry shoots me the bird.

3:01 P.M.

I sit down on my lab stool and look over at Georgia. We only speak when it's absolutely necessary, like for lab exercises. She opens her book and smiles at me, and for the first time since we stopped talking, I smile back.

Hearing that story has softened me. I've spent weeks building a wall between me and Georgia to protect myself. I listen to signs from the universe, and that tarot card with three swords through the heart was too real to ignore. Georgia has already thrust one sword into my heart. I can't imagine what two more will do to me.

I have the tarot card in my wallet to help me build that wall. And to remind myself of the danger of falling for her again. Also, that tarot card has a cute girl's number on it. I'm not ready to reach out, but it gives me a secret power.

Mr. Glover comes into the room in full lab coat and gloves, and then he flips the lights off. He scurries to his chem closet and turns around holding beakers filled with a pink liquid. There's white smoke pouring out the top of the beakers.

The class is quiet (for once). Everyone is watching and wondering if our punny chemistry teacher has finally lost his mind. He raises the beakers above his head. "Young Scientists! This is your time to shine! This is the kick-off of the yearly Science Hack Day! The rules are simple: find a problem and solve it . . . . *with science*! Ten-page paper and five-minute presentation!"

Mr. Glover pauses to make sure we're as excited as he is. (We are not.)

"Paper and presentation due Monday, October 7! Teams of two! Your partner is . . ."

Please don't say it . . . my walls are already weakened . . .

"The person at your table!"

Fuck.

In his own version of the mic drop, Mr. Glover accidently drops a beaker. The glass shatters, spilling pink chemicals all over the floor. The class gets loud as he recruits students to get up and help him clean.

I'm watching the drama unfold when I feel a tap on my shoulder. "Hello. I don't believe we've formally met. I'm Georgia."

I don't want to play along, but that story was so awful. No wonder she has trust issues. "Nice to meet you. I'm Pony," I say as plainly as possible.

"Pony? What an interesting name. I bet there's a good story behind it."

My brain is protesting, my body is tensing, but my heart is celebrating. "I'm glad you asked," I say. "When I was a young child, my heart stopped working."

"Oh, dear," she says.

I continue, "And the hospital was fresh out of human hearts."

"What on earth did you do?"

"Well," I say, moving closer like I'm telling her a secret. "My doctor called up his veterinarian friend, who, lucky for me, had a horse heart. So they put that in."

"Well, Pony, I'm happy that you survived, and that we are hack partners."

"Teacher-appointed hack partners," I remind her.

She continues, "And maybe we could be friends?"

There it is, the dreaded F word. I ignore it. I'm not ready to answer. "So, Georgia, is it? That's an interesting name, too. How did you get it?"

"My grandma's middle name," she says simply.

I shake my head, confused. "Really?"

"Why, yes, Pony. I've been thinking that if I want someone to be honest with me, I should be honest with them."

Without checking in on my brain, I say, "I'm sorry."

She looks at me, stunned. "Same," she says. "Friends?"

This is doomed. This is doomed. This is doomed.

"Friends," I say.

IPHONES, 11:21 P.M.

    GEORGIA: YO BRO U UP?

    PONY: Hi. Miss me already?

    GEORGIA: Lol. NO.

PONY: What you doing?

GEORGIA: Nothing

GEORGIA: Hey?

PONY: Yeah?

GEORGIA: I did miss you

GEORGIA: I'm glad we are friends

PONY: Thank you for not telling my secret

PONY: I appreciate it

GEORGIA: How is that going?

PONY: Good. No one knows, which is cool

PONY: I'm passing . . .

GEORGIA: Passing the test?

PONY: Haha. No.

PONY: Well, kind of?

PONY: Passing means to pass as your gender

GEORGIA: I have a lot to learn

PONY: Yeah you do

GEORGIA: And some questions . . .

PONY: Oh boy.

GEORGIA: Not now. Later.

PONY: I'm going to bed

PONY: Goodnight Georgia

GEORGIA: Goodnight friend.

ELEVEN

Sunday, September 29

GEORGIA, 5:55 P.M.

I'm putting the finishing touches on dinner when my phone rings. I turn down NPR and plug in my headset. "Hello, Georgia's Kitchen."

"Hi, sweetie," a soft voice says, laughing nervously.

I turn away from Dad and lower my voice. "Hi, Mom."

We haven't talked in weeks. I thought we'd found a good rhythm of me not reaching out and her not reaching out, and it seemed to be working out fine. Hearing her voice makes me miss her. And that pisses me off.

This moment's additional awkwardness is brought to you by the fact that my dad is at the dining room table finishing the *New York Times* crossword puzzle. The level of difficulty of the crossword increases during the week. Monday is easy, Sunday is ruthless. The frustration is all over my dad's face.

"How's life, honey?"

"Good. Busy," I say as I go back to cutting green peppers for the salad. My mom's special-recipe lasagna is simmering in the oven. The irony of the call is not lost on me.

"Great. The team is good this year . . ." she says, then trails off.

"Totally," I say through clenched teeth. Do I casually mention that I know she comes to the games? I don't want to be having this buddy-buddy catch-up with my mom, who should be here cooking this lasagna, but left us for money. I start chopping the peppers harder.

"And are you dating anyone special?"

"No," I say curtly. "Can we not do this?"

A couple seconds of silence pass.

"Georgie," she says carefully, "I called to invite you to Thanksgiving. Wayne is taking me to Paris, and I was wondering if, maybe, you want to come with?"

"I can't really afford the plane ticket," I say.

"Wayne would pay, of course."

I stop cutting the peppers. "My love isn't for sale."

"Georgie."

I sneak a look at my dad. He has set his pencil down and is watching me. Obviously, that sounds like an amazing trip minus hanging out with *Wayne*. But my dad would be alone eating from Kentucky Fried Chicken. Just because she left him doesn't mean I can, too.

"I can't . . ."

"Leave Dad," she says. "I know, sweetie, and that's so nice of you. But he will be fine. I promise."

That ticks me off. I feel a lump in my throat, the beginning of tears. I push it down and steady my voice. "Actually, I want to be here."

"I understand," she says. "OK. Then how about we have dinner? Just me and you?"

"Maybe," I say.

The alarm on the stovetop rings.

"Whatcha cooking?" she asks.

"Your lasagna."

"Don't forget the nutmeg."

"Already in," I lie, heading over to the spice rack. "Bye, Mom."

"Text me about dinner. I love you, babygirl."

"You too," I say, then remove my earpiece. I go back to searching through the spices, hoping my dad doesn't bring it up.

"Was that Mom?" he asks.

I keep my head in the spices. "What's the deal with paprika? I bet there's a spicy story behind that name." I'm trying to pun myself out of the conversation.

"What did she want?" he asks.

I look at my dad, sitting at the table in his favorite denim button-up shirt—a Sunday staple—and his glasses with frames that haven't been in fashion for years. His hair has thinned, but it's always neatly parted.

"She invited me to Thanksgiving."

He takes off his glasses. "Planning ahead?" he asks.

"Well, they're going to Paris," I add.

"Oh."

"I'm not going."

"Maybe you should, Georgie. Paris is beautiful."

I bring the salad bowl to the table and sit down. "Ugh, no, Dad. I'm going to have so many invites to Paris. Better yet, I'll take myself to Paris one day. But this Turkey Day, I'll be here with you watching the Cowboys lose."

"That's my girl," he says just as the doorbell rings. "And that must be our dinner guest!"

I bounce over to the front door, grateful to be done with that conversation. I swing the door open wildly, and Pony laughs at my dramatics. He looks cute in a black hoodie and jeans. We enter the kitchen and Dad asks, "What's an eight-letter word for heterosexual?"

"Straight," Pony says, and then smiles at me.

"Aha!" Dad scribbles the word into the crossword, proud of his progress.

"Dad, this is my friend Pony."

He looks up. "We met, I believe, on the porch?"

Crap. I forgot about that night. Well, I didn't forget that night. More like I have worked hard to block it out. I grab the lasagna from the stovetop and let Pony handle that one.

"Hello again, Mr. Roberts," he says, shaking hands with Dad. "Thanks for having me over for dinner."

"This is all Georgia. And you have a school assignment to work on?"

"Yes, we are attempting to cure the water depletion in Africa."

"No big deal," I say, peeling off the foil to reveal the masterpiece of bubbling sauce, pasta, and melted cheese. The smell of Parmesan and Italian sausage fills the air. I'm so proud I could weep.

Before dishing out squares, I sprinkle nutmeg all over the lasagna. Now it's ready. "Bon appétit!" I say.

"Bon appétit!" they repeat.

Dad puts his napkin in his lap. "So, how do you plan on saving the water supply?"

My spatula slices through the layers. "Oh! Pony had a great idea. Tell him," I say.

His face goes red. "That was a joke," he whispers.

"Just tell him," I chide.

"OK. We invent a bucket that you use, you know, as a bathroom. And the bucket makes purified water. Through *science*."

We both laugh. "This year's Nobel Prize," I announce.

"Goes to the Purify Potty," he says, and we both laugh again.

Dad catches my eye and lifts an eyebrow. "You always finish each other's sentences?" he asks.

Whatever, that's a normal friend thing.

We stuff our faces while recapping last night's *SNL* for my dad, who goes to bed too early to watch. I wonder if he can tell that Pony is transgender? Probably not. Pony passes the test with everyone.

"Mr. Roberts, how's the online dating going?" Pony asks.

"Well, don't want to brag, but I have been on three dates."

"All to the same bar," I add.

"The Mucky Duck is charming! I have a second date with Cynthia tomorrow. Got any dating tips for me, Pony?"

"Six thirty-one," I say and they both look at me. "Just noting the time of when this dinner officially got weird."

Pony wipes his mouth with his napkin. "Well, I don't have tons of experience, but I think you should compliment her. Listen to her." He looks at me. "Don't hide anything from her."

My face goes as red as the lasagna. Dad is eating it up. I was not aware of this second-date-with-Cynthia business. We haven't been talking as much lately.

"I'm inspired by your advice, Pony," Dad says, placing his napkin over his plate. "Thank you. And thank you, wonderful daughter, for the wonderful dinner. I'll leave you to cure the water problem. I'm off to watch *60 Minutes* and text Cynthia."

As Dad exits, whistling, I roll my eyes at Pony.

"That must be awkward," Pony says under his breath.

I cover my face with my hands. "Ya think?"

"Hey, at least you're close to your parents."

"Oh yeah, I'm really, really lucky," I say, then uncover my face.

Pony sits up straight, his move before getting serious. "My dad isn't cool with me being trans."

He whispers *trans* like it's a bad word. Pony is finally talking to me about this stuff. I have millions of questions but also don't want to say something insensitive.

"Because he's in the army?" I ask.

"That's part of it." Pony starts tapping his plate. "He thinks it's a phase, and I'll change my mind soon. He won't stop using my deadname."

"Your deadname?"

"That's when someone uses my birth name—my girl name—instead of my chosen name."

"That's awful," I say.

He shrugs. "It is what it is."

"If Pony is your chosen name, why did you choose it?"

He hides a smile and looks away. "If I told you, I'd have to kill you."

"Maybe someday?" I ask, making the biggest eyes possible.

"Maybe," he says.

"Ice cream?" I ask.

"Definitely."

I bring the plates to the sink and get the Blue Bell Vanilla Bean ice cream and chocolate syrup. We talk endlessly, high on sugar and good company. We just fit together in this way that's comfortable and exciting.

"This ice cream is good," Pony says, scraping his spoon at the bottom of his bowl. "Much better than the Hillcrest cafeteria ice cream that leaves a flavor in your mouth reminiscent of household cleaner."

My heart drops all the way to the ground and into the basement.

Those are my words. He read the cafeteria food review. He knows it's me. I'm out of words but manage to push out, "How?"

He looks down and smiles. "How did I know you were Anonymous? Maybe I know your voice."

I shake my head in disbelief. "You read the *Hillcrest Reporter*?"

"Sure," he says, shrugging. To be honest, I hoped Pony would read the articles. "Georgia, you are a good writer." *And I hoped he would think I'm a good writer.* My heart flies up from the basement and shoots off into the clouds.

"Thanks," I say.

"But why write under Anonymous?"

I rearrange the place mat, uncomfortable. Every molecule in my body wants to make up a story. I don't want to tell Pony the real reason, even though he probably knows. "It's against the rules of being a cheerleader."

He gives me side-eye. "Is it?"

"I don't know. But I do know that I don't want people to know that part of me. It's silly, but I don't want it to hurt my reputation."

"That must be exhausting," Pony says.

I kick his foot under the table. "You kind of inspired me," I admit.

"I did?"

"You did. But Pony? No one knows it's me. Can you keep my secret?"

"As well as you have kept mine," he says.

I check my phone. It's past nine. "It's getting late."

"I should go," he says, grabbing his bag. "Or I could spend the night?"

"You wish."

"Georgia, friends spend the night all the time. I'm just trying to be a good friend."

"Get out of here before I release the hounds," I say, then watch as he gathers his things. I secretly wish we could hang out longer. Before he heads out, I stop him. "Pony?"

He turns around, and I get to my feet. "Friends do hug, though," I say, then throw my arms around his him. He smells nice, like soap and Old Spice.

IPHONES, 10:01 P.M.

PONY: I made it home safe. In case you were worried . . .

GEORGIA: I was not

PONY: We forgot to do something tonight

GEORGIA: What's that?

PONY: Work on saving the water supply?

PONY: You were very distracting

GEORGIA: And you, sir, used me for my lasagna

PONY: And ice cream

GEORGIA: UGH

PONY: I don't have plans on Saturday

GEORGIA: I can't

PONY: Cheerleading thing?

GEORGIA: No

PONY: ??

GEORGIA: I have a date with Jake

GEORGIA: Pony?

GEORGIA: You aren't allowed to be mad at that!

PONY: I was brushing my teeth

GEORGIA: For seventeen minutes???

PONY: I have a lot of teeth

GEORGIA: Lol. Stop bragging.

PONY: Just trying to impress you

PONY: Friend.

GEORGIA: Consider me wildly impressed

GEORGIA: Friend.

TWELVE

Saturday, October 5

PONY, 5:59 P.M.

I tape up a box and label it *CLOTHING—GOLF PANTS*. How can one man have so many golf pants? I jump into a reclining chair and pop up the footrest. Time for a break. I shut my eyes.

Georgia has her date tonight. Not that it matters. We are just friends. But it's taking all my energy to not think about her. She must be getting ready right now. Jake will be over to pick her up soon. It's probably going to be romantic and perfect. This hurts more than I thought it would. I'm trying to keep busy—working late—hoping the distraction will relieve the pressure in my heart and mild panic attack.

The Science Hack Day has been a great excuse to text Georgia, to talk with her, to hang out and procrastinate together. But I want to be more than friends and can't make myself want less. I try to not forget the warning from the tarot card with the heart stabbed by three swords. Even made it my lock-screen image on my phone. Nothing works. Whatever this is between me and Georgia . . . it will end badly. I will get hurt again. I know that. Yet here I am.

Ted London gets sicker every day. His breathing is more forced, movements more painful. But he stays upbeat. Ordering Victor around and dragging an oxygen tank behind him.

I haven't been here all week. Ted had an infection, and the doctor didn't want anyone in the house. When I arrived this afternoon, Victor looked like he'd lost five pounds and hadn't slept in days. That guy was already small—a hundred pounds soaking wet. I haven't seen Ted yet, but Victor assured me he is on the up-and-up.

On the chance that I might be carrying around germs, I have been banished to sorting belongings in the pool house. I asked for $500, and Victor was too tired to negotiate. After the pool house, I'll have close to $3,000 saved up for my new chest.

I get back up to start sorting a pile of clothes on the bed. It's clear that no one has hung out in this pool house for years. There's a thick coat of dust everywhere, furniture covered in sheets, and it reeks of ghosts. This is where Ted kept all his fancy formal wear and crazy costumes. Suits worthy of *Mad Men* and costumes that could have been in *Gladiator*. There's so much to see out here, I'm having fun trying to sort this madness. I have my music up loud in my ears to drown out any thoughts about Georgia and her date.

I pull out a bright yellow women's one-piece bathing suit. My memories of being forced to wear these bathing suits when I was young come rushing back. I loved the water but hated these form-fitting girl suits. I would always wear a shirt over the suit and wish I could be in swim trunks.

For the past three years, I've skipped all pool parties and beach days. There are water binders, but I don't have one. Until I get my top surgery, I don't want to deal with swimming in public places.

I hear my phone ding. And ding. And ding.

MAX: DUDE I EMAILED YOU A LINK

MAX: SPOILER ALERT: IT'S A PETITION!!!

MAX: DUDE DUDE DUDE

I open my Gmail and read the online petition posted by Max, with fifty-one signatures so far. Two weeks ago, a sophomore transgender girl was asked to use the bathroom in the teachers' lounge instead of the girls' bathroom. Turns out, a couple concerned parents went to the school board and made a fuss about the safety of their daughters. Same story, different town. When the school treats trans students like they're different, it gives the green light for the other kids to do the same, but kids are way meaner. I sign the petition.

PONY: Done!

MAX: Great, now post it, my man.

MAX: We need to spread the word!

MAX: We need to help Ashley!

I knew he would ask me to share it. The passion of Max. He fights so hard for our community. There's just one problem: if I post that petition about a transgender girl, then my fifty or so new friends from Hillcrest are going to wonder about me. It would be a bad move right now.

PONY: I'm busy but later!

MAX: Pony! We need more trans visibility.

MAX: DO NOT HIDE ON ME!

I pocket my phone. I don't need a guilt trip. I'm dealing with enough right now. I check my watch for the hundredth time today. Has the date started? I am officially torturing myself with this friendship.

"Hey, boy, why are you doing nothing?"

I jump up, startled. Victor has snuck into the pool house.

"Yeah, I'm making good progress. Check it out." I show Victor that I'm wearing a fake armor chest piece from some Roman war movie.

"Do not break that!" he says in high alarm.

Poor Victor. This job has got be hard on him. Taking care of someone who's both sick and stubborn must be exhausting. The bags under his eyes are visible from across the room.

"Hey, V," I say, moving toward him. "How long has it been since you had some time off?"

"What month is it? Mr. London requires constant attention, as I'm sure you are aware."

I frown. "Well, it just so happens that I don't have plans

tonight. Maybe I could hang out here and you could go have some me time."

Victor starts speaking but stops. "Yes, I will take you up on your offer. Are you sick?"

"Of cleaning this pool house? Yes!" I say with a smile.

Victor finally smiles back at me. "Thank you, Pony. But you must promise to take good care of him! I have already prepared dinner. Enchiladas! Big man's favorite. You will need to heat them up for fifteen minutes in the oven. You know what an oven is, right?"

"I can google it later," I joke.

He looks at his watch. "I will be back at ten p.m. Is that OK?"

"Yeah, man. I'll head in soon. Get out of here and do you."

"Oh, I'm sure I can find someone to do me," Victor says with a wink. He turns around and exits with a skip in his step. It feels good to help.

As I'm exiting the pool house, a stack of photos collapses by my feet, old Polaroids spilling out all over the floor. I drop to my knees, gathering the photos into an envelope. I pick up a black-and-white photo of a blond man with a big smile, standing confidently in his swim trunks on the beach. His arm is around Ted in a very comfortable way. I flip it over and see Ted's handwriting:

1958. My Love.

Holy shit, what is Ted London hiding? I pocket the picture and head into the house.

In the kitchen, with the enchiladas heating in the oven, I take the photo back out of my pocket. Is this Ted's love? He's told me a few stories about his dates and relationships—all women. So who is this guy?

My phone starts dancing in my pocket again.

MAX: POST IT PONY POST POST POST IT PONY

MAX: TICK TOCK PONY

MAX: R U SERIOUS?

Sorry, Max, I'm dealing with more pressing issues now. I google Ted London and get his Wikipedia, which leads to his IMDb and a carousel of his movies' posters. Farther down the page I see:

"Is Ted London Gay?" from the National Enquirer, *1959*

"The Secret Sex Life of Ted London" from the New York Times, *1963*

"The Real Reason Ted London Left Hollywood," from People *magazine, 1987*

"Hey there, son," Ted London says, scaring the crap out of me. "How's dinner coming along?"

"Five more minutes!" I say, making up a number that felt right. Ted London leans on the kitchen counter. He's lost more weight than Victor.

"Aye, aye, aye!" Ted says. He snaps his fingers, then coughs. "Do you want a margarita?"

"Sure," I say.

"Just one for you, young man. I'll be in the dining room." He meanders off slowly.

Ten minutes later, I carefully balance the tray of enchiladas and plates and bring it into the dining room. It's a huge banquet hall, meant for lavish dinner parties. Ted is seated at the head of the long table with a margarita.

"How exciting is this?" he says. I set the tray down in front of him, steam rising from the light-green-and-dark-red casserole. Ted leans over the dish and laughs. "This looks like something that came out of *The Fly*!"

"David Cronenberg is one of my favorite directors," I admit.

"Ah, he was a friend! I was in one of his lesser-known flicks."

I listen as Ted unleashes one of his amazing stories while devouring too many enchiladas. They are green chili and black bean, spicy but not too hot, cheesy but not too much, and the sauce is perfection. Hollywood stories and good food—this is exactly where I should be tonight.

I take a big drink of my margarita to cool down the spice, leaving me light and silly. I try to keep a straight face, but Ted sees right through me. "I figured if you only have one drink, I better make it strong. Thanks for babysitting me, Pony."

"I wanted to hang out with you." I'm feeling warm from the alcohol and chatty. "I want to work in movies. Not as an actor. More behind the scenes. How did you do it?"

He sits back and crosses his arms. "Tinseltown is all about who you know. Don't forget that, Pony. Make connections with people.

That's what will pay off." He takes a big drink of his margarita. Does that mean he wants to help me?

I'm feeling daring. "Can we play another round of show-and-tell?"

Ted straightens up in his chair. "Certainly. What did you bring me tonight?"

I hand him the picture from my pocket. He pulls out the glasses from his shirt pocket and takes a look. His eyes go from curious to angry. He flips the picture over and reads what it says.

"Who is that guy, Mr. London?" I ask.

"That is none of your business, boy," he says, then pushes himself up using the table. "You shouldn't be asking me questions like this." He starts walking off. I watch him, eyes wide and mouth open.

Before leaving, he turns to me. "Get out of here." Then he coughs. It starts small but quickly builds to loud, booming coughs. I think he's going to pass out. I get up to help.

"Leave!"

"You know I can't, Mr. London. I promised Victor."

"Oh, Victor. I'm a big boy. I can take care of myself!"

I don't move an inch.

"Fine," he says, the coughing slowing. "After you're done clearing the table, go wait in the study until Victor gets back."

"Are you kidding?" I ask.

"No," he says, then takes off down the hallway.

A movie star just put me in time-out. I sit back in my chair, frustrated. My phone buzzes.

MAX: POST THE PETITION OR WE ARE DONE

Now it's official; this day is fucking awful.

After clearing the dinner table, I lie down on the couch in the study and scroll through my old texts with Georgia. I wonder how the date is going.

Ted comes limping into the study, palming the cane in one hand and his drink in the other. He sits down at the desk and begins digging around in the drawers. After a few minutes of shuffling papers and cussing under his breath, he pulls out a cigarette and immediately lights it up. "Don't you dare tattle to Victor about this, Pony."

"It's your life," I say.

He relaxes and puts his feet up on the desk. "I owe you an apology."

"No, I shouldn't have said anything. I'm sorry, Mr. London."

He waves me off. "Call me Ted, please. It's still challenging for me to talk about this stuff. But I'm dying, so la-di-da!" He laughs and takes a drag off his forbidden cigarette. "The movie I told you about, *The Gigantic?* That Oscar wasn't the only thing I won. I also met Lee Grayson."

"The man in the picture?" I ask.

"Yes, that's him. With a smile that could stop traffic."

"Are you gay?"

"It would appear so, Pony. Women didn't interest me the way men did. But back in the day, it was wrong. Being a homosexual was considered a mental illness until the seventies. So, I denied it. Pushed it down. I had big dreams, and I wasn't going to let anything get in the way."

"You had to hide it?"

"Had to hide it, yes." He frowns and looks away. "I traded in love for anonymous sex that left me feeling empty and full of shame."

If that time in history was contentious for gays, I can only imagine how hard it was for trans people. How many didn't transition, living life trapped in bodies that didn't feel like their own.

Ted continues his monologue. "That was, until I met Lee on the set of *Gigantic*. He had a small walk-on part. We fell in love almost instantly. You don't find that often in life, I can tell you that. Loving Lee changed every molecule in my body. I no longer cared about the fame and money. He made me insanely happy. I was ready to leave the business and start my life with Lee, but . . ."

I'm hanging on every word. "But?" I ask.

"But Hollywood wasn't done with me. My agent blackmailed me. Good old Roy James. Piece of shit, Roy James. He's dead now, so I can say that. I went to Roy to discuss my plan of quietly leaving Hollywood, naively thinking he would be happy for me, but his reaction was quite the opposite. He told me that if I quit, he would expose me for the *faggot* I was."

Cigarette puff, drink of whiskey, cigarette puff.

"If he ratted me out, it would ruin my life. And more importantly, Lee's life. I couldn't do that to him. Or my family. So

I ended things with Lee, giving no explanation. Broke his heart, which broke my heart even harder."

"And you went back in the closet?" I ask.

"Yes, deep back in that closet. I hated myself. My acting was piss poor. My heart wasn't in it. I did a string of wildly unsuccessful movies."

"And you married a woman?"

Big Ted London laugh. "Asking the tough questions, Barbara Walters! Did you look her up?"

"Yes," I lie.

"I married Roy's secretary. All for show. She's a lesbian, actually," he says, putting his cigarette out. "We never consummated the marriage, if you know what I mean . . ."

"Yes, please don't explain," I say. "But you got to live your dream?"

"Sure did, kid."

His words hang in the air, heavy. "I'm off to bed. This night has been a truly memorable one. I trust that you will keep what we discussed to yourself?"

"Yes, of course," I say, watching him exit the room slowly.

"Ted," I say before he gets out the door, "did you ever talk to Lee Grayson again?"

He turns around, and his face looks older than it ever has before.

"No," he says simply, then leaves.

My phone starts ringing. It's Max on FaceTime. I don't want

to pick it up, but I do anyway. I see Max's face and a party going on behind him. He finds an empty room and shuts the door.

"Hi, Pony. Are you for real not going to post that petition?"

This is a pickle. I want to post it for Max, but I don't want to cause suspicion with my new friends. They would wonder why I was so passionate about some trans girl at a different school. It was would raise flags, and I can't take that risk.

"I'm not going to post," I say, ready for the blowback. "It might out me at school. I'm sorry, dude."

Max kicks something. "We need you, Pony. Can't you see that? The trans community is tiny, and the war is big. We need every soldier on the field, and Pony, you are not on the field."

"It doesn't have to be a fight," I say.

Max shakes his phone until all I can see are blurry outlines. I can't make out what he's saying, but it doesn't sound complimentary. He calms down, and I can see his face again. "Pony, if we don't raise our voices and make ourselves known, then we will continue to lose our rights. You too, buddy."

"I'm sorry, Max. I don't want to be known as trans. That's not what I'm about."

"Pony, it's not *what* you are, it's *who* you are," Max urges.

As usual, when I need to say something, I can't. All my words are somewhere else.

"Pony-bro, I need some space from you right now."

"How long?" I ask, but he's already opening the door and heading back to the party. I can see queers standing around, having fun. Eventually, the phone screen goes black, and I look around, alone.

IPHONES, 10:59 P.M.

    GEORGIA: Hi Pony

    PONY: Hi Georgia

    GEORGIA: How was your night?

    PONY: I worked

    PONY: It was a very weird night

    PONY: How was your date?

    GEORGIA: Fine

    PONY: Just fine?

    GEORGIA: Idk. Yeah. Fine. Final answer.

    PONY: Ok

    GEORGIA: Good night, Pony

    PONY: Night

THIRTEEN

Tuesday, October 8

GEORGIA, 3:58 P.M.

"All right, class!" Mr. Glover yells with enough excitement that we actually listen. "It's time to announce the winning team of the Science Hack Day! There were so many great presentations yesterday! So tough to pick just one . . ."

Pony whispers to me, "The suspense is killing me!"

"Buuuuut before I reveal the team that's the winner, winner, chicken dinner . . ."

I whisper to Pony, "Stop trying to make 'winner, winner, chicken dinner' a thing!"

"I'm going to announce the grand prize! The winning team will get an excused absence on Friday!" Wild applause from the students. "To go to the science museum in Dallas!" Applause abruptly stops.

"OK! Drumroll, please! The winner of the Science Hack Day is . . ."

To be honest, I don't think we have a real chance to win. Our solution to the water shortage in Africa ended up being drones dropping bottles off and picking them up. We called it Project Droned. Some would argue it was all a ruse to buy a cheap drone from Walmart and fly it around the class, but those people would be dead wrong.

"Congratulations, *Project Droned!*"

No way. No *freaking* way. A few people clap, but I can tell they all feel shorted. The bell rings. Everyone gets up and leaves, but Pony and I remain seated in utter shock. Then we start laughing—it's all so ridiculous.

Pony walks me to cheerleading practice (because having every class together isn't enough time with each other). We head down the hallway, passing the basketball gym and coaches' offices, then pause outside the double doors leading to the dressing rooms. "I don't know if we should have won," I admit. "Our project wasn't that great."

"Well, I did secretly hide four puns in the presentation. Subliminal puns," Pony says proudly.

"Hide them? No sir, they were obvious," I clap back.

"Regardless," Pony says, "we are the winner, winner, chicken dinner!"

And just like that, we have another inside joke.

I spot Ms. Randolph as she comes around the corner. I can see the pencils poking out of her hair from ten feet away. Perfect timing—I need to run an article by her. "Hi, Georgia," she says with her warm smile. "And hello, Pony!"

"Hey, Ms. R," he says.

"You two know each other?" I ask, confused.

"From another school, actually. I knew Pony from Westlake," she says, removing her glasses.

"Eighth grade," Pony says, giving me a you-can-figure-out-what-that-means look.

"What an interesting coincidence," I say while connecting the dots in my head. That means Ms. Randolph knew Pony before he was Pony. I have so many questions about who Pony was before transitioning. It feels weird to think of Pony dressed like a girl. I have looked online (unapologetic stalker mode) but found nada.

"Georgia, are we in safe company?" Ms. Randolph asks, eyeing Pony.

"Yes," I confirm. "Pony is an avid reader of your paper. That makes two of those?" I kid.

"Very funny, Georgia. When can I expect your next article?"

"Soon," I promise. I had more time to write when Pony hated me and I wasn't going on predictable dates with Jake. "I was working on a piece about the garden in front of the school."

Ms. Randolph pushes her glasses up. "What about the garden?" she asks.

"It sucks? I don't know. I just started working on this one."

"Georgia, I urge you to dig deeper. You have bigger things to say. If it feels scary to write, you're on the right track."

"Ms. R, obviously you have not seen that garden. Truly horrifying."

"I'm late to a parent-teacher meeting. Can't wait to see what you send me, Anonymous."

We say goodbye to Ms. Randolph. I state the obvious: "Holy moly, Pony. She knew you before you changed."

"Before I transitioned, yes," he says with a quiet smile.

I look around, the hallway is empty. "Am I allowed to ask questions about before?"

Pony leans against a locker. "Sure. Yes. Ask me anything. But don't get offended if I don't answer."

"Deal," I say. We wait for some band kids to pass on their way out to the field.

"How did it feel? To be a girl?" I ask.

"I was never a girl," he says, curtly. "I just presented that way. 'Cause I had to."

"What did you wear? Did you have long hair?"

"I was all high heels and miniskirts," he says.

"No!"

"No," he confirms. "I wore baggy clothes. When I look back at pictures from before I transitioned, I don't look like a boy or a girl. I looked like nothing."

"I know it's your deadname or whatever, but can you tell me your real name?"

"Pony is my real name," he shoots back.

"I didn't mean to say that, I'm sorry. Sometimes I wish I had a two-second delay on my mouth."

"Nah, you wouldn't be as interesting," he says.

The dressing room doors fly open. Mia runs out, distressed. "GEORGIA!"

"Busted! I'm Georgia," I say to Mia.

"No time for that. Shit is going down. Seriously. Dressing room in two. Go. Go. Go!" She marches off, giving Pony an unhappy look. I turn to him and roll my eyes.

"Your friends are weird," he says.

"You're my friend," I say, then hug him goodbye.

I head back into the dressing room. It's typically madness before practice, but today it's eerily quiet. The benches and chairs are filled with cheerleaders on their phones, all whispering. I find a seat on the floor by Lauren. She sticks her tongue out at me and returns to texting her boyfriend.

Mia and Kelly walk in together, holding hands. Kelly looks upset, like she's been crying. Mia clears her throat. "Girls, the football guys have tried to get us back for the sick prank we pulled last week."

The girls all laugh, satisfied with our work. We sufficiently got the guys back for gluing our lockers shut by severely forking several guys' yards. Forking a yard is the oldest prank in the book, but we added a twist by covering the handles of the forks with Vaseline. When the guys went to pull a fork out of the lawn, their hands were covered in slimy jelly. The prank went without a hitch. We were dying at the pictures posted of football guys deforking their lawns with those yellow dishwashing gloves.

Mia raises her hand to silence the room. "The guys have stolen the mascot suit! Kelly, tell them."

"Well," Kelly begins, looking unsteady, "I was getting out of my car at lunch today, when Mac and Ryan came up to me."

Whatever comes next isn't going to be good. Mac and Ryan are supreme assholes. They are the two biggest meathead players on the team and have one job: destroy guys before they tackle the QB.

Kelly continues, "They started asking questions. Wanting to know where I kept Boomer. I was freaked out, so I told them my car trunk. They made me open it." She stops and folds her arms across her chest. "Ryan took the suit, and Mac pushed me down."

I can see red marks on Kelly's elbows from falling backward. Anger rises into my throat.

"Ugh, so unnecessary," Mia says, annoyed.

Kelly looks down. "And called me a lesbian."

Mia starts wagging her finger. "Girls, we need to find the suit and get them back for this."

I jump to my feet. "Mia, that wasn't a prank. Those jerks pushed Kelly and called her a lesbian. That's bullying."

She brushes it off. "Kelly, are you hurt?"

"No," Kelly says.

"And are you a lesbian?" Mia asks.

Kelly looks up and scans the room. "No," she says. "I have a boyfriend."

"See. Wait, what? Kelly, Jerry is officially your boyfriend? That is so great! I mean, it's Jerry, but still, so cute!" Mia gives Kelly a hug, and the girls start clapping. What is even happening? We should go to Principal Scott or at least Coach Harkins. This is bonkers.

Everyone settles down, and the prank brainstorm session begins. All the textbook pranks are suggested, and a couple weird catfishing, possibly illegal, online schemes. I am seething. A sophomoric prank won't stop these guys from being dumbasses. There's no cure for that.

"Just pants them," I say, and the room goes quiet, all eyes on me. "You know, show their manhood. Or lack of manhood."

"YES, GIRL!" Mia is clapping. "Let's expose those guys to the school. What a killer idea, Georgie. Even more impactful after what happened to you this summer."

"Wait, I was kidding," I say.

Lauren jumps in. "The Senior Dude Dance! At the pep rally this Friday! Let's depants them there!"

Mia is beside herself. "Yes, girls, this is beyond perfect!"

Hillcrest tradition #172,347: Every year, the senior football guys do a ridiculous dance at a pep rally. They hip thrust and grind somewhat close to the beat of the hottest song of the moment. Plenty of humping each other, weird faces, and taking off their shirts for the big finish. The crowd always goes nuts. Imagine what the school will do when they see more than their naked chests . . .

A whistle quiets the girls. "Girls, I have been waiting!" Coach Harkins says. She must have finally noticed that the entire squad was missing from practice. Mia takes the lead. "My apologies. We were discussing some secret stuff. Girls, let's hit the mats!"

Everyone heads out. I fast-walk over to Kelly and pull her sleeve. "Hey, I'm sorry, Kelly. Are you all right?"

"It's not a big deal, G. I'm fine."

"I know—you're tough as acrylic nails," I say. "Funny thing, I just remembered something."

Kelly smiles at me. "Oh, here we go."

"No." I stop her. "Anthony told me once that the football team has a secret storage closet. Maybe the suit is there?"

"Nice job, Private Investigator Roberts. You might have cracked the case."

We head down the hall, past the weight room and soda machines. I have never seen Kelly this quiet, no jokes, nothing. When something is wrong with someone as funny as Kelly, you can tell immediately. She's trying to hide it, but she's shook.

"I know you don't want to talk about it, but those guys were out of line. We should tell someone."

"Georgia, no way. Mac and Ryan might get kicked off the team, and I would be outcast. Snitches gets stitches," she says, pretending to shiv me.

"But what they did is, like, a hate crime." I am so hip to the lingo now that Pony is my friend.

"But I'm not a lesbian! And if this got out, I would have an even harder time convincing people I wasn't."

"Well, it's OK if you are," I say.

"Well, I'm not. Can we drop it?"

"Sure," I say, and we arrive at a door behind a broken weight bench. The sign reads *DO NOT ENTER*. I push the bench and open the door, no lock. Sure enough, there's Boomer. The suit is stuffed into a trash bin, safe and sound.

Kelly grabs it and walks off.

IPHONES, 8:56 P.M.

>**PONY**: So, Friday?

>**GEORGIA**: Yeah, what about it

>**PONY**: We have a date

>**PONY**: to the museum of science

>**GEORGIA**: Not a date

>**PONY**: ☹

>**PONY**: That's no way to talk to a fellow winner winner chicken dinner

>**GEORGIA**: Lol.

>**PONY**: Should we do this?

>**PONY**: Me. You. Science

>**GEORGIA**: Yeah just one problem

>**GEORGIA**: A pep rally

>**PONY**: Duty calls, I guess

>**GEORGIA**: But! Not until 3:30

>**GEORGIA**: And whatever. I'm over it

>**GEORGIA**: Long story.

>**GEORGIA**: Let's do this thing

>**PONY**: Great. It's a date.

>**GEORGIA**: NOT A DATE

>**PONY**: Ok.

>**PONY**: It's an undate

FOURTEEN

Friday, October 11

PONY, 8:50 A.M.

Today must be perfect. You don't get many chances at undates, so today actually needs to be beyond perfect. Epically perfect. It should feel like a movie montage of a couple falling in love. Profoundly perfect.

No pressure.

I'm amped without coffee, gripping the steering wheel tight as I head to pick up Georgia. I couldn't sleep last night, my mind running endless scenarios on how this day will unfold. Sometimes ending badly with awkward silences. Sometimes ending good with a kiss.

Here's the plan: remain calm, collected, and just indifferent enough about her presence. Flirt . . . but not too much. I have a list of things to do in Dallas, but I want to make today feel spontaneous.

I pull into her driveway at 8:30 a.m. on the dot and honk a few times while pushing empty water bottles and wrappers under the passenger seat. I tap on the air freshener that has never been re-filled. Change the song. Adjust the volume. Change the song again.

Georgia appears at the front door. She's got on black jeans, a bright red coat, big smile. And today, she's all mine.

I hand her a Starbucks cup when she sits down. "Pumpkin Spice Latte."

"My hero," she says, buckling up. So far, so good.

She removes the top and sips directly from the cup. I knew she would do that. I like knowing the little things about her.

"Pony, I am thrilled about our day, but I need to head back around two thirty to make it to the pep rally."

My heart sinks a bit. I wanted to spend more time with her, and now we have a hard stop in six hours. I'll just need to condense my charm. She changes the song, and we head out.

The traffic slows us down. We creep along the highway, bumper to bumper with people headed to their jobs. Georgia looks out the window at the other cars. "All these people, all dressed up and headed to their desks. Every day, Pony, they get in their car, drive to Dallas, drive home, and do it again and again. It's depressing."

"The American dream!" I exclaim.

She's lost in thought. "I guess if you love what you do, it wouldn't be bad."

"Or you hate your job but have a great carpool companion like me."

She looks at me and says, "You'll be in Hollywood."

"You could come with me," I offer. "We could move to East Hollywood, get jobs, and figure it out there."

She judges my seriousness. "I thought you'd never ask," she says. Not a yes or no, very clever.

I turn off the highway, confident. I know my way around Dallas. We drive down a street full of cool bistros and cafés. City life seems so cool. Always something going on, and you never have to eat at a chain restaurant. "Georgia, if you could live in any city, where would you be?"

"Addison, obviously. That town has it all."

I invoke Ted London's method of remaining quiet until the truth comes out. Eventually, she says, "I could see myself in New York."

"Cool. My sister lives there. She loves it."

"I think I would love it, too."

"OK, shut your eyes," I say channeling one of my mom's positivity exercises. Georgia plays along and shuts her eyes (after rolling them). "Now," I continue, "it's the morning in your dream life. Where do you live? Where would you work? How do you feel?"

She takes a deep breath. "OK, it's morning, so I'm running late. Scratch that, this is my dream life, so I'm on time and relaxed. I'm in my apartment in . . . New York! I'm getting ready for work. It's a small place but cute. And clean. Very clean. I have a great closet full of smart work clothes."

She opens her eyes. "And not one cheerleading outfit!" She closes her eyes again.

"I put my coffee cup in the sink, pick up my designer purse, and hit the subway. I walk into the *New York Times* building and go to my desk. The hustle and bustle of the office is addictive. I sit down and get to work on a story that will change the world forever."

She opens her eyes and looks at me, almost surprised.

"Breakfast tacos?" I ask.

"Don't tease me," she says. I pull into the drive-through of the Taco Joint, voted one of the ten best breakfast-taco places in Dallas by some website.

"It's almost like you had that planned," she says.

"Who, me?"

10:07 A.M.

We are eating tacos under the stars.

Well, fake stars in the planetarium at the Perot Museum of Nature and Science, but it's still the most romantic picnic with a friend ever. We snuck our breakfast into the museum.

I take the last bite of the bacon-egg-and-cheese taco and immediately miss it. Georgia sounds like she's making out with her taco, but I don't blame her—they were amazing. Sometimes the internet is right.

After breakfast is devoured, I recline my chair and look up at the stars. This place is like a movie theater with the screen on the ceiling. Georgia is typing away on her phone. "Sorry, this is so rude," she says. "Almost done."

"Cheerleading emergency?" I ask, hoping she isn't texting Jake.

"Something like that," she says, putting her phone back in her purse.

"Check it out: the Medium Dipper." I point at a random group of stars. "Always overshadowed by the Big Dipper."

She reclines her chair and leans over, our shoulders barely touching. "And there's the elusive My Little Pony configuration," she says, pointing at some other stars. "Speaking of stars, how's that actor you are helping? Get any good gossip?"

"None for you, Barbara Walters."

"I'm more Anderson Cooper," she says.

I look at her, stunned. "You and Ted should meet. I think he would like you."

"Why?"

"Just a feeling," I say.

"Answer me, weirdo."

"Is this off the record?"

"Completely."

I tell Georgia about my night with Ted London. He told me not to tell, but I trust Georgia with his secret. She listens attentively, living for the gossip. It's a relief to finally tell someone. My go-to would be Max, but he's done with me. Just thinking of him makes my heart heavy. I miss him. I'd do almost anything to hang.

"Wow," she says once I've finished, taking it all in.

"Yeah, it's heavy," I admit.

"What a sad life," she concludes, then rests her head on my shoulder.

"Sad? Why?" I ask. "He lived his dream of acting. He just had to hide one part of himself."

"But to not have love?" she says. "What's it all worth?"

I don't know the answer to that.

She picks her head up. "Pony? What about the man Ted loved, Lee Greatson?"

"Lee Grayson. That's all I know about him."

"Yeah, and that's why God invented the internet, Pony." She pulls out her phone, and two minutes later: "I have an address!" This feels like an invasion of Ted's privacy. He gets so weird about his personal stuff; I don't think he would be pleased to know that I'm stalking his long-lost love.

"He owns a store in Dallas," Georgia says.

"I think we just figured out why Ted moved to Texas. To be near Lee. He's lived in that house over ten years without getting in touch with him."

"And now he's going to die," she says.

"Where is Lee?" I ask.

"His Facebook page says he owns an antique shop on Richmond Street. How long does Ted have left?"

I think about his less-frequent breathing and his more-frequent visits to the hospital. The machines, pill bottles, oxygen tanks around the house. "Not long," I admit, and we both look back up at the stars.

My vision gets blurry as tears fill my eyes. I wipe them away, undetected. My heart hurts for Ted and everything he missed out on in his life. I don't want to waste any time with Georgia today, but maybe we can help Ted London get some closure. It's time to add something to the schedule.

"Georgia, how about we go antiquing?"

"I thought you'd never ask," she says.

We ditch the museum, snapping a few pictures as proof we were there, including a selfie of us in front of a huge cross-eyed frog. Half an hour later, we turn into the parking lot of an old church that's been renovated into a store. I park the car and read the large, rusty sign above the doors. "Thingamabobs?" I ask.

"Yeah, duh, from *The Little Mermaid.*"

"Any girl who combs her hair with a fork is a big red flag," I say.

She laughs. "You ready, Pony?"

"To be part of your world?"

"I'm done here," she says, then gets out of the car.

We walk up to the huge cathedral doors. I open them, setting off several chimes and bells. A dog barks from the back. This place is huge, with high ceilings and endless shelves. It's stuffy, like we're inside a snow globe of dust. And it does feel oddly like the Little Mermaid's cave, with gizmos and gadgets from floor to ceiling.

I'm tense. We shouldn't be here. Ted is going to kill me. Too late to turn back—Georgia has run off to the shelf of typewriters.

A man appears from the office dressed in a polo shirt and khakis. He's a bit younger than Ted, and slimmer and healthy. No oxygen machine at his side. "Good afternoon!" he says with a warm smile that I can see from across the store.

I'm frozen in place. I have no idea what to say. I look at Georgia with panicked eyes.

"My boyfriend has a question for you," she shouts, shrugging at me.

"Thanks, *girlfriend*," I say (and pretend it's real) as I walk toward the man. "Hi. We were just in the neighborhood and had to stop. We are freaks for antiques." I look back to Georgia, who is shaking her head and trying not to laugh. "Beautiful shop you have here. Are you the owner?"

"Yes, been open ten years."

"That's nearly a decade," I say, wasting more time.

"Sure is," he agrees.

"Is your name Lee Grayson?" Georgia says, now standing behind me.

"Why, yes," he says, taking a closer look at us. "Do I know you two?"

"No, but I know someone you know," I say, finally finding my words. "I've been helping an old friend of yours. His name is Ted London."

Lee takes off his glasses. I can see a shake in his hand. "I see," he says, leaning on the counter. "He lives here?"

"Just outside of Dallas, Mr. Grayson."

"Please, call me Lee."

"This is Georgia, and my name is Pony. I have some sad news. Ted is sick. Real sick." My eyes water, but I fight it back. "He's doesn't have much longer, and I think he moved here to be near you." Lee's face has grown white. His eyes look busy. I continue, "And I think he's going to kill me for doing this."

"*Honey*, he will have your head for this," Lee says, wiping his eyes. "That man is stubborn as a mule."

I pick up the pen on the counter and scribble on a receipt. "Here's his address. I don't know the whole story between you and him, but I do know that he cares about you more than words."

"That makes two of us," Lee says. "Thank you, Pony and Georgia. This was very brave of you." Georgia grabs my hand and squeezes. As we walk out, Lee yells, "And you two make a very cute couple."

GEORGIA, 12:41 P.M.

We sit in the car outside of Thingamabobs and decompress. Pony is looking at the window, thinking. "You did a good thing, Pony."

"Thanks," he says, then turns to me. "I couldn't have done that without you."

"I know," I kid.

He smiles and shakes his head. "We should get back to make it in time for the pep rally?"

"Actually," I say, "I'm skipping the pep rally. You're stuck with me until the game."

"Really?" Pony asks with big happy eyes.

"Yeah, the girls have a prank planned that I disagree with. It's an over-the-top, jump-the-shark prank. I don't want to be involved. So I'm not involved." I cross my arms, so very defiant.

"What is it?" Pony asks.

"Every year, the senior football players do a silly dance at the pep rally. It's a lot of humping the air and grinding on each other. During the dance, the girls are going to pull their pants down. Or shorts. Or whatever they are wearing."

"In front of the entire school?"

"Yeah. I hope to God they have underwear on."

He shakes his head. "I've got to be honest: the prank thing is weird."

To an outsider, all the traditions of Hillcrest must seem ridiculous. Especially the prank war between the cheerleaders and the football guys. We run around attempting to humiliate each other on grander scales. But this year, it's above and beyond.

Pony starts the car and pulls onto the road. I look around, unsure where we are headed. "What's the next stop on this undate?" I ask. He ignores me and tuns up the music. If circumstances were different, this would be a date. We are doing date things: eating tacos under the stars, reconnecting dying lovers. Ten minutes later, we pull into an empty car lot. I see an old playground.

"Want to swing?" he asks.

"Hell yes," I say, getting out of the car. Pony runs past me toward the swing set, and I catch up. Weeds wrap around the slide. The swing set is covered in rust. When was my last tetanus shot? Doesn't matter. I hop into a swing and go. Pony matches my pace, and we sync up our swings, laughing for no reason. I'm getting higher and higher until the metal frame creaks. We dig our feet into the gravel and come to a full stop.

He kicks a little dirt on my boots. "About the pep rally? I get it. After what your ex did to you at the party, you know how it feels to be exposed."

He knows about that? "Who told you?"

"Jerry and Kenji. At lunch the day that Science Hack Day was announced." He re-creates Mr. Glover's beaker dance, and it makes me laugh.

I think back to that day. Pony was finally nice to me. I should have known something was fishy. "Did you feel sorry for me? Is that why we're friends?"

"What? No. I mean, I did feel bad for you. That must have been awful."

"I'm sure your bro friends did a great job telling the actual story," I say.

"Kenji was there," he reminds me, *like I don't remember.*

"That was hard. I trusted Anthony."

Pony nods. "Maybe you could write about it?"

"Too personal," I admit. "The three readers of the *Hillcrest Reporter* would figure out that I am Anonymous."

"And that would be a bad thing?"

"The worst thing," I say. I get out of my swing and go behind Pony. "But maybe it's time for an exposé about pranks."

"Can't wait to read it," he says.

I give him a big push, sending him swinging. "You're like my muse, Pony." I push harder. With each push, I feel something under his sweater. Like an undershirt but textured and tight. What the frig is this? "Pony, what are you wearing under your sweater? Are you wearing Spanx?"

"No," he says, catching the ground with his feet. Without looking back at me, he says, "It's a binder. I wear it to hide my chest." He doesn't turn around. Maybe it's easier to not look at me.

I try to needle my finger in between the binder and his skin but can't get in. "It feels really tight, Pony."

"It's really tight," he confirms.

"Can you even breathe?"

"Most of the time."

"What kind of fabric is this? Duct tape?"

"Polyester, mostly."

"Wait, so all this time I was stuck in my polyester prison of a cheer outfit and you had your own secret polyester prison?"

He stands up and faces me, all serious. "Aren't we all in polyester prisons, hypothetically?"

I look at his body again with my new knowledge. His chest is completely flat. I have never once thought that he had boobs. Not even manboobs.

"For real, those things can't be healthy to wear?"

He pounds his chest like King Kong. "Me tough."

"There must be an operation. If they can get bigger, they can go away."

He steps closer to me. "There's a surgery. I found a good doctor in Dallas."

"Let's go now," I suggest. "We are getting *so* much done today."

"It's expensive. Too expensive. But I need to get it soon. I can't spend another summer in these binders. In this body. I need to get it done. That's why I took the job with Ted London, but it's not enough. Not even close."

"How much more do you need?" *Maybe I could help.*

"Twenty-five thousand dollars."

Never mind.

"Your parents won't help?" I ask. I'd like to think my parents would help me.

"Not a chance," he says. "Who cares? I don't need them. I'm going to postpone college until I can afford the surgery."

"You can't do that," I say, all of a sudden incredibly invested in Pony's studies.

"Georgia, want to go somewhere?"

"This sounds suspicious."

"Do you trust me yet?" he asks.

"No," I say.

"Great, let's go."

Fifteen minutes later, we pull into a run-down strip mall with a smattering of busted cars in the parking lot and a few shady characters walking around. "Pony, you really are going to kill me," I say, accepting my fate.

He points at the sign in front of us, and I read it out loud. "Ralph's VR World?"

"Virtual reality," he says proudly.

"Are you kidding me with this?" I'm not into video games. They have never been my thing. I didn't dip out on the second-to-last pep rally of my life to spend the afternoon in a desperate minimall wearing a dirty headset shooting CGI zombies.

Pony can tell I'm not happy. He laughs. "Will you just try?"

"Fine," I say, getting out of the car. I will go with the flow, but if I get pink eye, then Pony is a dead man. We walk in, and the front desk guy stands up.

"Ponyboy!"

"Ponyboy?" I whisper to him.

"Don't worry about it," he whispers back.

"Hey, Ralph! This is my friend Georgia. Georgia, this is Ralph. He owns this place!"

Ralph corrects Pony: "Co-manage." He is short and round, wearing an baggy SpongeBob shirt that has been washed too many times and cargo shorts. The small amount of hair left on his head is dyed light blue with black roots. All in all, Ralph is endearing.

"Hi, Ralphie. I am very happy to be here," I say with enough sarcasm that he thinks I'm sincere, but Pony knows I'm not.

"Ralph," Pony says, putting his hands on my shoulders, "we've got a VR virgin here!"

These guys have no room for virgin jokes.

"Cool beans," Ralph says, then heads over to the headset wall.

I'm silently questioning my life choices when Pony says, "Why do you immediately shut something down because it's different?"

"That's not true."

"Face it, Georgia, you live life in the comfort zone. Time to step out of it."

"With VR and Ralph?" I ask a little too loudly.

"With me," Pony says.

Ralph leads us to the room that Pony rented (*très romantic*). It's the size of a big closet. And smells like socks. The walls are white, with nothing on them but a flat screen with tons of wires branching out across the room. Ralph places the headset on me. The goggles cover my eyes, and I'm transported into another world. He places a controller in my hands and shows me how to work things.

"Pony?" I say, totally disoriented.

"I'll be right behind you," he says. "Push the button, and you'll be immersed in a quick video. Try to have fun!"

OK, I can do this. Comfort zone? That's ridiculous. What does Pony know about me? I lift my hand, push Start, and instantly transport to a medieval castle with drawbridges and a moat. I'm shook by the realness. I walk into the castle, one massive room with impossibly high ceilings. It looks like a cartoon but feels like

I am there. *Inside a freaking cartoon.*

A prompt starts flashing: *WALK NOW.* I move my legs in place, probably looking like a total idiot as the walls fall away. I'm in a meadow now. Hundreds of butterflies fill the air. They fly so close to me that I duck backward. I nearly fall on my butt when a short Viking man comes running at me. With no notice, I blast off into space. My body tenses up like it's actually happening. This is wild.

A prompt flashes *PONYBOY HAS ENTERED THE GAME.* We are now traveling in space together. "Hi, Ponyboy," I say.

"Come here often?"

I look over (in VR world) and see Pony's avatar standing beside me. He's got the same hair and general look but way, way more muscles.

"How much cyber currency did those muscles cost?"

He flexes his fake muscles and smiles big.

"Pony, I can't see myself. What do I look like?"

"You're not going to love this. New players always get the default avatar." A mirror appears in Pony's hand. He holds it up to my face.

"I'm Ralph," I say.

"Aren't we all Ralph, really? Can I give you a tour?"

"Do I have a choice?"

"No," he says, then grabs my virtual hand. We blast off back down to earth and straight into the ocean, landing on the ocean floor within seconds. Hundreds of brightly colored fish swim by as a dopey turtle crawls across my feet.

"Should we find the Little Mermaid?" I ask.

"Look behind you," Pony says. I turn around, and I'm face-to-face with a huge manatee. I scream, but just a cute amount. I pet the sea cow, and she smiles back at me, blowing colorful bubbles.

Pony calls over two dolphins. We hop on—never say no to a dolphin ride—and take off through the fake sea, cruising past football field–size whales and squid that light up the water.

The screens all go black, and then we are in a war zone with a gun in each hand.

"Ew, no thanks," I say. Killing isn't my thing. The screen flashes again and I'm standing over a huge kitchen stove. I look up, and we're in a busy CGI restaurant. Who the hell wants a virtual job?

Pony walks over and cracks a couple eggs in a skillet. I grab a handful of bacon and set it on the pan. I feel silly cooking fake food, but it's cool to hear sizzling bacon and chatter from the customers. Only thing missing is the smell.

Virtual Ponyboy is cooking right beside me. I toss some pancake batter on him. He laughs and picks up and throws a CGI egg that hits me in the CGI face. "Oh, we've got beef now," I say, then throw some virtual hamburger meat at him. "Get it?" I shout between laughing.

We're having a food fight that I won't have to shower after—this is genius. Eggs are flying, and so are avocados, carrots, bread, and anything we can get our fake hands on. Pony flips a bowl over, and flour goes everywhere. I am about to break a rib from laughing so hard.

When the flour fog finally clears, Virtual Pony is standing right in front of me. He puts his arms on my shoulders and pulls me in. No words, just a busy restaurant not getting their fake food. I run my hand down his chest. I put my arms around him. We are embraced without touching. Right now, we are just two bodies uncomplicated by our limitations.

A prompt flashes *SESSION ENDS IN 10 SECONDS.*

We take off our headsets, back to reality. My eyes adjust to the real world. It feels like I've been crossing my eyes for thirty minutes. Pony is standing just out of my reach, staring at me.

"Georgia, will you ever be able to trust me?"

"I don't know," I say.

He drops his headset. "Did I tell you about my grandma?"

"You did. She passed when you were a freshman?"

"That's her. Growing up, my parents would ship me and my sister off to Nana's house in Montana for two weeks every summer. Cheaper than sleepaway camp, they said. She lived by a ranch with horses. I would spend hours watching the horses running, fast and free. So strong and confident."

Pony is standing about three feet away. I can see his hand shaking.

"For me, choosing my new name was one of the hardest parts of transitioning. One late night of googling names, I wrote down the characteristics that I wanted most: strength, confidence, freedom."

"Like a pony," I say.

"Like a pony," he confirms.

He takes a step closer. I still feel off-balance from the headset.

He continues, "I won't keep secrets, Georgia. You can know everything."

He takes a step closer. Our faces close. "My birth name, *my dead name*, the thing you want to know so bad, I'll tell you. it's Sa—"

I lean forward and kiss him.

I don't want to know that name. That's not him. I forgot how soft his lips are, how nice. He pulls back, just a little, stunned— but he figures it out. He kisses me back, wrapping his real arms around me. It's perfect. I run my fingers through his hair and down his neck.

Eventually, I pull away. Pony is frozen.

"Friends kiss sometimes," I say.

IPHONES, 11:35 P.M.

> **GEORGIA**: I didn't see you at the game.
>
> **PONY:** I told you I wasn't going
>
> **GEORGIA**: You are a terrible friend
>
> **GEORGIA**: Kidding. Thank you for today. It was perfect
>
> **PONY**: A successful undate?
>
> **GEORGIA**: . . . .
>
> **GEORGIA**: Sure
>
> **PONY**: Aww.

PONY: How was the game?

GEORGIA: Fine

PONY: And did The Great Pep Rally De-Pantsing happen?

GEORGIA: Yes. And they said it worked. Makes me nervous about payback.

PONY: Good luck. Nice knowing you!

GEORGIA: Ugh

PONY: I was thinking maybe we could have another undate?

GEORGIA: Pony.

GEORGIA: We are friends

PONY: ::steps back in friend zone::

GEORGIA: Good night, Pony

PONY: Good night, girl friend

GEORGIA: Pony . . .

PONY: Girl that's a friend = Girl friend

FIFTEEN

Friday, October 18

PONY, 4:50 P.M.

It's Friday, but there's no football game. It's something called a "bye week." There's only one reason that matters to me, and she's sitting in my kitchen. Georgia could be anywhere in the world, but she's in my kitchen. I cooked for her. We're eating Totino's Pizza Rolls.

A week has passed since the undate and our very real kiss. Sadly, the stats aren't on my side:

Number of texts since undate: Hundreds, easily.

Times we have talked about the kiss: nada.

Times we have kissed again: nope.

I have attempted to create moments in which another kiss would be appropriate, but it's been an exercise in futility. I bite into the first pizza roll too soon out of the oven and burn off all my taste buds. Georgia is scrolling through her phone. "Pony, look!" she says, putting her phone too close to my face. "It's up!"

I read the headline on the *Hillcrest Reporter*: "*Has Pranking Gone Too Far?*" *by Anonymous*. She hands me the phone, and I scan the article. I don't need to read this thing because I already have; I helped on two edits. I was happy to help, of course.

The article questions the pranking tradition and how it could be dangerous. I guess the pants-pulling prank crossed a line for her. "It's amazing," I say, looking up. She's glowing. "I'm proud of you."

"I couldn't have done it without you, my muse," she says, dipping a pizza roll in ranch dressing. Maybe this would be a good time to kiss again. I lean closer and put my foot on her stool. Instead, she grabs her phone back and scrolls to the bottom of the article. Probably checking for comments.

"You aren't worried about the blowback from your team? Or the football guys?" I ask.

"No one reads this paper. I just needed to say it."

"And you said it. Or Anonymous said it, rather."

She leans her shoulder into mine. My body warms up. "How's your dad?" I ask.

"He's good. Dating helps him move past the divorce, but it's too freaking weird, watching my dad 'playing the field.'" She rolls her eyes. "He *texts* with ladies. I tell him to put his phone down during dinner. Watching my dad flirt over text. *Flirt over text, Pony.* It's hard to wrap my head around."

"Do his lady friends spend the night?"

"Once," she says darkly.

"Well, you can always spend the night here when that happens," I say, raising my eyebrows. It's a bluff, of course. My parents would never allow a girl to spend the night.

"OK, I might take you up on it," she says, upping the ante. We are fully engaged in sleepover chicken.

"Great. In my bed," I suggest. *Checkmate.*

"OK," she says, squaring off, "but I snore."

"OK," I say, returning her stance, "but I'm little spoon."

Our laughter is disrupted by the front door slamming shut. *Shit.* One of my parents is home early. They shouldn't be home. This is parent roulette, and I don't know which option is better: Mom will embarrass, and Dad will harass.

"Hello?" I ask, hoping it's a robber.

Nothing. Total silence. Creepy. Georgia and I look at each other with big eyes.

My sister jumps from the doorway. "DADDY'S HOME!"

Rocky runs up and hugs me so hard I almost fall out my chair. What is she doing here? She rocks me back and forth and kisses my head. "Let me have a look at you, baby brother," Rocky says, placing her hands on my face. She turns it from side to side like she's examining me. "You are turning out quite nicely. Yes, a fine young lad. Wouldn't you agree?"

"He's not too bad," Georgia says, even though she has no idea who this person is, why she's attacking me, or what she will do next.

"Georgia," I say, "this nut is my sister, Rocky. All the way from New York City."

"Hello, Georgia. You're as pretty as Pony described you."

I'm out-of-my-skin excited to see my sister, but I didn't plan for an incidental meeting of my crush and my chatty sister who knows all about said crush. Rocky doesn't really believe in conversation boundaries. "Making a surprise visit?" I ask.

"Surprise? Pony, it's Mom's birthday? I'm here for dinner tonight, as promised." I forgot about Mom's birthday. Of course Dad didn't remind me. He pays for Rocky to come home on Mom's birthday so we can have dinner as a family. I wonder if he'll do the same for me when I move away. Rocky sits on the stool beside Georgia and ogles the spread. "You kids having a pizza-roll date?"

I look at Georgia. "Something like that," I say.

"Or something more casual than that," Georgia says.

"Cute. So, Georgia, what's the deal with Jake—"

I stand up and get real nervous, start stuttering and laughing, anything to not have this talk. Georgia gets up, too. "I should get going. Y'all must have so much to catch up on."

"Girl, stay! Hang out for a few. I want to get to know you." Rocky grabs Georgia's hand. "And those nails."

Georgia looks at them and frowns. "I know."

Rocky opens her bag and pulls out a bottle of bright red nail polish. My sister is never far from nail polish or makeup. "Want me to touch them up?"

Georgia claps excitedly. "Yes, girl."

My dining room table turns into a beauty shop. I sit as still as possible and pray that Rocky doesn't embarrass me. Lucky for me, she's busy telling stories about living in New York. Georgia is at the edge of her seat, eating them up. She looks at me. "I think I could move to New York. What do you think?"

"Let's go," I say. I'm probably more serious than she is.

"Rad! But you can't stay with me. Glad we got that talk out of the way," Rocky says and winks at me.

"Rocky, how's the dating going? Still seeing the flame eater?"

"Pony, he is a flame *dancer*. And no. Too hot for me."

Totally dumb joke, but Georgia laughs. She's got big doe eyes for Rocky. It's fun to watch Georgia get charmed by my sister. This happens to everyone who crosses Rocky's path.

"I actually have been taking a break from all of that." Rocky blows on Georgia's nails to quicken the drying process.

"Oh," Georgia says. "You're on a Men Cleanse?"

"Men, couples, but yes. Ding, ding, ding."

"I was, too," Georgia admits. "Well, just guys."

Rocky leans in. "And then a handsome Pony came galloping into your life?"

"Something like that. But we're just friends now."

My sister sneaks a look at me. "Anyway, G, want me to thread your eyebrows?"

"Sounds scary. I'll pass. I do really need to go," Georgia says while carefully collecting her things, trying not to ruin her new nail polish. "Rocky, you are amazing."

"Girrrrl," Rocky says, and they hug. Georgia comes over to me for my hug. Another kiss-less day. Like those signs on construction sites counting the days of injury-less days, mine says: 7 DAYS WITHOUT A KISS.

6:47 P.M.

I put my fork and knife down. "Mom, that was amazing."

I have guilt about Mom cooking on her own birthday, but she insists every year. And it truly was one of the best meals of my life. She slow-cooked a brisket in a Crock-Pot. We stuffed the meat into sweet Hawaiian mini rolls that are soft as clouds and poured in savory barbecue sauce. With creamy mac and cheese and buttery green peas.

Dad hasn't said much, opting for the occasional grunt and whiskey—it's usually beer, but he's in a mood. I'm always stiff and guarded around Dad. It's like dining with a wild animal that could attack at any moment.

"I'll go get the cake," Mom says in her happy-the-whole-family-is-home voice. Once she leaves, Dad eyes Rocky.

"Rachel," he says.

"Rocky," she corrects.

"Whatever." He rattles the ice cubes in the empty drink. "You think I don't see the credit card statements?"

Here it comes. He waited until Mom left the room before going in on my sister.

"Yes, Father. New York City has proven to be more expensive

256

than my salary. I work all the time but need your occasional help. And for that, I thank you."

"Typical," he says, then stands up abruptly. Rocky and I both brace ourselves, thinking he's coming at us. He's come at us before. Instead, he shuffles over to the bar cart for a refill. "No college. No ambition. You think I don't look at your social media, but I do. I see you, working hard." He laughs, but there's no joy in it. He pours a stiff drink.

"I'm an artist," Rocky says. "I don't expect you to understand what I do."

"Head in the damn clouds—that's what I understand."

She yawns, trying her best to act ambivalent. "And you wonder why I don't come home more."

Dad grips his glass tight and sits down. "And this one?" Motioning to me. "This one wants my money to cut her tits off. Just look at both of you. Bunch of—"

"DAD." Rocky slams her hands on the table.

"Freaks."

"Who's ready for cake?" Mom returns singing but immediately picks up on the tension like a whiff of foul odor. "Norman?"

"He called us *freaks*, Mom." Rocky is pissed. I'm frozen, as usual.

"Norman," Mom repeats with way more downward inflection. "It's my birthday."

"What? Our kids have new names, new nose piercings, new genders. That's not freaky?"

He finishes the drink he just poured. My body is tight, ready for any sudden movements. On nights like tonight, I go into protector mode.

"Same old drinking problem for you, Dad," I say.

He stands back up with enough force that the chair flies backward, hitting the ground with a *thud*. I match him with the same intensity. *Thud*. Our eyes deadlocked.

"Oh, you want to be a tough guy? Look at you. You're a coward. No one will ever see you as a man."

I flinch. His words hit harder than a fist or palm or belt. He's right. I'm not a real man. And I'll never be one. My dad removes the Jenga piece, and I come crashing down.

"JUST STOP, YOU ASSHOLE," Rocky screams, standing up and knocking her chair to the ground, too. *THUD*. She digs the credit card that caused this fight out of her purse and hurls it at Dad. "There. You no longer own me. I am done with you. I am free. Come on, Pony." She takes my hand and leads me away. Before I am out of the room, I look back at my mom and mouth, *I'm sorry*.

8:32 P.M.

Rocky puts her feet on my dashboard. "Pony, I didn't expect to spend my night out in Addison at Sonic."

"Not my fault. Addison is no Dallas. Nothing going on." I hold up my phone. "But I can probably find a party in the woods?"

"Yeah, I'm not doing that."

"Maybe this will help?" I pull out a flask from under the seat. It's half-full of cheap vodka. Rocky snatches the flask and dumps most of it in her Blue Raspberry Slush. She reclines the seat and hits her vape pen.

"Are you vaping pot?"

"CBD. It's cannabis minus THC. I get all the medical benefits without feeling stoned. I need something to take the edge off after that shitshow."

I drum the steering wheels. "Aaaaaand that concludes another episode of Jacobs Family Shitshow!"

Rocky laughs. We take care of each other on nights like tonight. Dad Rage doesn't happen often. Maybe once every couple of months. But when it happens, it happens. Drinking is like a Duraflame log to his anger. It's messy. And scary.

"Pony, you need to get out of there," Rocky says.

"I know."

"I know you know, but do you have a plan, man?"

Man.

"I have no plan," I admit. "Guess I'll have to survive on my good looks."

"No, you won't last a day! You need a plan. Maybe two!" She nudges me. "But seriously, my exit might have looked spur-of-the-moment and flawlessly executed, but I had that plane ticket for three months. And I found an apartment before I kissed the tarmac at JFK."

"Please say you didn't actually kiss the ground," I beg.

"Moral of the story, having that plan was how I survived. Things happened in high school, Pony. Things I haven't told you about. But that exit plan was my light at the end of a dark tunnel. I needed it. And you do, too."

"I started thinking about it, but I have been busy . . ."

"With?" she asks.

"With Georgia, and my job, and figuring out how to get enough money to cut my tits off," I say, calling back my dad's harsh words. We both cringe. "I was thinking of staying at home until I can pay for the surgery."

"Pony, respectfully speaking, that's the dumbest thing I have ever heard."

"I can't wear binders for much longer. They squeeze me into nothing. I can't take a deep breath without full concentration. And Texas summers? The sweat just traps inside."

"Then move to New York and get a job with health insurance."

"I didn't think of that," I admit.

"Or find someone rich to ask for the help. I don't know, like an old dying actor?"

"He doesn't know I'm trans."

"Pony," she says, disappointed. "I'm not going to comment on that."

"I'll tell him at the funeral."

"You have options. There's more than one way to get from here to there."

"You always know the right thing to say."

Rocky pulls a nail file out of her purse. "Don't walk around thinking I'm perfect. You heard about the credit-card thing. New York is no joke. It will beat you down. But I get back up every time because I'm a stubborn Taurus."

I look around at the nearly vacant Sonic lot. "Georgia wants to move to New York."

Rocky takes the last pull of her slush and tosses the cup into the backseat. "You really like this girl, don't you?"

I pause. "Yes."

"But do you *love* this girl?"

I pause again. I have never been in love, but the feelings I have for Georgia are consuming, obsessive, overwhelming. "Yes."

"Pony, she likes you. I picked up on the vibes. You finish each other's sentences. You have so many inside jokes. Too many inside jokes. A little advice here—when you lovebirds aren't alone, use your outside jokes."

"Noted," I say, proud that we are annoying.

"Pony, I'm being as serious as Grandpa's heart attack right now. You are a special dude. Either way, you need to know the truth. Shit or get off the pot, right?"

My heart starts beating. "A movie-magic grand gesture to say I love you?"

"Whoa," she says. "I was thinking coffee?"

"Oh," I say, feeling silly.

"You know," Rocky says, "if you love this girl, you should go big. What are you thinking?"

I look out my car window and think. I remember that night in the golf cart playing Truth or Truth. "Her favorite movie is *Love Actually*."

Rocky starts bouncing up and down in the seat, shaking the car. "Yes! Let's re-create the poster-board scene!"

She's referring to the scene where the guy from *The Walking Dead* professes his love to his best friend's wife on Christmas by showing up at her door and standing with poster boards that say cute things. While his best friend is in the house. Really messed up if you unpack it.

"Tomorrow! And, you'll come with me?" I ask.

"Oh, Pony. No, sorry, baby. I'll be on a plane putting many miles between me and this place." She grabs my hand and squeezes. "You don't need me there."

My heart sinks. "You're already leaving?"

"I promised to show up for Mom's birthday. One day. And what a day it has been!"

My phone buzzes. Probably Georgia, so I check it immediately. It's Dad. I read it out loud: "'I'm sorry. Tell your sister I said that. Mom wants you to come home.'"

"He always had a way with words," Rocky says, rolling her eyes. "Ugh. Fine. Let's go back. For Mom. But first we need to make a quick stop at Walmart to buy them out of poster boards and Red Bull. We have a long night ahead of us."

"You're the best sister ever," I say.

"And you, sir, are the kindest, sweetest brother."

Brother.

"And Pony," she says with her serious voice, "I will always come home if you need me."

"Thanks," I say.

IPHONES, 11:39 P.M.

 GEORGIA: PONY

 PONY: Hey you

 GEORGIA: Where's my text buddy?

 PONY: Here! But busy with Rocky

 GEORGIA: ☹☹☹☹

 GEORGIA: TALK TO ME

 PONY: I'm sorry, Rocky leaves tomorrow so we are hanging out.

 GEORGIA: Np. Good night.

 PONY: Goodnight actually.

 GEORGIA: Weirdo.

SIXTEEN

Saturday, October 19

GEORGIA, 5:55 P.M.

I wake up on my couch, confused about time of day or purpose of life. I check my phone. I have been out cold for two solid hours. The house is dark, cold, and quiet. *Like my heart.* Dad went to the movies with his new lady friend. I was invited, but no thanks.

I sit up and stretch my arms. My eyes slowly adjust to the darkness of the living room. Growing up, we were the Saturday-night-hot-cocoa-cheesy-movies-buttery-popcorn kind of family. I pretended like I hated it, but I didn't. And now I miss it.

I'm on my feet and headed upstairs to change and maybe even shower when the doorbell rings. *Sonofabitch.* I open the door and see my girls. Mia stomps inside without invitation (guess she's not a vampire). "You have not been looking at your phone," she says. Lauren follows closely behind Mia.

I shut the door. "I have been napping. To what do I owe this visit?"

Mia sits on my couch. "Did you read the *Hillcrest Reporter*?"

My heart jumps into my throat. "The school paper?" I need to play this cool. "Why would I read that?"

"Right," Lauren says, sitting on the footstool. "Mia, no one is reading that thing."

"What thing?" I ask.

Mia tosses me her phone. "See for yourself," she says.

I sit down on the floor, my back against the couch, and read my beautiful article. "Wow," I say.

"Wow is right," Mia repeats. "How dare someone write that crap?" Her hands are shaking. "It's not even good."

"And to not put your name? What a coward," Lauren adds.

The realness of this situation hits me. My best friends are upset about an article that I wrote, and they don't know I wrote it.

Mia looks at her phone. "I hate this part the most: 'The outdated tradition of football versus cheerleading prank wars needs to stop before someone gets hurt.'" Mia cracks up, and Lo joins. She continues reading. "'The pranks are setting a bad example for the underclassman and allowing for bad behavior.'" They bust up laughing again.

And then the doorbell rings. How could this get worse?

I open the door to something even more surprising: Pony holding a stack of poster boards, wearing a Santa hat. Saturday has officially lost its mind.

He *shhhh*s me and reveals a poster board: *SAY IT'S CAROL SINGERS*

"Pony, no one is here," I lie.

"Just say it," he whispers.

I turn my head in and yell, "It's carol singers." I catch a look at Lauren, more confused than ever.

"Who is Carol Singers?" she asks as I close the door. Pony bends down and pushes play on an old-school boom box. It's some Christmas song. *OMG*, he's *Love Actually*-ing me.

Pony smiles and reveals the next poster: *WITH ANY LUCK,*

And the next: *SEEING HOW YOU AND I ARE ONLY FRIENDS*

I'LL SOON BE GOING OUT WITH ONE OF THESE GIRLS . . .

He shoots a cute look at me and flips to the next poster. It's a bunch of old ladies in bathing suits. I laugh. This is so cute I could melt, but it's leading to something that makes me both excited and uncomfortable.

Pony flips another poster board: *BUT FOR NOW, LET ME SAY,*

BECAUSE IT'S CHRISTMAS*

He raises his eyebrow and flips the next card: *(*NOT REALLY. GO WITH IT)*

(AND AT CHRISTMAS YOU TELL THE TRUTH)

YOU HIDE THE BEST THINGS ABOUT YOU

BUT I SEE THEM

I SEE YOU, GEORGIA

AND TO ME, YOU ARE PERFECT

He pauses on this card. My heart is exploding. Nobody has

ever done something so sweet. He turns over the next card: *I*
WANT TO BE WITH YOU

UNTIL YOU LOOK LIKE THIS

The next poster has the same old ladies in bathing suits.

GEORGIA,

We lock eyes.

I LOVE ACTUALLY YOU

Pony drops the last poster board and gives me the double
thumbs-up like the movie. I step closer to him and hope the girls
aren't watching from the window. "You love me?"

"Yes, Georgia. I can't be just friends. I can't stop how I feel
about you." He takes a step toward me. "And I think you feel it,
too."

"Pony, it doesn't matter," I say.

"See! You love actually me, too."

I step away from him. "I can't do this."

"I know I lied at first, and I'm sorry. Forgive me. Let's try
again."

The front door opens, breaking our intensity. Lauren peeks
out. No doubt Mia sent her. She is stunned. I'm guessing she
didn't expect to see this scene.

"Hey," I say to her, "I'll be back in two."

Without comment, she closes the door.

"Pony," I say, shutting my eyes. Of course this would happen.
I led him on. I kissed him. It wasn't fair of me, and I need to be
honest. "I can't date you."

He steps away. "Because I lied?"

"Not because you lied to me," I admit. "It didn't help, but . . ."

"But why?" he asks again.

"Because you're transgender."

"What?" he says with an anger that I have never seen from him. "Is that true?"

I wish it wasn't true. I wish I didn't care about it. But I do. I lower my voice, worried they can hear. "Pony, people will find out about you. And if we're dating? I can't be connected to that kind of thing. People wondering if I'm gay or whatever."

"Are you attracted to girls?" he asks.

"No," I say. "I'm into guys. But you—"

Pony cuts me off. "Then you are straight. You like guys, and I'm a guy. Body parts don't define the gender, the person does."

"But everyone at school won't know that," I counter.

"Who cares what people think?"

"I do. I need to look after my image," I say.

"Image?" he scoffs. "This is high school, not Hollywood."

I run my hand through my hair. He's right. But I made my choice. Pony collects the poster boards and looks at me with hate in his eyes. "So, this is it?" I ask.

"Yeah, this is it," he says, then walks off for the second time. And again, I don't stop him.

Before I can go back inside, Mia and Lauren come outside. "Pony? Georgia, really?" Mia says, taking a seat on the patio couch. Lauren does the same.

"No."

"I don't believe you."

"Come sit down," she demands. My heart feels like it has been cracked open. I want them to leave so I can curl into a ball and wake up next year. I hop up on the patio railing. Mia continues, "Girls, this article. Georgia and this Pony guy? *The secret lesbian?*" She stops and shakes her head. "We are out of control."

"What do we do?" Lauren asks. I watch the sun setting behind my neighbor's house and think of Pony. I want him in my life.

Mia stands up. "Monday morning, I'm going to the principal about the article."

I'm about to explain why that's unnecessary, but she's already off to her Mustang with Lauren trailing behind her. *Thanks for stopping by?*

IPHONES, 11:18 P.M.

ROCKY: JUST LANDED. BACK IN NYC. THANK GODDESS.

PONY: Did you kiss the tarmac?

ROCKY: Not this time.

ROCKY: HOW DID IT GO

PONY: Bad

ROCKY: How bad?

PONY: Bad bad bad

PONY: She said no.

ROCKY: Ugh. I'm sorry Pony

PONY: I don't get it.

PONY: Rocky your advice is always right. And this time I listen, and it's wrong?

ROCKY: Oh Pony

ROCKY: You were a smitten kitten

ROCKY: You needed the truth. Good or bad.

PONY: I could have facetimed her for that

ROCKY: Go big or go home, I think that was your idea . . .

ROCKY: You had to try. That's all we can ever do

PONY: She says it's because I'm trans

ROCKY: That's going to happen

ROCKY: You need to be tough about that

PONY: Easy to say

ROCKY: When your heart breaks, my heart breaks

ROCKY: You needed an answer, and you got it.

ROCKY: Just because it didn't end happily doesn't mean I was wrong.

ROCKY: Sometimes the ending isn't happy

ROCKY: Be sad and then put on your big boy pants and move on

ROCKY: Pony?

SEVENTEEN

Sunday, October 20

PONY, 2:10 P.M.

On days like today, I think about *it.* Would I have the balls to actually do *it?* I would hate to add to the statistics on the posters in the LGBTQIA Center, but when things get hard, that's where I go. And right now, ending my life feels like the only way out of this body.

And that scares me. My family would be so sad—not Dad—but my mom and sister. They are the reason I don't think about doing *it* more.

Who knows what happens when you do die, but I like to believe in reincarnation. That way, I have a shot at coming back in the right body. And I'll never get rejected like I did last night. I can hear Max in my head saying, *I told you so, bro.* I wish I could hear him saying it to my face. I miss him.

Rocky was right: I needed to know the truth.

I get my ass to Ted London's to bury all my troubles in his piles of crap. I walk in with my large coffee and am immediately greeted by Victor, more anxious than his usual anxiousness. "Pony! Be quiet! Hush hush hush!"

"Will do," I say in a whisper. "Why?"

"Mr. London has a guest!"

This is unusual. He hasn't had a guest in months, or ever maybe? At least not while I have been here, though by the looks of Victor, I'm guessing this doesn't happen often.

"His name is Lee!"

My heart drops into my stomach. "Lee Grayson?" I ask.

"Yessssss," Victor whisper-sings, and then continues down the hall damn near skipping.

I hit the bathroom and shut the door. I feel a panic attack creeping in. Maybe I should get out of here? Ted London will be angry. I put my hands on the sink and look at myself in the mirror. There's a good chance he will fire me.

"Mr. Pony," Victor says from the other side of the bathroom door.

"Ted wants to see me?" I yell back.

"How did you know?"

A couple minutes later, I take a deep breath and knock on Ted's bedroom door.

I hear a couple coughs, then, "Enter."

This is my first time in Ted's bedroom. It's surprisingly clean and sparse compared to the rest of the hoarder headquarters.

The bed looks like two king beds pushed together with a massive headboard.

"Come sit down," he says, gesturing at a chair beside his bed. The mighty Ted London is propped up on pillows in bed, an oxygen machine beside him, looking weak. I sit down and try to read his face. Is he mad? Happy? Sad? He reveals nothing.

"Pony, why don't you take a guess at who was sitting in that chair before you?"

"Lee Grayson," I say. No reason to beat around the bush.

"Lee Grayson," he confirms.

"How did it go?" I ask.

"How is that your business, my boy? Who gave you permission to reach out to Lee? I don't remember asking you to do that. Yet here we are."

I tighten my grip on the sides of the chair and steady myself. Sometimes I think about how I would do *it*. Pills seem like the easiest option, but there are none around my house. Jumping out of a window or falling off a ladder seems extreme. I would probably cut my wrists. Messy for someone to see, but maybe I could call the cops, and they could find me instead of my mom.

"Pony, you are a naive high school boy. How could you have any idea what I have been through?"

He glances over, challenging me to speak. The thing about cutting my wrists would be the pain. I would hate that pain.

"I'm trans," I blurt out.

Ted raises his eyebrows. "You're what?"

"Transgender."

"So, you were born a girl?"

"I was assigned the gender of female at birth."

"And now you are a boy?"

"I have always been a boy," I say.

Ted shakes his head and laughs but not in a mean way. It was a the-world-sure-has-changed laugh. He clears his throat. "Pony, back in my day, it was hard for the gays, but it was nearly impossible for the trannies."

I channel Max. "That word has been retired. We just say transgender now."

"Why are you telling me this?" he asks.

"Because you shouldn't say that word anymore."

"No, son, why are you revealing your secret to me now?"

I didn't really have a reason to tell him, it was more of an urge. "No one knows at school. I'm hiding it."

"I see," he says, thinking. "I suppose we both know something about hiding who we are to protect our image."

I scoff. "I don't care about my image. I just want to be normal."

"Normal isn't an image?" Ted asks, laughing one of his famous laughs, followed by a cough. "Pony, you see how hiding who I was turned out for me? I kept lying and lying until I didn't know who I was anymore."

Victor enters with a tray of medicine. I take my cue and get up to leave.

"Pony," Ted says, then finds my eyes. "You are stronger than you think."

"Thanks," I say, not believing him.

6:39 P.M.

I get into my car and take a deep-ish breath. Sunday night and I have nowhere to go. I could go home, obviously, but my thoughts have been so dark. I could hit up some Hillcrest friends, but I can't tell them about my *Love Actually* fail. I start my car and feel completely and utterly alone. How about that car exhaust thing? People take their lives like that in movies all the time. I'd need to google it. Seems peaceful.

My thoughts are disrupted by my sister FaceTiming me. I don't have the energy to pick up, but I do. I see her face, but it's dark. And loud.

"Rocky?"

"Hello, Pony," she says, holding her hand to her mouth like it's a reporter's microphone. "Reporting live from Metropolitan Bar in Brooklyn. It's happy hour, and I'm surrounded by queers."

I laugh (maybe for the first time today?) and ask, "What are you doing?"

"I wanted to introduce you to a few of my new friends." She swings the phone around, revealing a table of awesome-looking people, all waving at me.

"Pony, this is Tuck," she says, handing the phone to a hipster guy with a light beard wearing a Yankees cap.

"Hi, Pony, cool name. I'm a trans guy, just like you. Rocky told us about that girl. What you did was brave as hell. Good for you, my man."

Someone grabs the phone. She's beautiful, like a young Indian punk rock singer. "Pony, you're adorable! I'm Sai. Tuck is my partner." She kisses him on cheek. "Get yourself to New York. There are great girls here that would love to hang out with a guy like you."

The phone is passed to an older man with thin gray hair and a gray beard wearing a Hawaiian shirt, like gay Santa on vacation. "Hello, Pony. I came from a small town, just like you. It was a battle every day. You keep your chin up. Be brave, my boy."

"I will," I say.

The phone is passed to a guy with huge piercings in his ears and a neck tattoo. "Hey, kid, you be you. If they don't like it, *fuck them!*" He laughs loudly and chugs his beer.

"Yeah, fuck them," I echo. Tears build in my eyes. I wipe them away.

A beautiful trans woman comes on the screen. She's glowing like an angel. "Honey. I wish I could hug you. Life for you and me, it ain't easy. Lucky for us, we're built tougher than others, so we can handle all the *bullshit.* You hang on, fam. And promise me something?"

"Anything," I say.

"Get the hell out of Bumfuck, Texas!"

I promise her I will, and the phone goes to a 1950s pinup girl.

She's got oil-black hair and bright red lipstick. "Hi, Pony. I'm Zoe."

"Hi, Zoe," I say, my voice cracking.

"Your sister is something else." I can see Rocky sitting very close to her.

"She's one of a kind," I confirm. I really hit the sister jackpot.

Zoe lowers her voice. "Is Rocky single?"

"For you, I'm sure," I say.

"Fantastic. Thanks, sugar." She winks, blows a kiss, and hands the phone to Rocky.

"Pony, you are not alone. All these people love and support you without even meeting you. This hard time will pass. You just be strong."

"I will," I say, fighting the tears back. "I love you, Rocky."

"Love you, bye, Pony," she says, then hangs up.

I shut my eyes and say *thank you thank you thank you* to the universe for giving me a sister like Rocky.

IPHONES, 9:18 P.M.

PONY: Hi Gretchen, it's Pony. We met at the fundraiser for the Center.

PONY: You read my tarot cards . . .

GRETCHEN: Three of Swords?

PONY: Right in my heart

GRETCHEN: Ouch.

PONY: I survived

GRETCHEN: Good to hear

PONY: Do you have plans tomorrow night?

GRETCHEN: Not yet

PONY: Want to get dinner?

GRETCHEN: Yes, Pony. And I'll leave my swords at home.

PART THREE

HOMECOMING

EIGHTEEN

Monday, October 21

GEORGIA, 3:59 P.M.

I'm sitting in an empty classroom with the lights off. I got an email from Ms. Randolph around lunch. She wanted to talk to me after school. So here I am. I lay my head down on the desk.

When I close my eyes, I see Pony standing with those poster boards. The hope in his eyes. The smile on his face. A shiver runs up my spine.

Pony wasn't at school today. I was forced to look at his empty chair in every class. I'm worried about him but can't reach out. I tried to check his socials for any clues, but he blocked me again. Maybe forever this time.

I pick my head up and check the clock: 4:03. I'm going to be late to cheerleading practice (and get another demerit). What could Ms. Randolph want to talk about? Hopefully my next article. Spoiler alert: I don't have any ideas. I put my head back down.

Homecoming week is a big deal for Hillcrest. One could argue that it's more important than prom. It's an entire week of school pride. We wear silly clothing to school like pajamas (today) and country-western clothes (tomorrow), have a pep rally on Thursday, then the football game on Friday and the dance on Saturday. And if that isn't enough, we have our first cheerleading competition on Sunday. It's only Monday, but I'm already fully over this week.

Luckily, cheerleading competition season has just kicked off. We are only at semi-regionals, four rounds away from nationals. The competition at this level isn't tough. Even if every hungover cheerleader hurled during our performance, we'd still advance to the next round. The most difficult part of Sunday will be waking up for the bus that leaves at nine a.m.

I lift my head when I hear Ms. Randolph walk into the classroom. She doesn't notice me. "You're late," I say, watching her jump.

"Georgia! I didn't see you there."

"I guess I'm Anonymous in life too," I kid. Ms. Randolph laughs, and her glasses slide down her nose. She pushes them back up and leans against a desk. All teachers do the same desk-lean thing. Do they give a course on it at teacher college?

"Georgia, your article about pranking was great. It raised good questions and exposed some outdated traditions that should be addressed. I'm proud of you for digging deeper, just like I asked."

Her words are a ray of sunshine hitting my dark heart.

"Thanks," I say like a flower opening to the warmth. "I have some ideas for the next Anonymous banger," I lie.

Ms. R raises her hand to stop me. "I have good news and bad news. The good news is your article has caused a stir. Got people talking. Principal Scott is going to review the prank traditions. Bad news: some parents complained about an op-ed article with no name attached. They demanded to know who wrote it."

"Did you tell them?" I blurt out.

"No," she says. "But Principal Scott won't allow me to publish any articles without a byline."

"Oh," I say. I can't have my name in the paper, so this is a moot point.

"But Georgia, don't let this stop you from writing. I can talk to Coach Harkins and get approval for you to freelance?"

"No, please don't," I say. She would find out I lied about the cheerleading bylaws. Besides, it's not Coach Harkins I want to hide this from. It's Mia. It's Lauren. It's the school. I stand up to leave. I'm so annoyed and angry. "I really need to get to practice."

Ms. Randolph puts a hand on my shoulder. "Georgia, I hope you will still write. There's no reason to hide. And you just learned a valuable lesson."

"What's that?" I ask. "Never try to do what you love?"

"That your words have power."

I drag my feet down the empty halls of Hillcrest. Everyone has split or is at after-school practice. No Pony, no paper. What do I have left? Cheerleading, my friends, Jake. I have everything

I wanted but nothing I want. What else have I lost because I've been worried about what people think of me?

I push open the doors to the dressing room, expecting it to be empty. The girls should be in the gym doing stretches, but the place is packed. Girls huddle around someone on a bench. Has there been an injury?

I make my way through (gently) and find Lauren curled up on the bench, having a meltdown. Waterworks on high. Mia leans over and whispers in my ear, "She thinks Matt is cheating on her."

"He's a lying piece of crap," Lauren says.

We all stay quiet. No agreement or disagreement in accordance with the one rule of counseling relationship troubles: Don't talk crap about your friend's boyfriend until completely certain the relationship is done. *Done done.* Otherwise, when they get back together, your friend will never forget what you said and will hate you for saying it.

"Lauren, you do what's right for you," Mia says, obeying the rule. "Chad and I never fight, but I have read that it's healthy." She's so full of it. I witnessed a blowout between them in the school parking lot just last week.

Lauren buries her head in her arms and weeps.

"Lo," I say, putting my hand on top of her head. "The way he's been acting, you deserve better."

Lauren shows her agreement by crying harder. Mia signals to Kelly, who cares even less than me, to say something. She looks up from her phone. "Lauren, you deserve better."

"Georgia just said that," Mia says under her breath. Kelly shrugs and walks off. We all know Lauren and Matt will get back together. No couples break up this close to homecoming.

"I can't go to homecoming alone," Lauren wails.

The homecoming dance creates an insane amount of drama. Trending panics are dresses, dates, after-parties, alcohol procurement, and getting laid. It's about the pageantry, the dancing, and the homecoming court. Jake and I have a decent chance at homecoming king and queen. Although it's an open-ballot vote by the students, I'm betting that my competition is Mia and Lauren. Which is conflicting.

Lauren grabs her phone. "Girls, let's look up the hoes that liked his posts on Insta."

This is too much. I scoot out and head to the bathroom stalls. Kelly is there, washing her hands. "How much longer will Lauren drag this out?" I wonder out loud.

"Years? Decades? The rest of our lives?" She dries her hands off. "I think we might need to take her out back and put her down. Old Yeller style."

I laugh. "I miss you, Kelly. Why haven't we been hanging out?"

"Because you have a boyfriend," she says with a sly smile.

I look around. No one is listening. "Jake is not my boyfriend."

"Well, good thing I'm not talking about Jake," she says in a bad British accent.

I tilt my head, confused. She gives me that you-know-what-I'm-talking-about look.

"Pony," she whispers.

I feel dizzy all of a sudden. How the hell did she know?

"Don't worry, dude. Lauren and Mia don't know, just me."

"There's nothing to know!" I spit out finally.

"Georgia, chill," she says, laughing at my freak-out. "You kept it secret for a reason. I won't tell anyone."

"There's nothing to tell." I look down, sad again. "We aren't even friends anymore."

"Want to talk about it?"

"No," I lie. The problem is that I was more into Pony than I care to admit. He was the person who I didn't even think about because I was always just passively thinking about him.

"I miss you, Georgia," Kelly says in a rare moment of sweetness from her.

"Same," I say, putting my arm around her shoulder. "We have grown apart. I hate that. Let's do something about it."

"*Abso-fucking-lutely*," she says in an Australian accent. It must be accent day in Kelly's weird head.

"Are you in love with Jerry?" I ask.

She laughs. "Not quite."

I look at Kelly. "You're different."

"Gee, thanks," she says.

"No. Not in a bad way. I can't put my finger on it."

"Please don't put your finger anywhere near it," she says.

"There's my Kelly," I say.

She waits for me, and we head back to Lauren cry time. She's being so extra today, and I'm over it. "Lauren, listen to me. Matt is a douchebag," I say, watching the girls recoil in shock. I'm breaking the code. Why stop now? I continue, "He's probably an alcoholic. He's not great at soccer, he's a terrible dresser, and last week in class he thought avocados were called guacamoles."

I look at Kelly and Mia frantically, my eyes saying *HELP ME*, but they take the fifth and stay silent. "Lauren, you're the full package. There's going to be more Matts. But only one you. Move on."

Lauren's face is frozen. We're waiting for her reaction. And then she starts crying again. Mia rolls her eyes at me. "What?" I ask. "Don't you agree that we need to be honest with each other?"

"Georgia," Mia says with major tone, "we never know what's *true* with you. We just gave up on believing anything that comes out of that mouth."

I am off-balance. That was harsh. *Gave up?* Oh, hell no. I am on a roll. Why stop now?

"Mia, you need to chill. You can't control our lives. Especially Lauren's."

Kelly leans over. "Not cool, dude. Apologize. Claim temporary insanity."

I ignore her. I feel alive. All my anger and helplessness has a place to go. "Want to know what else? I wrote that article about the pranks."

Every eye is on me. And then Mia starts laughing. And then Lauren. And the rest of the girls. They think I'm lying. I shut my eyes and curse my ways. "Let's get out to the mats," Mia says.

On her way out, Mia whispers in my ear, "You are on very thin ice."

IPHONES, 9:03 P.M.

> **PONY:** Dude. Talk to me. Please.
>
> **MAX:** No
>
> **PONY:** Come on . . .
>
> **MAX:** No
>
> **PONY:** I'm sorry, Maxy
>
> **MAX:** Apologies don't matter.
>
> **MAX:** Action matters
>
> **MAX:** And visibility
>
> **PONY:** This is how I want to live my life
>
> **PONY:** We should support each other's choices
>
> **MAX:** Why do I have to deal with the discrimination? Judgmental looks? Dumb opinions said right to my face? While you get to slide through life with no problems?
>
> **MAX:** WHY IS IT ON ME TO BE OUT HERE AND NOT YOU?
>
> **PONY:** You are not alone, dude. I'm here.
>
> **MAX:** Then meet me Saturday night at Ft Worth City Hall
>
> **MAX:** We're protesting the place down.
>
> **PONY:** That's Homecoming
>
> **MAX:** And when have you ever cared about school dances?
>
> **PONY:** SUPPORT MY CHOICES!

MAX: Just emailed you link to petition, post it and we can be friends again

PONY: Dude

MAX: Dude

PONY: You know I can't

MAX: WFT WHY? Caring about another human won't out you to your new friends. Just post it.

PONY: No.

MAX: Then I can't be friends with you

PONY: Come on

MAX: Support my choices.

NINETEEN

Thursday, October 24

PONY, 4:52 P.M.

"Sir, which side do you dress?"

Jerry and Kenji snicker behind me. A cold sweat covers my forehead. I should have seen this coming. I should have come alone.

The tailor looks up at me as he cuffs my dress pants. "Right or left, sir?"

He makes a small chalk mark on the pants and clears his throat, waiting for an answer on which side I put my dick. If I had one, I'd put it everywhere.

"Right," I mumble. I'm guessing, I don't know.

"No one dresses right, weirdo." Jerry says, confirming my worst fear. There were only two choices; of course I pick the wrong one.

We managed to procrastinate on getting suits for homecoming.

We skipped the pep rally and headed to Dallas. Just some dudes, shopping. We started at Men's Wearhouse but found affordable tuxedos at Al's Formal Wear.

This tailor—suggested by Tex at Al's Formal Wear—looks like he was around when clothing was invented. He's wrapped in measuring tape and wearing thick glasses, pulling at my pant leg, probably wondering why my pants don't fit right. And why my hips are a little curvy. And where my dick is. Or maybe he's too old to care.

"OK, you are done. Move out of the way. Next," he demands. I'm excused and relieved.

Jerry jumps up in front of the mirrors and grabs his junk. "Buy me dinner before putting your hand on my family jewels."

Before my transition, I went to one dance in a red dress my freshman year. I was in love with Amanda, and Amanda was in love with Trevor. She said yes to his invitation to the dance on one condition: they double date with me. So, Trevor found a date for me because he wanted to go with Amanda, and I said yes because I also wanted to go with Amanda.

She demanded that we do all the girly things to get ready for the dance, like pick out dresses (pure torture) and get our nails done (more torture). Everything felt wrong about that day, but I would have done literally anything to spend time with Amanda. She was my first real crush. My feelings for her were loud and complicated. She made me want to write poetry. *Poetry.*

But today, buying suits and getting them fitted with my dudes feels so unbelievably right. I'm nearly giddy from the simple moments that a cis guy would never think twice about.

After Jerry is measured, Kenji jumps up, and the tailor runs off to get a longer measuring tape. (They both hang left.)

The tailor hobbles over and jots notes in an old book. "If you can wait one hour, I can do these now!"

With time to kill, we head over to the Hooters in the Oak Lawn strip mall. The place is empty and smells like old carpet, old beer, and sadness.

Our waitress, Candy, passes out the menus and tries not to look directly at us.

"The table will start with a pitcher of your finest ale," Jerry says, trying to sound as twenty-one as possible.

"ID, please?" the waitress asks with severe indifference.

"Scratch that. We have church later," Jerry says. "We'll have chicken wings, fried pickles, nachos, and hamburger sliders. Thanks, Candygirl."

Kenji and I hold back our laughs as we hand back our menus. Jerry is famous for ordering for the table. "It's Candy," the waitress says, and then walks off.

"Yelp will be hearing about the service at the Hooters in Oak Lawn strip mall," I say.

Kenji has been buried in his phone most of the afternoon. "Kenji, who you sexting?" I finally ask. He looks up and notices that we're both staring at him.

"I signed up for Tinder."

I laugh out loud. "Yeah, right. You're too young."

"And innocent," Jerry adds.

"I lied about my age. I've been talking to some girls."

Jerry pats him on the back hard. "Hell yes, bro! Let's see those sweet honeys!"

Kenji rolls his eyes. We huddle around his phone, swiping through the girls. Jerry is not giving too much thought to each girl. "Too old. Too sad. Too nerdy. Oh yeah, look at this one, Pony." He shoves the phone in my face. She's a beautiful blonde in front of the ocean in a tiny bathing suit. "Hubba, hubba."

It's so unrealistic to think we'd have a chance with her, but I confirm back, "Hubba, hubba."

Jerry pushes the phone in Kenji's face. "Look at this one. She's a tranny for sure. I can see the Adam's apple!"

In one split second, everything around me disappears. There's no music, no sports games blaring from the TVs, no Hooters. All I hear is Jerry's word over and over: *Tranny tranny tranny.*

Kenji flips through the pictures. "Yup. See the bulge in her pants? Definite shemale."

I should speak up. I should punch them. They can't talk like that. But I can't say something without revealing my secret. I focus on keeping any emotion off my face, but all I hear is *tranny, tranny, tranny, tranny.*

I stand up. "I need to piss."

Kenji gets up as well. "Me too, let's go."

"Scratch that, I'm going outside," I say. I can't deal with the bathroom thing right now. Once outside Hooters, I sit down on the steps and put on my sunglasses. I try to take a deep breath but can't. The harder I try, the less air goes in. My binder feels like it's closing in on me. I need to hold it together.

Some days, I barely think about being trans. And other days, it's an obstacle course. I should have said something. You don't have to be trans to correct someone. I could have just been an ally. But I didn't. 'Cause I'm a chickenshit.

Max is right.

What I'm doing is wrong.

But I'm in too deep.

I pop in my EarPods and put on my favorite playlist, entitled *Georgia On My Mind.* I made it on the first week of school. I thought maybe I could play it for her someday. Instead, I haven't stopped listening to it. This playlist is the last little secret thread connecting me to her.

Seeing Georgia in class has been so awkward, so sad. We politely pretend we never met and know nothing about each other. Truth is, I miss her like crazy. I've tried to move on, but I seem to be stuck. I played sick on Monday to avoid it altogether. I stayed in bed all day and watched movies. I was supposed to work, but Ted went to the hospital.

After one song, I get to my feet and dust myself off. I head back in and hop on my stool. There's a feast of fried and greasy food on the table, untouched. That's nice of them to wait. And highly unusual. Normally, they are complete food monsters, and

I'd be left with scraps.

"Sorry about that," I say, and grab a nacho.

"You don't have to apologize," Kenji says.

"What's your deal?" Jerry asks, then takes a bite of chicken wing.

"It's stupid," I say. "I'm bummed that I don't have a date to homecoming."

They look at each other, relieved. Kenji has decided to take Tina to the dance. He had three viable candidates, but Tina is the captain of the salsa dance team and one of the most beautiful girls at the school. He made a good choice. Jerry is taking Kelly, of course.

"Didn't you have a date on Monday?" Jerry asks with a mouthful of hamburger slider.

I had dinner with Gretchen the tarot reader. It was nice, but she was too into crystals, and I was too into Georgia, so that didn't work.

"Not a match," I admit.

After we have devoured every morsel of food in the red plastic baskets, Kenji stands up, farts, and says, "I'm going outside to call Tina."

"Tell her thanks for last night," Jerry shouts, always the wiseass. Once Kenji is gone, he gives me a curious look.

"What, dude?" I ask him.

"I might have a solution to your little homecoming date problem."

"I'm listening," I say.

"What if I could get you a date with one of the hottest girls in school?" Jerry has taken on the air of the Godfather, making me an offer that I can't refuse.

"Tell me more," I demand.

"I'll do you one better," Jerry says, swiping through his phone. "I'll show you." He smiles and turns the phone around, revealing a pretty girl, indeed.

"Taylor?"

"Taylor, man. Her and Kelly are good friends, and they want to do a double-date thing."

Just like me and Amanda at freshman dance.

Could Kelly and Taylor be a couple? Poor Jerry. On the bright side, I have a hot date, even if she doesn't like me. And Taylor is Georgia's mortal enemy. Revenge runs through my veins, making me feel high.

"Set it up," I say.

11:01 P.M.

FROM: PonyJacobs@gmail.com

TO: GeorgiaRobertsTX@gmail.com

DATE: Thursday, October 24 at 11:03 p.m.

SUBJECT: [TRASH][DRAFT][UNSENT] Homecoming Dance

Hi Georgia!

How's life? Hope it's great. I just wanted to give you a heads up,

I'll be attending homecoming dance with Taylor. Unless you say no?

FROM: PonyJacobs@gmail.com
TO: GeorgiaRobertsTX@gmail.com
DATE: Thursday, October 24 at 11:06 p.m.
SUBJECT: [TRASH][DRAFT][UNSENT] Deal with it

I'm taking Taylor to homecoming. Didn't want you to be blindsided.

FROM: PonyJacobs@gmail.com
TO: GeorgiaRobertsTX@gmail.com
DATE: Thursday, October 24 at 11:10 p.m.
SUBJECT: [TRASH][DRAFT][UNSENT] What's up

Georgia, hi.
Look I know this isn't ideal but I'm going to the homecoming dance with Taylor. Please know this is to make you crazy jealous.

TWENTY

Saturday, October 26

GEORGIA, 6:56 P.M.

This dress is everything.

I bust out a couple dance moves in front of my mirror to confirm my theory. And confirmed: this dress is pure fire. I named her Stella. We met at a high-end vintage shop, and it was love at first sight. She's dark red, like expensive wine, tight and silky. You better believe my girl Stella has a wild side.

I check my face in my bedroom mirror. I've got some time to kill before Jake picks me up. I'm not looking forward to the obligatory before-dance photo session with my dad struggling to take a picture while explaining why "cellular phones" confuse him.

But I think it will cheer my dad up. He's been down and out since quitting online dating last week. I was up late reading one night when he came stomping into my room, demanding that I remove his "dating advertisement." I put up a fight but eventually deleted his profile.

I finish off a tall can of sugar-free Red Bull and burp. I'm already dreading having to be at the bus tomorrow at nine in the morning for the cheer competition. Things are still awkward between me and my girls. We haven't been talking much. Did they start a new text thread and not include me? Do they go to Sonic without me? I'm hoping things will blow over soon. I wish we were prepartying right now.

To put it bluntly, things suck. I want to take to my bed and never come out, but I know that's not healthy. Still, so damn tempting. Instead of depression city: population me, I'm going to have fun. Even if it's forced fun. This is my senior year—the last homecoming dance—and I have my eyes on that homecoming crown.

"Honey?"

I turn around, startled to death.

"Mom?"

My body tightens up, and anger rises inside me. I'm sorry, but you can't parent by absentee ballot and show up on the big days. No way. She covers her mouth, and I can see a tear run down her face. "Sweetie, you look absolutely stunning."

And just like that—without my consent—the need for my mom extinguishes the anger flame burning in my belly. I start picking up clothes like she's going to lecture me. Instead, she gives me a big mama-bear hug.

"You look good too, Mom," I say. I'm not blowing smoke up her butt; she really does look good. Stylish outfit, healthy hair, and her skin literally glows. I think about Dad and feel a thumbtack of guilt poke into my heart.

"Thanks, darling," she says, pushing a piece of hair behind my ear. "How have you been?"

Well, I fell for a guy, found out he's trans, and broke his heart (twice) because he's different. Quit my writing job. And lost all my best friends.

"Groovy," I say. "My grades are so high they're trying to invent a letter better than A to give me and plan on naming a wing of the school after me. In my free time, I've been teaching orphan kittens how to read!"

Mom laughs her small laugh. "You know, I used to do that."

"Teach orphan cats to read?" I ask.

"No, tell stories. Funny little stories."

"I didn't know that," I say. "Why did you stop?"

She shifts on her feet, probably deciding how honest to be with me. "I don't know, dear. People never knew when I was telling the truth, so no one took me seriously."

Highly relatable. "Well, good thing that never happens to me."

"You sure?" she asks.

"How's being rich?" I ask, then watch her mouth fall open. She didn't see that coming.

"Honey, I didn't mean to upset you. I should have called. I just wanted to see you on the big night."

"Makes sense that you would come here, Mom. There's no way

to watch me secretly from the bleachers at the dance."

She looks at me. Shocked again. "You knew I was there?"

"Duh, Mom," I say. "I spotted you last night, too. Why didn't you wait for me after the game, or, I don't know, text?"

She hesitates. "Because."

"Because why, *Mom*?"

"Because, *Georgia*, I didn't know if you wanted me there. But I wasn't going to let that stop me from seeing my baby shine."

I sit down on the bed and lower my head. "I wanted you there," I admit. "I miss you."

She stands over me and rubs my neck like she did when I was little and had a fever. "I know, baby. I think about you all the time. Worry about you. You were so mad at me. I wanted to give you the space you needed."

I shut my eyes to block any tears from falling.

"I have something for you, Georgie," she says, taking my hand, leading me over to the mirror. I watch her in the reflection as she carefully drapes a necklace over my head. "Close your eyes," she says softly while fidgeting with the clasp.

I shut my eyes and have immediate déjà vu to playing the game with Pony in Dallas. I wonder who his date will be tonight, if he even shows up.

"OK, Georgie, open 'em up!"

I step closer to the mirror to get a better look. There's an expensive gold necklace with an expensive diamond charm around my neck. "Do you like it?" she asks nervously.

"This looks . . . expensive."

"It wasn't cheap," she confirms.

I turn around, so we're face-to-face. "Mom, you can't buy my love."

"I'm not trying to *buy* your love. I'm trying to *show* you love. I wanted to get you something nice for homecoming. Please don't be so dramatic."

Dramatic? How dare she?

"But that's exactly what you did, Mom. You picked money over your family."

She steps back a little. "Is that what you think?"

"Yes," I say, feeling very small.

"Honey, me and your dad, we hadn't been in love for years. We tried. We tried so hard, mostly for you, but we are different people in different places. I was unhappy, Georgie."

"Thanks."

"No, no, no. Never with you. You are my greatest achievement."

"No pressure," I say.

She ignores me and continues, "I didn't choose money. I chose happiness. We only get one chance at life. I couldn't spend another day stuck because I was worried about what people thought of me."

"But didn't you lose all your friends?" I ask.

"You bet I did. You think leaving your husband for a rich man makes you the toast of the town? I knew that everyone would have opinions about my life. But you know what, sweetie? It's my life. And I chose to be happy despite what people think."

For once, I have nothing to say. I just hug my mom. Like, really hug her. We have a long road back, but this feels like a step forward.

"Now," she says, letting go of me, "how is Jake?"

"How did you know about Jake? Oh my god, are you full-on stalking me?"

"Just enough."

"He's OK. Rich like your boyfriend," I say, trying to impress her.

"And? Who cares? Does he make you happy?"

PONY, 7:13 P.M.

I attempt a few moves in front of the mirror. My dancing looks terrible, but the suit looks great. For being a thousand years old, the tailor nailed it. He even left some room in my pants to dress right. I ordered a new binder for the dance. I wanted it to be *tight* tight. I haven't taken a deep breath in an hour, so it must be working.

I straighten my bow tie. Jerry's bathroom is the size of my bedroom. I knew Jerry's dad worked in tech, and that means they're loaded, but I didn't know they were *this* loaded. We should hang here more often.

I'm psyched for homecoming. Wearing this suit, hanging out with my dudes, with a hot date? That's the trifecta of manhood. I have arrived at the paramount of high school masculinity. The fact that my date has no interest in me doesn't even get me down. Nothing will get me down tonight.

I head back to the living room and find the beer I've been nursing. Kenji is snuggled up on the couch with his date, Fiona. She was his backup date after Tina didn't make the final cut. Jerry is smashing his fingers against the Xbox controller and yelling at the flat screen. About an hour ago, he ate a pot cookie that we all decided was too much.

We're waiting on the arrival of Kelly and Taylor. They're coming together, which is suspicious. I'm thinking I'll have a better read on what's going on with them after tonight.

My phone starts vibrating in my blazer jacket. I pull it out and answer.

"Pony? It is me, Victor. I have some sad news to share with you."

"OK," I say and steady myself.

"Ted London passed this afternoon."

And just like that, all the air is sucked out of the room. I feel nothing. Stillness. I can hear my breath and Victor crying softly. I look at things around the room: vase with flowers, can of Bud Lite, wooden knob on a cabinet.

Ted was in the hospital for pneumonia, but it didn't seem serious. My heart starts pumping, and my eyes go blurry. I guess it was more serious than they thought. I can hear Victor blow his nose. My legs are too heavy to stand.

"I am so sorry, Victor."

"Oh, Pony, we knew this day would come. The world has lost a great man. He was a great, great man."

"He was," I confirm, and he starts wailing. My heart breaks for Victor. He loved Ted London. My lip quivers; tears are coming. I shut my eyes and try to will them away. Not while my friends are watching.

"Will there be a funeral?" I ask.

"I am afraid not. I will be sending the ashes to his old manager in California to be spread around the Hollywood sign."

"That's what he wanted?"

"Yes," Victor says, steadying himself. "The request was explicitly stated in the will."

I'm not sure what to say. "I'm sorry. I really am."

Victor takes a deep breath. "Me too. I devoted my life to helping that man. I don't know what's next for me."

"You'll figure it out. I know it," I say.

"Thank you, sweet boy. Your job is complete. You did good."

That's the first time that Victor has ever complimented me.

"And Pony, thank you for reconnecting him with Lee. I know it gave Ted peace."

Peace, I think, and tears run down my cheeks. There is no way to stop it.

"Speaking of, I need to call Lee now." He pauses. "Goodbye, Pony, and best of luck to you."

"Bye," I say, but Victor has already hung up. I drop the phone like my fingers forgot how to work. Sadness covers me like a weighted blanket. I knew this would happen, but that doesn't stop the emptiness.

I remember one day, I was on the chair beside his bed, shooting the shit. He said, "Pony, when we first met, you asked if I had any regrets. I lied to you, son." He told me more about that night at the Academy Awards—what it felt like to get on the stage and receive the statue, how overwhelming the audience and cameras were. He remembered "like it was yesterday." It was the highest point in his career but the lowest point in his life. He regretted not using that stage to come clean about his sexuality. All he needed to say were "two words" into that microphone.

I assume those two words were "I'm gay," but Ted still—even on his literal deathbed—struggled to say those words out loud. He could have been free from his agent's blackmailing. Free to love Lee. But he never said those two words.

I snap out of it and look up. All eyes on me, asking for an explanation. "The guy I worked for, the movie star. He died today," I say, wiping away a tear.

Kenji gets to his feet and walks over. "Bro, I'm sorry. I lost my grandpa last year." He puts a hand on my shoulder.

"It's OK," I say, standing up. Kenji wraps his giant arms around me in a Bro Hug. It's a sweet moment. Kelly and Taylor walk into the room, confused.

"Who died?" Kelly asks, and we laugh at the glorious timing. Taylor is wearing a short black dress with her curly hair pulled back in some bun thing. I can't believe she's my date. Kelly looks awesome in her suit and tie.

Everyone looks at me, not sure what to do next. Honestly, I'm not sure what to do next either. What do you do when someone dies? Ted London wouldn't want me to sit at home, crying over him. He would want me to party even harder.

Their eyes ask: *Should we go? Are we allowed to have fun? Did I eat too much pot?*

I answer with a smile and say, "Let's do this."

GEORGIA, 8:11 P.M.

Jake helps me out of his truck. The air is crisp as hell. I guess the humidity took a night off. My date is easily the most dapper gent in all of Texas, with his fitted dark blue suit and black lapels. Jake would make a great politician someday.

Every Hillcrest homecoming is at the Hyatt Regency in downtown Dallas. Only the best for us! Jake and I enter the ballroom like we own the place. It's dimly lit (romantic), and awash with gold balloons (fancy), candles (dangerous), and a buffet table covered in appetizers from the Piggly Wiggly (gross). The DJ—approved by the school board—is on the stage, and no one is dancing.

We hit the dance floor and make our presence known. There's some sexy and silly dancing going down. By the time the song is finished, we're surrounded by people dancing. This is my homecoming. Jake and I dance it out for a couple songs and make our rounds, saying hellos and fawning over dresses. I spot Lauren and Mia, looking fantastic. I pretend to ignore them and have more fun.

During a slow song, Jake sneaks me into a corner of the ballroom and pulls out a flask. We are pressed up against each other, hiding from the adult chaperones. Laughing. I take a swig of warm, expensive whiskey. "You're nicer than you look," I say to Jake.

He scoffs at me, taking offense. "Georgie, I am so nice. And thoughtful. And charming. You had your mind made up about me from day one. I didn't stand a chance." He takes a drink and puts his hand on my hip. I reflexively shove it away.

"See?" he says.

"Jake . . ." I trail off, unsure of what I want from him.

"Here's the deal, gorgeous," he says, pulling the hotel key card from his pocket. "I have a room here—penthouse, actually. My parents don't want me to drive home. I'm not expecting anything, but if you wanted some time alone . . ." He takes the flask out of my hand and replaces it with the key card. "I think this could be a really special night."

"You only want me because you can't have me," I blurt out.

"Truth comes out at homecoming," he says, then takes a drink.

"Truth comes out with expensive whiskey," I say, taking another drink myself. My body warms up.

"I can't have you, Ms. Roberts, because you aren't haveable. You might be standing here, but you aren't here." He finds my eyes. "Still, I keep trying because I like you."

I grip the hotel key card in my hand, unsure what to say next. I look over Jake's shoulder and spot Pony walking in with a big smile, confident. He looks handsome. Kelly and Jerry enter right behind him. Then I see his date.

Taylor Malone. Are you kidding me? Pony is dating Taylor? *Fuck that times one million.*

My face is as red as my dress. I'm seeing blood. And carnage. I want to destroy things. Seriously, I asked Pony for one thing. One thing. *One damn thing.*

I need a pillow to scream in.

"I'm going to find the bathroom," I say to Jake, then scurry off.

PONY, 8:29 P.M.

The floor of the ballroom is littered with hundreds of balloons. There's dancing, cheesy music, awkward flirting. It looks like all the high-school-dance movie clichés have thrown up on the Hyatt ballroom. It's beautiful.

I'm wearing a tux with a pretty girl on my arm. Just another guy—no big deal—literally living my dream. There's a tug at my heart for Ted London, but it's overshadowed by excitement and nerves. We find an empty table to accommodate our triple date. Once seated, Taylor leans in and says, "You look handsome, Pony."

"Stop trying to get in my pants," I kid.

"Never on the first date, sir."

I lean in closer so only she can hear. "Who are you really here with?"

She smiles at me playfully. "You wouldn't understand."

"Try me," I say.

"The real question is, why would you agree to take me to the dance? I know Georgia hates me. What's your end game?"

"You wouldn't understand."

"Try me," she says.

GEORGIA, 8:29 P.M.

I find Mia and Lauren holding court at a packed table by the dance floor. I'm pushing pause on our fight. I need some girl time. Mia's dress is bright blue and edgy, like she stole it off a fashion-week model in New York (which I wouldn't put past her). Lauren looks like a celebrity in a dark green dress that perfectly matches her eyes. They both seem pleasantly buzzed.

"Did you see?" I ask.

"Let me guess," Lauren says with a slight slur. "Taylor is here with Pony."

"Dun dun dun," Mia says, and they cackle.

"Ugh, yes. It's killing my mood."

Mia grabs my shoulders and gives me a playful shake. "KEEP IT TOGETHER, ROBERTS."

"Yes, Captain, my captain," I say, glad to be back on Mia's good side, even though it's because she's tipsy. We spend the next ten minutes throwing shade on the bad dresses and embarrassing dancing until we laugh so hard our stomachs hurt. It's mean. And doesn't feel great. But I'm happy to be back with my girls.

I'm fuming at Pony. How dare he date Taylor? I have the urge to return the favor and reveal his secret—the one thing he asked me not to do. Mia and Lauren would explode at the juiciness of his secret. It's on the tip of my tongue.

Before I get it out, our dates swarm the table and grab our hands. We hit the dance floor and wild out. The music slows down. Jake turns to me and half bows. "May I have this dance?"

"Fine," I say, wrapping my arms around his neck. He puts his hands on my waist, and we find the beat together. Jake smells nice, like sporty, spicy cologne. Out of the corner of my eye, I catch Pony and Taylor dancing. I hate it. So much.

"Jake, important question—does the hotel room have rose petals on the bed?"

He smiles. "Of course not."

"Correct answer. I'd like to see it later," I say, laying my head against his chest and trying to forget Pony. When the song ends, the lights brighten up. It must be time to announce the homecoming court. My palms and pits immediately start sweating.

I grab Jake's hand and drag him across the dance floor. I want to stand next to Mia and Lauren for the announcement of homecoming king and queen. We all have a chance to win . . . and I'll be happy for whoever does win . . . but I really hope it's me. Why do I want that crown so bad? Maybe for the validation that the past four years weren't a complete waste of time.

Principal Scott takes the stage and grabs the microphone.

"Students of Hillcrest, what a beautiful homecoming! And how about that win last night!" The audience goes nuts. It wasn't even a close game—the football team won by thirty points. "Let's thank the planning committee and DJ Blaster!"

"More like DJ Douche Blaster!" Kelly says from behind me. I turn around and hug her hard. Now the gang is complete. Perfect timing.

Principal Scott continues, "And the time of the night we have all been waiting for . . ."

"Sex!" someone yells, and everyone laughs.

He clears his throat. "It's time to announce second runner-up, first runner-up, and the homecoming king and queen."

On cue, a line of six students walk onstage with fancy envelopes containing the names of the winners. The golden envelope must be homecoming king and queen. My heart is beating out of my dress.

"They're really going for an Oscars feel this year," Kelly says. "Surprised the accounting firm isn't here with a briefcase handcuffed to their wrists."

Two kids walk up to the microphone—nervous out of their minds—to announce second runners-up. "Erin Collins and Joseph Rabb," they say in unison. The wildcard couple. She's on the dance team and he's the baseball star. The next two kids step up to the mic to reveal first runners-up. Lauren and Matt. This is not a surprise. Good thing they made up before tonight! They hug and head up to the stage, pretending not to be pissed they didn't win. Mia and I make eye contact. It's got to be her or me.

Two football jocks approach the mic with the golden envelope. "OK," Tim says, yanking the microphone until it screeches. "The award for SECRET SCISSOR SISTERS goes to Kelly Daniels and Taylor Malone!"

Randy follows it up with "Come up and get your fish tacos, lesbos!"

The entire room goes deafening silent. Confusion settles in. I look back at Kelly and Jerry—they are motionless, with panic in their eyes.

Principal Scott jogs back from the buffet table yelling, "STOP! STOP! STOP!" but it's too late.

Tim grabs the mic back. "Come on up here, Taylor! Maybe you just need some of this," he says, then grabs his junk while Randy yells "PRANKED!" over and over.

How is that a prank? This is exactly what I didn't want to happen. Or, Anonymous didn't want to happen. The ballroom breaks out in complete chaos, everyone talking and yelling. I watch Tim and Randy flee out the back doors like the cowards they are. In the middle of the madness, someone jumps onstage and grabs the microphone.

PONY, 9:03 P.M.

The spotlight burns my eyes.

What the hell am I doing up here?

Is this what Ted London felt like when he accepted that Oscar?

The crowd goes silent. Principal Scott has stopped just offstage. He must want to hear what I am about to say. *If only I knew what I was going to say.*

I hold the microphone close to my mouth. "Hi, I'm Pony."

I clear my throat, and the mic releases a shriek of feedback. "As many of you know, this is my first year at Hillcrest. And, I like it. But I hid something because I wanted you to like me. I wanted to feel normal." I pause again. My binder feels two sizes too small. "But what is normal?"

I think of Ted London's regret. Of the two words he couldn't say. And how he can never say them again.

"I'm transgender," I say into the mic.

My body feels like it's on fire. I watch the faces in the crowd register my two words with shock. I need to keep going, but all my other words are bottlenecked in my throat. I can't move. I can't talk. I find Kelly in the crowd. I push my words out for her.

"I'm coming out to stand with Kelly and Taylor. And all the LGBT people here. Hiding something suggests that it's wrong. You might think people like me are different. You might even call us freaks."

"FREAK!" someone yells from the crowd.

I stop and take a breath. "But there's nothing wrong with me. Or Kelly. Or Taylor. And now that I think of it, there's no such thing as normal. We are all different. So, I'm not hiding anymore."

I back away from the spotlight in disbelief. I didn't know I had that in me.

My speech is met with blank faces. I start to walk offstage—feeling mortified—when one person starts clapping. I look up. It's Georgia. Then, more clapping. A whistle. Cheering. Nothing overpowering, but support. I head offstage and out the back door, not sure what happens next.

GEORGIA, 9:07 P.M.

This dance floor is in end-times chaos.

Everyone is running in every direction and loudly discussing what just went down. I'm still in the middle of the dance floor, completely shook. That's a new side of Pony. His bravery has blown me away. He protected Kelly and Taylor by sharing his truth.

Taylor walks past me, probably headed to Kelly, and stops. I guess we're doing this now. "You and Kelly?" I ask.

"Yes, Georgia," she says, very upset. "I tried to talk to you. And Kelly wanted to tell you, but—"

I cut her off. "But you hooked up with Anthony?"

"Hardly," she says. "Look, that was super shitty of me. I was going through a breakup with Patti. I take responsibility for what I did. I'm sorry, Georgia. I really, really am."

Patti from the dance team. That's scandalous.

"So you're into girls?" I ask.

She shrugs. "I don't get hung up on gender. I fall for people's hearts," she says, then smiles. "And I have fallen hard for Kelly's big, beautiful heart."

My brain is officially overloaded. "How many people are

LGBT at Hillcrest?" I ask.

She seems annoyed. "Enough to make what Pony did really special."

"But aren't you worried about what people think about you?" I ask.

She touches my shoulder like I do when people don't understand something. "I need to go find Kelly. Can we talk more later?"

"Yes, of course. I'm sorry," I say, then surprise myself by hugging her. And while we're hugging, I surprise myself again by forgiving her.

The music starts back up, and people begin eating and talking and laughing. No one really cares that Kelly and Taylor are dating or that Pony is transgender. I mean, there will be plenty of whispers and gossip, but those are just words. I think of my mom, following her heart. I think of Taylor, following her heart. I think of my heart, and how terribly unfollowed it must feel.

I hear Pony's voice in my head: *Close your eyes.*

Doesn't matter that I'm standing alone in the middle of an empty dance floor as the music pounds in my ears; I close my eyes. Block out all the noise. And for the first time, listen to my heart. It only says one thing, over and over.

I open my eyes, and I go find that thing.

PONY, 9:10 P.M.

I splash my face with ice-cold water. And again. And again.

I turn the water off and dry my face with a scratchy paper

towel. The reflection in the mirror looks like a new guy. It's like we're meeting for the very first time.

The men's bathroom is empty. I'm sure everyone is too busy talking about what just happened. The endorphins running through my veins make me feel like the human equivalent of a Fourth-of-July sparkler. I could run a marathon. I could dunk a basketball. I could be president. First transgender president? Could you even imagine?

I can't believe I did that. I already feel lighter. This high will wear off soon enough, and I will surely descend into a spiral of regret and depression. But for now, I'm on top of the world.

Max will be so proud of me. Finally, I have done right by my friend. I pull out my phone to text him. Maybe I can sneak out of here and meet him at the center.

As I unlock my phone, I hear the bathroom door open.

GEORGIA, 9:11 P.M.

"Jake, I'm glad I found you."

"It's good to be found," he says, getting up from the table. "Quite the night."

"Did you know about that little stunt?" I ask with fire in my eyes.

"No," he says. "Georgia, no. What Tim and Randy did was fucked. But what Pony did was pretty cool."

I feel relieved. *But just a little.*

"Jake, I need to be honest with you. There's someone else. And tonight, I need to be with him."

His eyes soften. "Georgia, I had a feeling. I was hoping you would come around, but I get it."

That is not how I saw this going. He even seems sad. "Why are you so nice?" I ask.

Jake smiles, revealing his million-dollar dimple. "Because," he says, "believe it or not, there are good guys out there. Now, go get yours."

PONY, 9:12 P.M.

"Well, look who it is," Mac says to Ryan.

"Just who we wanted to run into," Ryan says to Mac.

Terror moves through my body. I'm stuck in the bathroom with the two most ruthless football dudes. Georgia told me about them pushing Kelly down, stealing her mascot suit, and calling her a lesbian. I can smell alcohol on them and see hate in their eyes.

This is my fault.

I shouldn't have come in here. I haven't had to worry about my safety in the men's bathroom in months. I let my guard down, and I'm about to pay for it.

"I was just leaving," I say, grabbing my jacket off the plastic paper towel holder.

Ryan steps closer to me. "What are you doing in here?"

Mac steps closer to me. "You're in the wrong bathroom."

Drunk guys, empty bathroom, threatening words. Welcome to my nightmare. I don't know what to do. I've never been in a fight.

I want to run, but men don't run.

I puff up my chest. "I'm exactly where I *should* be," I say.

Mac steps toward me, but I don't move. Men stand their ground. "You *should* be in the girls' bathroom, freak." He puts his hand over my face and pushes me backward. I go stumbling but stay on my feet. I drop my jacket. It's useless to me now.

This is not a fair match. Both guys have a hundred pounds on me. I need to get out of here, but they're blocking the door. I take off running and try to pass them like we're playing a fun game of Red Rover.

But nope.

I hear the thud before I feel it. One of them clotheslines me in the chest, sending me to the ground. I pull myself back up—men get back up—and throw a punch in the direction of Ryan but miss. Mac approaches me, puts his hand on my shoulder, and delivers a hard punch to my gut. I double over in pain and crumple to my knees. While fighting for a breath, I look up and see big smiles on their hateful faces.

"Fucking freak," Mac says, then grabs my arm, pulling me up on my feet. "I know you aren't supposed to hit a girl, but . . ."

A meaty fist connects with my cheekbone, tearing my skin open. I can feel my brain shake in my skull. I'm bent over, holding my face until a hand grabs my hair and pulls my head up. Another fist connects with my face, this time right in the eye. I stumble around, punch drunk. I lunge toward the door, but Ryan sticks out his foot and trips me. I fall to the ground, belly down on the wet bathroom floor.

I'm going to die tonight.

Mac flips me over and pulls my arms above my head. Ryan sits on top of my legs facing me. I'm pinned down but keep fighting against them. "Stop," I yell over and over.

"Shut up," Ryan says, and slaps my face.

Will anyone miss me?

"Let's see the freak's tits," Mac suggests. "I bet he has girl tits."

"Good idea," Ryan says, leaning forward and grabbing my shirt collar with both hands. He rips it open, buttons flying everywhere.

Will my dad be glad that I'm dead?

"What the hell is this?" Ryan asks, confused at my binder.

"Take it off," Mac screams while digging his nails into my wrist.

Rocky will miss me.

"Another good idea," Ryan says. He gets up from my legs— I'm not fighting anymore—and grabs the bottom of my binder. Yanking it hard up my body and around my head. I feel the cold and sticky bathroom tile against my back. My chest is exposed. They are looking at my boobs. They are laughing and talking, but I can't hear them.

I'm not a man.

My eyes get heavy. I don't want to be here anymore. Next time, I hope I'm born in the right body. A foot digs into my rib cage. And another. And another. But none of it matters anymore. My body goes limp, and my eyes shut.

The last thing I think is: *Georgia.*

TWENTY-ONE

Sunday, October 27

GEORGIA, 12:01 A.M.

The hospital waiting room is empty, quiet, sad. My nostrils burn from the pungent bleach-based cleaning products. My eyes burn from crying so much. The TV bolted to the wall blares a news channel with the same report on loop every fifteen minutes. I almost have the words memorized.

And I can't stop shivering.

My blood ran cold when I heard what happened to Pony, and I haven't been able to warm up. I was looking for him the exact moment he was jumped. The news about the beating spread through the crowd like wildfire. Half the crowd went looking for the fight, and the other half split to the after-parties.

I ran to the hotel lobby and called my dad. I was mad, confused, frustrated, guilty, and scared. Having too many emotions at once is like mixing too many colors together—everything turns to a grayish nothing. That's me. I'm a grayish nothing.

While waiting in the hotel lobby for Dad to drive from Addison to Dallas, I watched Pony get loaded into the ambulance. Cops everywhere. That's something I can never unsee.

Dad showed up soon after with a change of clothes and hot coffee. Bless him. I spilled my guts on the way to the hospital. Rambling on about Pony being transgender, how I felt about him, and what happened at the dance. We sat in the Dallas Methodist Hospital parking lot, and I cried until I was out of tears. But every time I think of Pony getting beaten up, I seem to find more. Everyone is talking online like they know what went down in that bathroom. They say Pony will never walk again. They say he will never see again. That he's dead.

It became too much. I had to put my phone away.

I tried to get an update on Pony from the hospital staff, but I'm not family. Good thing I'm resourceful and gathered intel from overhearing chatter at the nurses' station. Pony has a couple broken ribs and possibly a concussion. They are monitoring for internal bleeding. He's shaken, one nurse said, and won't talk to anyone—not even to his parents.

"I know you."

I snap out of my thoughts and look up. There's a short guy wearing baggy jeans with a gold nose ring and a leather vest covered in rainbow buttons.

"Probably not," I say.

"Yes, I do. You're the cheerleader. Pony's cheerleader. I've seen plenty of pictures of you."

"That's creepy," I say.

"Max," he says, extending a hand. "I'm one of Pony's nearest and queerest friends. Pronouns are him, he, his."

I shake his hand. "Georgia. But you knew that."

"Any updates?" he asks.

"Not really. I heard broken ribs."

Max sits down beside me and lets out a sigh. "And a broken spirit."

I nod. That's probably why he isn't talking.

"Do you know who did this?" he asks.

A shiver goes up my spine. "I think so," I admit.

Everyone suspects Ryan and Mac. I wouldn't be surprised. Those guys are awful ogres, but I had no idea they were capable of something this heinous.

Max shakes his head, defeated. "This is so fucked. And all my fault. I feel so guilty," he says, wringing his hands. "I pushed him too hard. Told him to come out. And when he does, this happens?"

"You heard what he did tonight, right?" I ask.

"I heard he came out at the dance," Max says. "And about the bathroom."

"He did much more than come out. Two girls, my friends, were outed for being gay during the awards ceremony. Pony was trying to protect them. He didn't want them to be alone in that moment," I say, my eyes filling back up.

I give Max the blow-by-blow as he listens in awe. I show him a video of Pony's speech that some kid posted on Instagram. When the video ends, I look over and see tears falling down his face. "Max?" I ask, putting my hand on his back.

"I'm so proud of him." He wipes away the tears.

"It was something else," I admit.

"And got his ass beat for it," Max says darkly. "Those guys are going down."

"You going to rough them up?" I ask, imagining a queer social justice league out policing the streets.

"What? No, that's not my style," Max says. "I like to hit people with community action and reform."

I don't mean to laugh, but I do. "Really?" I ask.

"Violence doesn't solve anything, and never makes it better. I'm all about action and change."

"Damn," I say, letting the thought sink in that Mac and Ryan might go to jail.

Max looks over at me, tears in his eyes. "No one hurts my Pony," he says.

I heard sneezes are contagious, but I think crying is too. My nose starts to tickle, and tears blur my vision. Apparently, I have a Costco amount of tears in me. Max hugs me, and we cry together, total strangers. After a couple minutes, we separate and take a deep breath. Things feel a little better with Max here.

He flashes a big smile. "You know how Pony feels about you, right?"

My heart warms. "I know. And I feel the same way."

"Sure," he says, then leans back in his chair, crossing his arms.

"What?" I ask. This night has left me with zero fucks to give.

"Don't you have an image to uphold?" he asks.

I also cross my arms and lean back in my chair. I feel very tired all of a sudden. "Max, you don't have to be mean."

"Not sorry, sis."

I'm about to state my case with Max but get interrupted when Pony's parents come around the corner with a doctor. Looks like they're heading home for the night. The group pauses by the exit—near us—to talk. We eavesdrop as they discuss Pony.

"But his ribs, they should heal, no problem?" his mom asks the doctor in a quiet voice.

"Yes, but I will advise Pony that he should discontinue wearing chest-compression clothing."

"Oh shit," Max whispers.

"What?" I ask.

"The doctor just said Pony can't wear binders. That will destroy him."

With no words exchanged, Max and I jump up and book it over to them. I rudely interrupt their conversation. "Hi! We're Pony's friends. Can we see him tonight?"

Pony's parents exchange looks with each other and then the doctor. They're having a nonverbal adult conversation. The doctor turns toward us. "Kids, Pony is resting. He will be fine, but it's past visiting hours. You can come back tomorrow morning." Then he flashes his everything-will-be-OK smile. Am I supposed to feel comforted by that crap?

"Please," I beg. "Please, please, please." I say please until there are tears running down my face. I say please until it's no longer a word, only a sound. I say it over and over like I don't care who's watching because for the first time in my life, I don't care.

The doctor throws up his arms. "OK. Fine. I can bring one of you back to say good night." He shoots Pony's parents his everything-will-be-OK smile and says, "It might make Pony feel better."

I look at Max with wild eyes. I need to see Pony. I don't want to fight, but I will. Max smiles at me. "Get back there, Georgia. And send my love."

I give him a hug and follow the doctor back, unsure I'm ready for all this. We walk silently down the long hallway. "This is his room," the doc says. "Remember, he's on pain medication, so he'll be out of it. And he hasn't been speaking. I'll wait out here. Two minutes?"

"Sure," I say and hold up two fingers, revealing how badly my hands are shaking. I walk into the dark hospital room. My eyes adjust as I approach Pony's bed, the only light coming from the television above. As I move closer, I get a better look at his face. It's cut, bruised, and puffy. His body is hooked up to a beeping machine and wrapped in bandages. He's awake but has that thousand-mile stare going on.

"Hi," I say to get his attention. He looks over, and his eyes go wide. "I don't have much time, so I'm going to talk, and you're going to listen, *for once*."

I clock the smallest smile in the whole world on his face.

"Oh, Pony," I say as a couple tears spill out of my eyes. "What you did tonight was so brave . . ." I trail off to avoid busting into an ugly cry. I sit down and center myself. "I've missed you. I think about you. Like, all the time. I shouldn't have pushed you away, but I was a chicken. I'm not brave like you."

There's a knock at the door. I'm guessing that's my one-minute warning. I speed up.

"After you went onstage, I went looking for you. I want to be brave like you."

I pause.

"I wanted to be brave with you."

I hold his hand, wrapped in tape and connected to an IV tube. I wait to see if he says anything. But he doesn't. I continue, stubborn as always. "Pony, it took me longer to get here, but I'm here now."

And nothing.

"And I'm not going anywhere."

Say something.

"And if you can forgive me, I want to be with you."

Talk, dammit!

"I love you, Pony."

My body relaxes like I was holding my breath for days and finally exhaled. That is my truth, and I don't care who knows.

"Georgia," he says with a scratchy, low voice. "I can't go back to Hillcrest. I wish they had killed me. Maybe I should just finish the job."

"Pony," I say, ready to spew feel-good bullshit, but his eyes are the saddest thing I have ever seen. My heart crumbles right there.

The doctor opens the door. "Tell Pony good night."

"I'll be back tomorrow morning."

"No, you won't," he says, but I don't have time to convince him otherwise.

Once out of the room, the doctor points me to the exit and takes off in the opposite direction. I should have thanked him, but my mind is scattered. I drag my feet down the hospital hallway, hugging myself. I want a warm bath and a warm bed. I don't want to live in a world where something like this would happen.

I have so much anger, so much sadness. I have nowhere to put it. I stop walking. My head is pounding. I'm too dizzy to keep my eyes open. My stomach cramps up, unsettled and angry. The foul taste of bile rises up in my throat, and the hallway starts spinning. I'm overheating. A thin sheet of sweat covers my skin. My body is rejecting this moment, this pain, and the contents of my stomach.

I barely make it to the drinking fountain before throwing up. I haven't eaten in hours, so only sour yellow liquid comes up, burning my throat and nostrils. I retch several times into the fountain and then sit down on the ground.

This is the lowest I have ever been.

A nurse rushes up, and Max is right behind her. He slides down beside me, wraps his arms around me, and rocks me back and forth like I'm a little baby. The nurse leaves to get the janitor. "It's too much," I say between sobs.

"It happens to trans people every day, Georgia."

"Will the guys that did this get charged with a hate crime?"

Max shakes his head. "No, honey, not now. Gender identity isn't protected by Texas laws."

"It's not fair," I say.

"It certainly isn't," he says, handing me a handkerchief from his back pocket. "That's why we need to fight."

I wipe my face with the hankie. My mouth tastes terrible. I think I am finally out of tears.

Max gets up and extends his hand to help me up.

"Max, will you help me do something for Pony?"

"For my horse? Of course."

PONY, 7:52 A.M.

The sun is bright. It's morning. I'm alive.

But how long was I asleep? It's hard to tell. There's a sharp pain behind my eyes, like an ice pick stuck in my brain. I struggle to keep my eyes open. Nurses came in every hour last night to wake me up and drop pills in my mouth. And when I did fall asleep, my dreams all took place in that bathroom.

I try to take a deep breath, but my chest is full of broken glass. My head weighs too much. My body is weak. I am weak.

I feel broken.

Powerless.

Done.

"Pony?"

Mom and Dad are standing at the door. They look disheveled and tired. Mom comes over with a basket. "I baked your favorite muffins, banana chocolate chip!"

"Thanks," I say, but I'm not hungry. They served breakfast before the sun was up. I haven't touched whatever is fermenting on the plastic tray. It smells old.

"Glad you got your voice back," Mom says sweetly.

Dad is doing the same back-and-forth pacing thing that he did last night. He won't sit, or lean, or stay still. He also won't talk or look at me. I know he cares—it's all over his face—but he can't bring himself to look at his little *freak*.

My mom, on the other hand, is trying to smother me in love. She's good at it, and right now, I need it. "Did you sleep?" she asks while straightening my sheets.

"A little," I say.

"Well, they say we can bring you home this evening. Then you'll get to rest."

That's a relief. I do not want to spend another night in this hospital. "Did you bring my phone?" I ask.

"Oh shoot, sorry, it slipped my mind."

"Mom, I need my phone," I say, frustrated. I feel cut off from the world.

Dad steps forward. "Your mom was up all night worried about you. Don't you dare talk to her like that."

"Norman, it's all right," Mom says, then sits down in the chair by my bed. "Honey, I told you last night, but I'm going to say again—I love you. More than the moon and the stars. And your dad does, too."

She shoots a look, inviting him to chime in, but he doesn't.

"Dad is upset," she adds. "And scared for you."

He grunts. "Those little a-holes better be glad they're in jail."

"They're in jail?" I ask.

"Yes, sweetie," Mom says, smoothing my hair. "They did a bad thing."

I don't know why I'm surprised. Of course Mac and Ryan are in jail. And it's my fault. A wave of guilt washes over me, trying to pull me deeper into the darkness.

Dad walks over, finally looking at me. "So, are you going back?" he asks.

I'm not going back to Hillcrest. I can't face everyone after last night.

"No, I can just get my GED or something."

"No, that's not what I meant," he says, frustrated. "Back to being a girl."

Any part of me that wasn't broken is now. Mom is saying something to him, but I can't hear. I shut my eyes and try to disappear, secretly wishing those guys had finished me off.

But they didn't.

I open my eyes and do what I should have done a long time ago. I fight back.

"I. AM. NOT. A. GIRL."

My dad's eyes light up, happy to have somewhere to put his

anger. "Look at you. People don't accept this. Keep this going and you'll end up back here again. Or worse."

"I'm a man," I say.

He laughs, making me sick.

A fire in my belly ignites.

I lived.

I didn't die.

All my life, I have been too scared to fight back at the dinner table, or car, or wherever Dad decided to belittle and dismiss me. He made me feel wrong. He never accepted me. Maybe that's why I tried to hide who I am.

My dad is a bully. Just like Mac and Ryan. It's so obvious, but I couldn't see it until now. It's time to stand up to the first bully in my life. It's time to say what needs to be said. It starts right here.

"Dad, I was born in the wrong body. I'm not a girl. I have never been a girl. And I will never be a girl. You don't have to accept that, but I also don't have to accept you as my dad."

The room—maybe the entire hospital—goes quiet and cold.

Nurse Becky peeks her head in the room. "Pony, you have a couple visitors. Can they come in?"

Mom hops up. "Yes! Pony should see his friends. We need to run errands anyway." She gives me a kiss on the forehead. "We'll be back. You will be out of here soon. Love you, my brave angel."

Dad doesn't look my way as he stomps out. I'm rattled and want to nap. Nurse Becky picks up on the tension and pinches my foot, showing kindness. "You ready to see your friends? They said their names are Harry and Dick?"

It's obviously Kenji and Jerry. My best friends at Hillcrest found out my secret with everyone else last night. I should have told them before, but I didn't want our bromance to end. Too late now.

"Send them in," I say, even though I'm not ready. I tense up. Maybe they want to kick my ass, too? Nurse Becky leaves and Jerry and Kenji walk in, cautiously. They don't move far from the doorway, both looking at the floor. They're scared.

"Hi," I say.

Kenji looks up. "Hey, man," he says.

No reason to beat around the bush. "Guys, I'm sorry I didn't tell you I'm transgender. I understand if you don't want to be friends."

"Pecker," Jerry says, and then heads over to the chair. "We don't give a shit about that."

Kenji makes his way to the food tray. He'll eat anything. "Those asshats are lucky we didn't catch them."

"You went looking for them?" I ask, touched.

Kenji takes a bite of muffin. "Hell yes we did, but they split. We would have ended them."

I'm flattered. Tears try to form, but I push them down. "You guys aren't mad that I didn't tell you I was trans?" I ask.

"We kind of had a feeling," Kenji admits.

"Why didn't you ask me about it?"

Kenji starts peeling an orange. "We figured you would tell us when you were ready, or whatever."

"It just wasn't a big deal," Jerry says. He perks up. "Oh shit, *Judge Judy* is on."

"But you make fun of transgender people?" I ask.

They exchange a look, like they thought that might come up. Kenji takes the lead. "That was crappy of us. We never meant harm by it. Dumb jokes. That's all Jerry knows, right? We won't do it again. Sorry, man."

Man.

"Pony, we're glad you came to Hillcrest," Jerry says in a rare moment of sincerity. "You're a good dude."

Dude.

"Thanks for showing up here," I say, wiping away a couple tears. They pretend not to see. "Can we focus on *Judge Judy* already?" I ask. We watch TV, and they give me the blow-by-blow of the rest of the night and the after-parties.

I stop them. "So people aren't mad at me? For Mac and Ryan going to jail?"

"What?" Kenji asks, shaking his head. "No, they were worried about you." He gives me a look like that should be obvious.

"And," Jerry adds, "did you see what Georgia wrote about you? That was pretty dope."

"No," I say.

"You haven't checked your phone?" Kenji asks.

"I don't have my phone."

Kenji holds his up. "Do you want to see the article?"

Article? My heart kicks into high gear.

"Not yet," I say.

GEORGIA, 8:37 A.M.

The loud beeping from my phone wakes me up. It's my seventh alarm to snooze. I am an hour late.

Shitty shit shit.

I sit up, and last night smacks me in the face. I have vague memories of closing my laptop around five a.m. after posting my article on the front page of the *Hillcrest Reporter* without approval or editing. Ms. Randolph gave me the password when I started my freelance work. Wonder if she regrets that now? I shared the article on my socials and passed out.

I scroll through the notifications on my phone—lots of heart emojis and shares. No time to read; there's too much to deal with in the real world. I throw on some floor clothes, grab my stuff, and run out to my car.

I make it to the school parking lot in under ten minutes. The cheerleaders are standing in small groups around the bus. "Georgia, you're late!"

The sea of girls parts to reveal Mia, looking beyond annoyed. Lauren is near her with bags under her eyes. She has been crying all night. Kelly is absent.

"Mia, can we talk?" I say, looking around. "Anywhere but here?"

She's firmly planted, not going anywhere, and looking for a fight. "Don't you think you said enough in that little article?"

"Fine," I say. It's time to tell the truth. No more stories. "Mia, I can't go to the competition today. I need to be with Pony."

She scoffs. "Georgia, are you kidding me?"

"If your boyfriend was in the hospital, would you be here right now?" I ask.

"Excuse me, boyfriend? Do you love him?"

My skin gets itchy. I want to lie. "Yes," I say.

Mia doesn't even try to hide the horror in her face.

"Listen, Georgie, the thing you wrote was cute and moving. But you need to think about what people will think of you."

"I don't care," I say. "I have spent too long caring what people think. I'm over it."

Mia makes a face like I just slapped her. "OK, wow," she says in her favorite tone. "I guess Little Miss Anonymous wants to stand in the light?"

I shut my eyes so she can't see me roll them. "Yes, I tried to tell you that I was Anonymous. I said the pranks went too far, and last night they did. Can't you see that, Mia?"

"Well, bravo, Future Teller. Now get on this bus."

"I'm not going."

I brace for impact as hellfire breaks out in Mia's eyes. "Don't board that bus, and you are off the squad."

"You can't do that," I say.

She crosses her arms, defiant. "Do you even know how many demerits not going to a competition will get you?"

I look at Mia in disbelief. "A bad thing happened last night.

And our pranks were part of the problem. Do you even care about Kelly? I'm going to be with Pony, my *boyfriend*. Go ahead and kick me off the team."

I turn around and walk into the school. No one stops me. They just watch me go. I'm shaking so bad that I might collapse. I walk down the empty hallways and try to keep steady. It's dark, the only light coming from the occasional window outside. I pass by Ms. Randolph's room on the off chance that she's here. My blood sugar is low. I don't remember the last time I ate anything.

I'm about to exit the building when I see the lights in the admin office. I walk in and see Principal Scott at his desk. He looks up from his computer. "Georgia, hello!"

"I'm so glad you're here," I say. He takes off his glasses and rubs his eyes. Last night has taken a toll on everybody. "Georgia, that was a lovely article in the *Reporter*."

How many people have read it?

He opens a box on his desk. "I have too many donuts. Want one?" he asks, literally saving my life.

"Thanks, Mr. Scott," I say before grabbing two (glazed and chocolate icing). "I need your help with something for Pony."

He motions for me to sit down. "I'm all ears."

PONY, 1:30 P.M.

I open my eyes and see the most unbelievable thing.

Georgia.

She's in the chair next to me, head down in her phone. She's here. She's really here.

I've spent the morning falling asleep and waking up and falling asleep again. These pain meds put me in the clouds. I'm ready to be off them. Maybe this is a dream.

"Hi," I say.

"Hey, sleepyhead." She drops her phone, opting for my hand.

"Georgia, I can't believe you're here."

"I'm here," she says, and nothing sounds sweeter than her voice, and nothing feels better than her hand holding mine. "I told you I would be," she adds.

I think of my hospital gown and ground-beef face, ashamed. "Why?" I ask. "Do you just feel sorry for me?"

"No," she says flatly.

"This doesn't feel real," I admit.

"It's real, Pony. You have just been through a lot."

"But you didn't want me, remember? 'Cause I'm trans? And now you have a change of heart?"

"Pony, my heart hasn't been the problem. I had some things to figure out. But that was then, and this is now," she says, squeezing my hand.

I desperately want to believe her, but she lies. "How can I trust you?"

She gets up and sits on the bed. "Watching you reveal your truth onstage last night changed me. I saw how far away I was from my truth. I was miles away from the real me." She pauses to find her words. "I have spent too long keeping an outdated image intact at the expense of what I really want. I lost the real me. The me who loves to read and write. The me who never wanted to date Jake." She finds my eyes. "The me who wants to be with you."

"And you're back to the real you?"

She laughs. "God, I wish. But I'm on my way. I'm here with you. And I wrote something for the *Hillcrest Reporter* last night. Something I put my name on. Something about you."

"Kenji and Jerry told me," I admit.

"Did they show you?" she asks.

"No. And my parents took my phone home last night." I nod over to her phone on the chair. "But yours hasn't stopped vibrating."

"Yeah, you could say the article has been well received."

"It has?"

She shrugs. "A couple likes and shares."

My heart is pounding. What could it say? Why are people reading it?

"Pony, do you want to see it?"

I'm a joke—that's why people are reading. I never want to see another person from Hillcrest again. "Could you read it to me?" I ask. "My head is still a mess."

She grabs her phone from the chair and slides into the hospital bed, lying down next to me. While pulling the article up on her phone, she rests her head on my shoulder.

"You ready?" she asks.

I am not ready, but I say yes.

She clears her throat and begins.

STAY GOLD, PONY

by Georgia Roberts

Hillcrest is not about hate. Hard stop.

What happened on the stage at homecoming and later in the bathroom is completely and utterly unacceptable at this school or any place on planet Earth. Let's not shy away from the facts: Two of our fellow students were publicly outed, and another was severely beaten. There will be no tolerance or leniency for these acts of hate.

What was going through Pony's head in the bathroom? Did he wonder how people could be so cruel? So full of hate? Did he think he was going to die?

Sadly, what happened to Pony last night happens to transgender people all the time. The Trevor Project's latest research paints a dark picture:

- *71% of LGBTQ youth reported discrimination due to either their sexual orientation or gender identity.*
- *47% of transgender and non-binary youth were physically threatened or abused in the past year.*
- *58% percent of transgender and non-binary youth reported being discouraged from using a bathroom that corresponds to their gender identity.*

And the most staggering:

- *39% of LGBTQ youth seriously considered attempting suicide in the past twelve months, with more than half of transgender and non-binary youth having seriously considered it.*

These numbers are alarming. Frightening. Disgusting. But after tonight, is there any question about why they are so high? We need to do better. And it starts right here. Right now. With us, the students of Hillcrest and citizens of Addison.

I can't help but think of The Outsiders. In my opinion, one of the better of the required reading selections in seventh grade. Set in the late '60s, centered around a gang of boys who fought and fought and fought. Back then, fighting equaled masculinity and maturity. Do you remember Johnny? He was the friend who died, the sacrificial lamb. On his death bed, Johnny wrote Ponyboy a letter urging him to "stay gold." A motto inspired by the famous line in a Robert Frost poem, "Nothing Gold Can Stay." Johnny's final request for Ponyboy was that he remain innocent in a world of toxic masculinity. And to enjoy watching the sunrise.

I like to think our view on violence is shifting. Manhood is no longer measured by aggression and force. Not saying violence doesn't exist—it literally happened in the bathroom of the hotel last night. Rather, violence and masculinity are no longer synonyms.

If that's true (and obviously it is), then what does "stay gold" mean now? What would Johnny say to our Pony tonight? From where I sit, the transgender community isn't striving for innocence. There's no time to be innocent when the stats above suggest constant threats against their lives.

Nowadays, we need truth. The struggle is not to stay new to the world, it is to remain true to oneself, no matter what. To stand tall against intolerance and inequity. Rejection. Hate. Discrimination. Even violence.

Pony hid his truth of being transgender from us for months. He wanted to feel normal. Average. Nothing special. Things that no one strives for anymore. Pony wanted to worry about homework and dating instead of bathrooms and bullying. He didn't want the first thing people thought about him to be his gender. It breaks my heart that he needed to hide such an important part of him to experience these things.

We need marginalized people, like the LGBTQIA community, to be louder and more visible. And they need our help to feel safe enough to shine. That's on us.

All this talk of honesty must seem like one big joke coming from yours truly. And that's fair—the truth and I have had a complicated relationship. But getting to know Pony and seeing what he went through last night has changed me. His courage to stand up and speak his truth has inspired me. Right here and right now, I am done with the lies.

So, stay gold, Pony. Stay true to yourself when the world pushes against you, when your family doesn't accept you, even when the girl you want doesn't want you back. Stay gold because you are exceptional, and everyone will catch up someday. It took me time, but I am here beside you now.

Stay gold, Pony. The world needs you. Stay gold when it's hard. When it's lonely. When it's scary. Especially when it's scary. Stay gold, Pony, because there are so many people who want to help you shine.

And enjoy watching sunrises.

She looks up at me.

I blink, and tears roll down my face. "That's beautiful."

"And it's been shared three hundred and sixty-seven times."

She runs her hands through my hair, sending goose bumps all over my body. I lean over and kiss her. And she kisses me back. And for one moment, everything feels like it might be OK. We talk for a bit but eventually fall asleep in that tiny hospital bed. I can't turn on my side, so we decide that we are two spoons lying flat in a small drawer.

"Hi, honey." I wake up to my mom's voice and immediately panic. I don't want her to see me napping with a girl, but Georgia is safely back in the chair on her phone again.

"Mom, this is Georgia."

"We met last night. She was very passionate about seeing you. It was sweet," Mom says with a smile. Georgia stands up, and they hug.

"Good news, Pony. No internal bleeding and no concussion. How about we get out of here?" She starts straightening up like we're checking out of a hotel room. *Some vacation this was.*

"Get me home," I beg. I am ready to get out of here. My body feels broken, but I'm good enough to walk. Slowly.

"Soon, sweetie. The doctor needs to talk to you before we leave. I'll go sign you out, and Dad is waiting in the car."

Of course he couldn't even come back in here. Couldn't face his failure child. I'm out of that house the day I turn eighteen and never looking back. I'll miss my mom, but I can't do this anymore.

Georgia does a quick stretch. "I'm going to hit the bathroom before we leave," she says, following my mom out.

And then it's just me.

GEORGIA, 4:22 P.M.

I walk outside the hospital and immediately spot Pony's dad inside their green van. He's reading a newspaper that's resting on the steering wheel. I knock on the window and startle the shit out of him. *This is nuts. What am I even doing?* He rolls down the window. With great hesitation.

"Hi," I say, hoping to fully acknowledge the weirdness in this moment in one word.

"Hi," he says. His eyes light up. "Oh, I know you from last night. You're Sarah's friend."

And there it is: Pony's deadname. Why did I want to know it? That name has nothing to do with him anymore.

"Pony's friend," I correct him, frustrated that he can't get his name right. "Actually, I'm his girlfriend."

"Oh," he says, shocked. Pony would be equally shocked. We haven't really had time to discuss labels.

"Can we talk for a minute, sir?"

He unlocks the door. "Sure," he says cautiously.

I hop in the passenger seat and take a breath. Old me would start spinning a tale right now. I fight against it.

"Did you know," I ask, "that forty percent of transgender teenagers attempt suicide?"

"No," he says.

"Did you know that Pony thinks about it?" I ask. I am breaking Pony's confidence by telling him that, but he needs to know.

"No," he repeats, gripping the steering wheel.

"In the military, you break someone down, so they can grow stronger?"

He grunts. "Something like that."

"Well, that's not what Pony needs from you. He can't grow strong with you breaking him down. He needs your support. And love. He needs you to accept him. And he needs you to use his correct name and pronouns."

He grunts again and takes off his reading glasses. "It's hard for me to change. I keep forgetting. We named her Sarah. We had a girl named Sarah."

"Well, now you have a son named Pony, and if you don't accept that, you will lose him. Maybe we all will."

He shakes his head slowly, staring out the window. It's unclear if any of this is getting through to him. I borrow his phone and pull my article up.

"Read this?" I ask, handing him the phone.

PONY, 4:24 P.M.

I wiggle my body to test out the pain. It's there all right, a throbbing pressure along my sides, but better than last night. When it gets too quiet in this sterile white room, I can hear the crack of my ribs from the kicks. Over and over, I hear that awful cracking sound.

I kind of thought that Max would have come to visit. He writes petitions and disrupts school board meetings for queer kids he has never met, but he can't even come by the hospital and see me? It's crystal clear: Max must be done with me.

"Knock, knock," Dr. Sanders says, standing in the doorway.

"Come in," I say. I don't really have a choice.

"Time to break you out of here, Pony," he says, flipping through papers on a clipboard. "OK, everything looks good. A couple days in bed, and you'll be feeling better."

"No problem," I say. I could sleep for a decade.

"But Pony," he adds, "your ribs need time to heal. Lots of time. I'm going to ask you to stop wearing chest-compression binders."

"For how long?" I ask.

"A year, at least."

That felt like another kick to my side. "No," I say. "You don't understand. I need to wear them."

"Pony, you could cause permanent damage to your body."

I'm about to explain why this is impossible when Mom returns with a nurse. Dr. Sanders gives my mom instructions on medicine and care as the nurse helps me change into jeans, shirt, and hoodie. They fold me into a wheelchair, and my mom pushes me out.

"Where's Georgia?" I ask as we head out the door.

"She's out in the car with Dad."

"Mom, why do you stay with Dad? He's a bully," I say.

She stops wheeling me and puts a hand on my shoulder. "Your father acts like that because he loves you so much. This is killing him."

She starts pushing again. "He has a funny way of showing it," I say.

The van is waiting for us in the pickup zone. Dad helps me out of the wheelchair and into the back seat with Georgia. What could she have possibly been talking to him about? Sports? She buckles me in and gives me a kiss on the check.

The car ride back to Addison is quiet. I watch people in cars as they pass by, some doing double takes at my busted face. It's so easy for Dr. Sanders to tell me to stop wearing binders; he doesn't live in this body. Binders aren't an accessory; they are a necessity. I'm going to ignore his advice. Doesn't matter that it might cause permanent damage; I can't leave the house without a binder.

We pull onto the highway and pass a Sonic. I am never going back to Addison's Sonic. Or Hillcrest. I'll start researching my options when I get some strength. My eyes get heavy. I lean my head back, fall asleep, and dream of nothing.

I wake up to Georgia nudging me. I look around, confused. We aren't home. The car turns into the only place I don't want to be, Hillcrest High. My heart jump-starts. "What are we doing here?" I demand.

Before anyone can answer, I see why we are here.

A small group has formed on the front lawn of the school—

maybe twenty people—standing around holding signs and pride flags. A few people have also gathered across the street from the school with signs that read GOD HATES TRANS, NOT MY BATHROOM, and other hateful things.

What the hell is happening?

Dad parks the car and kills the engine. My heart is beating hard against my broken body.

"All these people are here for you," Georgia says. "Max and I planned it."

"Max?" I ask, connecting the dots of why he didn't show up at the hospital.

"And there's a part of my article that I didn't read you," she says, pulling out her phone. She clears her throat and reads out loud:

"To help show Pony that we accept and love him, I ask that you donate to the GoFundMe page below. The money will go to funding Pony's gender-affirming chest surgery. The goal is twenty-five thousand dollars."

I'm floored. "How much have you raised?" I ask.

Georgia smiles at me, her eyes wet. "In twelve hours, we've already raised six thousand dollars."

I start doing the math in my head. "I have four thousand in the bank, so I'm almost halfway there."

"At this rate, we should reach the goal in a couple days."

A lump grows in my throat. I am overwhelmed by the kindness.

Her phone dings. "Holy crap, Pony. You are halfway there now," she says. "Someone just donated two thousand dollars."

"Who?"

"Me," Dad says from the driver seat, phone in hand. "And your mother."

"But you said you would never give me—"

He cuts me off, "I know what I said. Pony, I have spent years trying to be the father I thought you needed. I wanted to protect you. And when you got hurt last night, I hated myself for failing you."

He turns around so we are face-to-face. I can see tears in his eyes. "I want to be a better dad for you." He pauses, figuring something out in his head. "I love you, son," he says.

Son.

My heart bursts in my chest. I want to believe what he said. I want to believe that he will be better. Time will tell. "We love you very much," Mom says, holding Dad's hand with tears in her eyes.

Someone approaches my side of the car—it's Max—pretending to pound on the window. Someone else approaches the other side of the car—it's Rocky—waving at me with a handful of flowers. It looks like she grabbed them from the garden around the school sign.

I open the car door, and they help me out. Rocky gives me a gentle hug, barely touching my body. "Rocky, you flew here for me?"

"I told you that if you needed me, I would be here," she says, and for the first time in my life, I see Rocky cry. She wipes the tears from her face.

"Thank you for being here," I say, trying to keep it together.

"No, Pony, thank you for being here. I love you, bro."

Bro.

I turn to Max. He's smiling at me. I missed him so much.

"Pony-baby, I'm sorry for pushing you to come out. And then pushing you away. I'm sorry—"

I cut him off. "Max, I love what you do for our community. I want to be there with you."

"I'm so freaking proud of the courage it took to get on that stage and stand with Kelly and Taylor." He looks me in the eyes. "I love you, dude."

Dude.

We walk, slowly, toward the group of people on the school's front lawn. There are students and parents with signs that read STAY GOLD and TEAM PONY and LOVE TRUMPS HATE.

We make it to the curb, the same spot I stopped at on the first day of school, and my legs freeze up again. I can't do this. I'm not strong enough.

Georgia senses my hesitation. "You OK?"

"It's too much," I confess.

"Pony, all of these people are here for you. You can do this." She puts her arm around me. "And I won't leave your side."

"But what about those people?" I ask, pointing to the group across the street protesting.

Max shakes his head. "That same group is at every LGBTQIA event. I know most of their names! We can't change those people's minds. We just love louder and harder than they can hate."

I return my focus to the group gathered on the lawn. All smiles, warmth, and love. My stomach turns over. Max pinches my butt. "You got this, Pony."

I hear Ted London in my head: *Fake it until you make it, kid.*

Rocky messes up my hair. "You the man!"

Man.

I put one foot in front of the other, and we walk into the crowd, together.

GEORGIA, 5:49 P.M.

I can't believe we pulled this freaking thing off. I catch Max's eye, and we exchange a smile. We are on either side of Pony, protecting his tender body. We are his tender bodyguards.

My heart cracks open wide as we walk through the group of people that came out to support Pony and the LGBTQIA community. Couldn't be more than thirty people, but not a bad showing for announcing at noon today. People do care. This feels healing for Pony and the school.

We pass by Kenji and Jerry. They snap a selfie with Pony.

Kelly and Taylor run up, and I give them both hugs.

"How are you doing?" Pony asks them, concerned, which is cute.

"We are better than ever," Taylor says, holding Kelly's hand with no worry about who's looking.

Kelly smiles big. "He's the one with broken ribs, and he's worried about us."

"You've got a keeper, Georgia," Taylor says to me, winking.

"You did pretty good, too," I say.

"Pretty good?" Kelly asks, offended. I haven't seen Kelly this happy in a long time. She's practically glowing. "Double date?" she asks.

"Hell yes," I say.

Without notice, we're surrounded by cheerleaders. I look at Pony with wide eyes. I didn't tell him that I quit the squad. He had enough to worry about.

"What are you doing here?" I ask Mia. They should be at the competition.

"We skipped the award part to be here," she says, forcing a smile. She turns to Pony. "On behalf of the cheerleaders, we are so sorry for what happened last night, Pony. That is not what Hillcrest is about."

"Thanks," he says.

"You are a wonderful guy, and Georgia is lucky to have you," she adds.

I cut in. "Excuse me? What changed?"

Lauren pushes her way up and puts her arm around Mia. "We had a little heart-to-heart."

"I came around," Mia admits.

"Damn right, you did," Lauren says with a sly smile. "Or else we all would have quit the team this morning with Georgia."

"You quit the team?" Pony asks me. I look over at Max. He's watching like it's an episode of *Riverdale*.

I turn to Pony. "I wanted to be with you today."

Before Pony can say anything, Mia jumps in. "Georgia, it's my bad. I was out of line. Please don't quit. I need you there, G."

"I could clear my schedule up, as long as I can keep writing for the *Reporter*."

"Are you—" Mia starts, then Lauren gives her a gentle nudge. "Fine. We can make it work." *This must be killing her.*

"Then I unquit the team," I announce. Mia hugs me like I've agreed to give her my kidney. I hug Lauren and whisper in her ear, "I'm proud of you for standing up."

"I learned it by watching you," she says with a wink.

Pony and I keep moving toward the steps leading up to the school's entrance. We lost Max somewhere along the way. I stop Pony. "I'm going to run into the school. I'll be back in two minutes. Will you be all right?"

"Yes," he says, but he looks unsteady.

I hop up the steps; I need to be quick. I push the doors open and immediately see Principal Scott adjusting his tie and smoothing out his hair while chatting with a couple students.

"Georgia."

I turn around. "Jake."

"How's Pony?" he asks, worried.

"Not great," I admit. "But he'll get through this, I'll make sure of it."

Jake lowers his head, probably not wanting to hear me talk about another guy. "Jake, what you're doing is above and beyond. You sure you want to do this?"

He finds my eyes. "One hundred percent. What my ex-teammates did, on stage and in that bathroom, was terrible. Anything I can do to help you and Pony."

"Thanks," I say, then give him a hug.

Ms. Randolph comes up behind me. "Georgia?"

I turn around, happy to see her. "Ms. R," I say, throwing my arms around her neck.

"Georgia," Ms. Randolph says, "I'm so proud of you. Your article was important. And the truth. I knew you had it in you."

"Thanks for helping me find my truth," I say.

"Let's talk Monday about your next article," she says with a smile.

Dad busts frantically through the doors. "Georgie! So glad I found you." He gives me a half hug. "I am so proud of you for turning this moment of hate into love. Remarkable."

"She is an impressive young woman," Ms. Randolph agrees.

"Hello there," Dad says with his sly smile. "I'm Robert, Georgia's dad."

"Nice to meet you. I'm Kerry. I teach English and run the paper here."

It's so weird that teachers have first names.

"The *Hillcrest Reporter*? I read it online every week," Dad says, fanboying out.

I look down and see no ring on Ms. Randolph's hand. I never clocked that before.

"Georgia," Ms. Randolph says, not taking her eyes off my dad, "do you mind if your dad escorts me outside?"

"Not at all," I say.

Is Ms. Randolph my new stepmom?

Dad hands me the box that I asked him to bring. "Thanks for this, Dad. You kids have fun out there," I say, watching them head outside. Dad sneaks a big dopey grin my way, and I give him a thumbs up.

PONY, 5:54 P.M.

Georgia returns with a small box. She opens it up and pulls out a flower boutonniere. The rose in the middle has been painted gold.

"What's this?" I ask as she pins the flowers to my hoodie.

"I just want to make sure you're ready." She smooths out my hair and kisses me. "Look at my handsome boyfriend."

Boyfriend.

Principal Scott walks out the doors and picks up the microphone connected to a small speaker.

"Thank you all for coming this evening. As you know, there was an inexcusable act of violence at the homecoming dance last night. We are here today to let Pony, Kelly, Taylor, and everyone out there from the LGBTQIA community know that those boys do not speak for Hillcrest. We are a strong, diverse, and proud school. We welcome and encourage all ethnicities, sexual orientations, and genders equally."

The group cheers.

"Pony," Principal Scott yells, "I hope that when you are ready, you will return to Hillcrest to finish the year."

They cheer again, louder.

"Now, on to the business of this evening. Jake?"

There's polite applause as Jake walks out the school doors, wearing a tux, and takes the microphone.

"I'm here to finish the awards ceremony from last night. Hillcrest High homecoming king and queen for the class of 2020 goes to . . ." He opens a big gold envelope and reads the card. "Pony and Georgia!"

Georgia grabs my hand to lead me up the steps, slowly, as the sun sets behind the school. Jake puts the crown on my head.

"But this should be yours," I say to Jake.

"We took a revote," he says, then winks. "You're the man."

Man.

I turn to the crowd. It's all smiles, tears, and phones recording the moment. I can see the faces of people I care about, caring about me. Jake hands me the microphone. Everyone goes quiet.

"Thank you. For all of this. And thanks to Georgia and Max for making it happen." I smile at Georgia. She smiles back. "Last night, I was going to withdraw from school." I stop and steady my voice. "But after this, I will be back to finish the year."

I catch my breath. I want these words to be clear.

"I'm going to say something that I have never said before. You'll be first to hear it. But not the last." I find Max in the group. He gives me a thumbs-up. "I'm proud to be transgender."

The crowd cheers. I hand Jake the microphone. I don't want it anymore.

I turn to Georgia. "You know, this is exactly where I was standing when I spotted you on the first day of school."

She holds my hand. "Right here?"

"Right here," I confirm. "I wondered what kind of guy I would need to be to date you."

"And did you figure it out?" she asks.

"Turns out, all I had to do was be myself."

"I love actually you, Pony."

We kiss. In front of everyone.

After the clapping quiets down, Georgia picks up the microphone.

She yells, "Let's hear it for the homecoming king!"

King.

THE END

ACKNOWLEDGMENTS

I'm sitting in a hotel meeting room. The year is 2018. I work at HarperCollins, and we're at our yearly sales conference in Miami. While listening to a speaker at the podium, my attention drifts and an idea for a book comes to mind. The title, characters' names, parts of the storyline. This has never happened before. And it was happening fast. The next day, like a madman, I pitch the book idea to the senior vice president of sales and editor in chief. Who does that? Me, I guess. Andrea Pappenheimer and Kate Jackson didn't laugh at me, didn't dismiss me; they believed in me. If they hadn't, I might have left the idea in Miami alongside my forgotten phone charger. Thank you, Andrea and Kate, what you did for me was life changing.

Overwhelming appreciation and endless gratitude to Andrew Eliopulos. It's an honor to call you my editor. Creating this book together was pure joy. Your direction is calm and careful, smart and thoughtful. Thank you for helping me tell the story in my heart. Also, you have the best smile.

And, tremendous thanks to Rosemary Brosnan. I've always thought we connected instantly, like maybe I knew you in another life. You are the kindest. And the coolest. Don't ever change. Special thanks to Bria Ragin, Laura Harshberger, Maya Meyers, and Gweneth Morton. I'm immensely grateful for your careful eyes, sharp notes, and actually testing the cinnamon roll recipe (Maya Meyers).

Big thanks to my literary agent, Tina Dubois. You are wonderful. I often think of you as my boxing coach—encouraging and helping me grow, giving me water, dabbing the sweat off my forehead, then pushing me back into the ring. Thanks for giving it to me straight. And enormous thanks to Nicole Borrelli Hearn, my supporter from day one. Alicia Gordon, thank you for believing in this book. Jennifer Knisbell, thank you for helping launch the Stay Gold Fund. I'm blown away by the support and talent of the Stay Gold team at ICM Partners. Thank you for caring so much.

Standing ovation for the cover, amazingly designed by David DeWitt with awesome art from little corvus. Thanks to Allison Michael Orenstein for my author photos. How do you make me look that good?

Forever indebted to HarperCollins—my first employer and first publisher. Thank you for taking a chance on me in 2003, when I interviewed for a sales assistant position, and thank you for taking another chance on me with this book. In so many ways, I learned by standing on the shoulders of giants.

Unending love and appreciation to the best sales team in

publishing (and my friends). You are smart with a bunch of heart, and that's hard to find. I am, and will always be, house proud. Josh Marwell, Andrea Pappenheimer, Kerry Moynagh, Susan Yeager, Andrea Rosen, Jessie Elliott, Jennifer Wygand, Megan Pagano, Frank Albanese, Kathy Faber, Heather Doss, Fran Olson, Lillie Walsh, Casey Coughlin, Deb Murphy, and Jessica Malone. Road warriors: Mary Beth Thomas, Ronnie Kutys, Kate McCune, Anne DeCourcey, Eric Svenson, Cathy Schornstein, Gabriel Barillas, Jennifer Sheridan, Jim Hankey, Robin Smith, Ian Doherty, Michael Morris, Richard Starke, Dawn Littman, Kim Gobar, Bob Alunni. Special acknowledgment to my Harper digital fam: Jessica Abel, Lauren Esser, Bethany Johnsrud, Serita Patel. Thank you to first reader, Anna Montague. Extra super special acknowledgment to anyone I accidently omitted from this list . . . I'll mention you twice next time.

To booksellers and librarians, I'd like to acknowledge your dedication and devotion to books. Thank you for everything you do: handselling, cheerleading, and creating space for diverse voices to be heard. Can't wait to meet you.

I'd be nothing without the emotional support of my cats, Buster and Bananas. Writing a book can be lonely, especially late at night. My cats kept me company—napping on my lap, demanding pets, and rooting me on. Several months after finishing this book, Buster passed on to the rainbow bridge. Goodbye Buster, my forever familiar; I miss you every day.

Extra-large serving of gratitude to my writing partner, Bob

McSmith. After creating eight musicals together, writing this book without you felt like cheating. But you never once made me feel that way—always encouraging, listening, reading drafts and scribbling illegible notes in the columns, and supporting me. That's a true friend. Bob, you are the best friend I will ever have.

So much love to my family and friends. There's not enough room to list who you are and why I love you. Also, I'm bad at spelling last names. If you are my friend and/or family, thank you for accepting me for me. That's the most perfect act of love. I wouldn't be here, and this book wouldn't be in your hands, without you.

Love and gratitude to my girlfriend, Amanda Berger. I swore off dating while writing this book which allowed us to become friends first. When I wrote The End here, our love story began. Thank you for the patience, love, and support.

Finally, I'd like to acknowledge the bravery and beauty of all transgender and nonbinary people—past, present, and future. This book is my promise to make the world better for our community. This book is my love letter to you.